THE
WAYWARD DAMNED

WRITTEN BY
S.M. MITCHELL

Copyright © 2024 by S. M. Mitchell

All rights reserved. No part of this publication may be reproduced, stored or transmitted in any form or by any means, electronic, mechanical, photocopying, recording, scanning, or otherwise without written permission from the publisher. It is illegal to copy this book, post it to a website, or distribute it by any other means without permission.

This novel is entirely a work of fiction. The names, characters and incidents portrayed in it are the work of the author's imagination. Any resemblance to actual persons, living or dead, events or localities is entirely coincidental.

ISBN: 9798876872111

DEDICATION

To all the other
volatile, opinionated, loud, & unapologetic feminists out there.
Keep yelling.

S. M. Mitchell

VAERNY

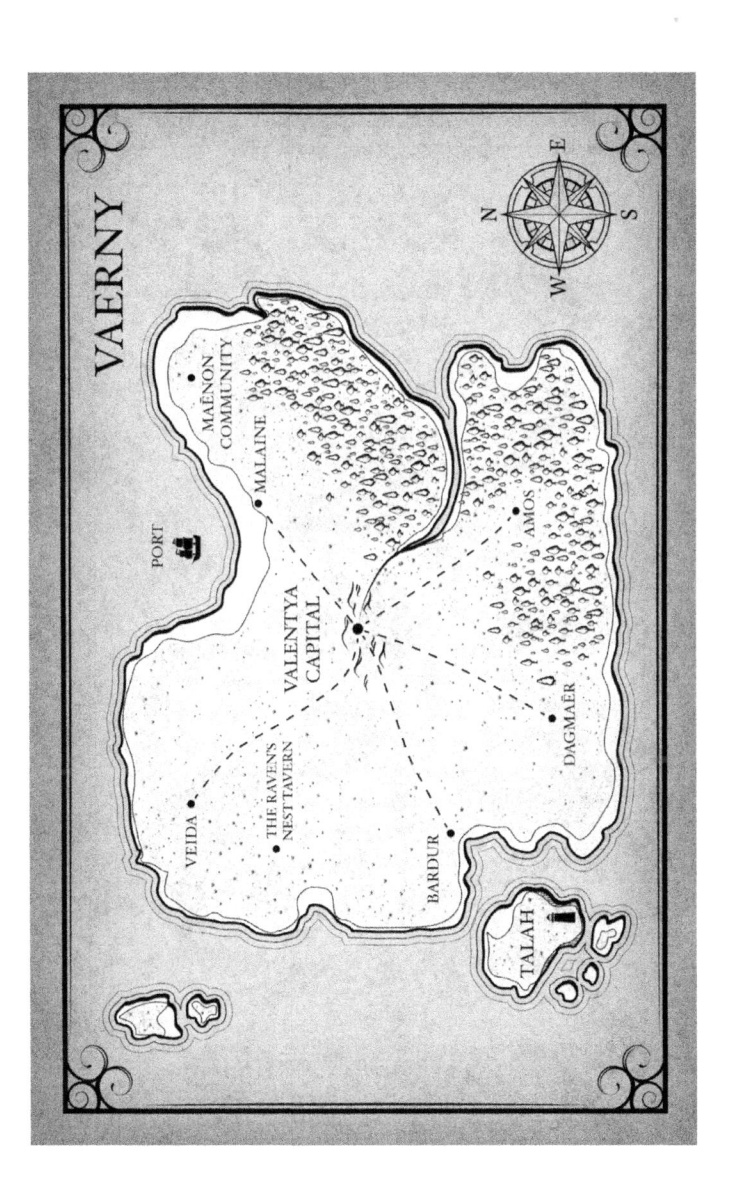

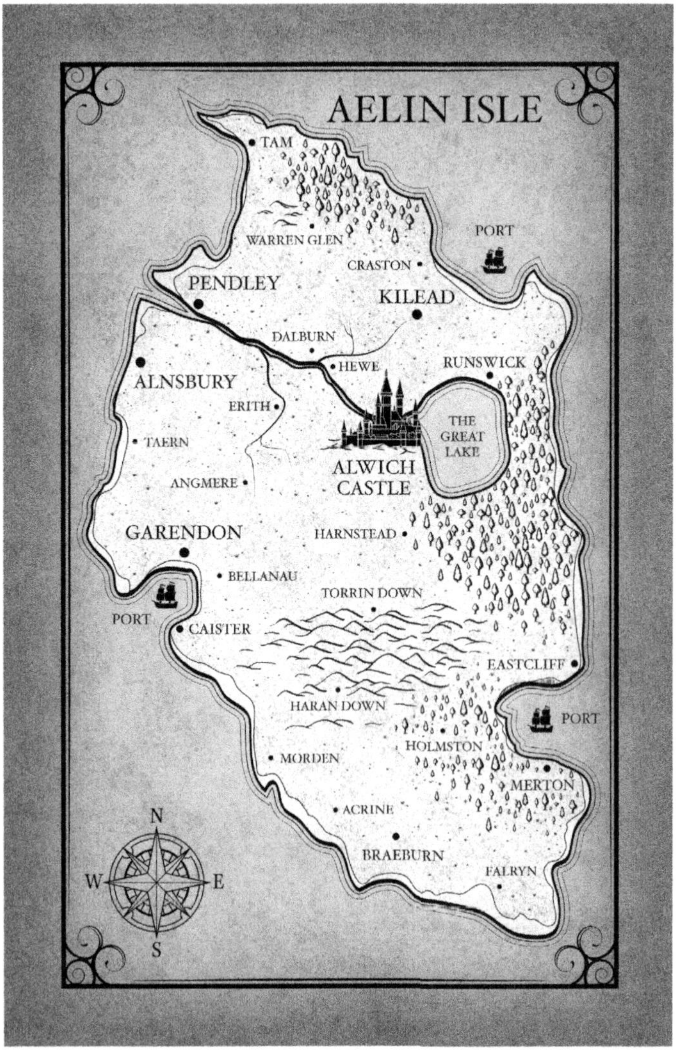
AELIN ISLE
TAM
WARREN GLEN
PORT
CRASTON
PENDLEY
KILEAD
DALBURN
HEWE
RUNSWICK
ALNSBURY
ERITH
THE GREAT LAKE
TAERN
ALWICH CASTLE
ANGMERE
GARENDON
HARNSTEAD
BELLANAU
TORRIN DOWN
PORT
CAISTER
EASTCLIFF
HARAN DOWN
PORT
HOLMSTON
MORDEN
MERTON
ACRINE
BRAEBURN
FALRYN
N
W
E
S

ALWICH CASTLE
THE GREAT LAKE

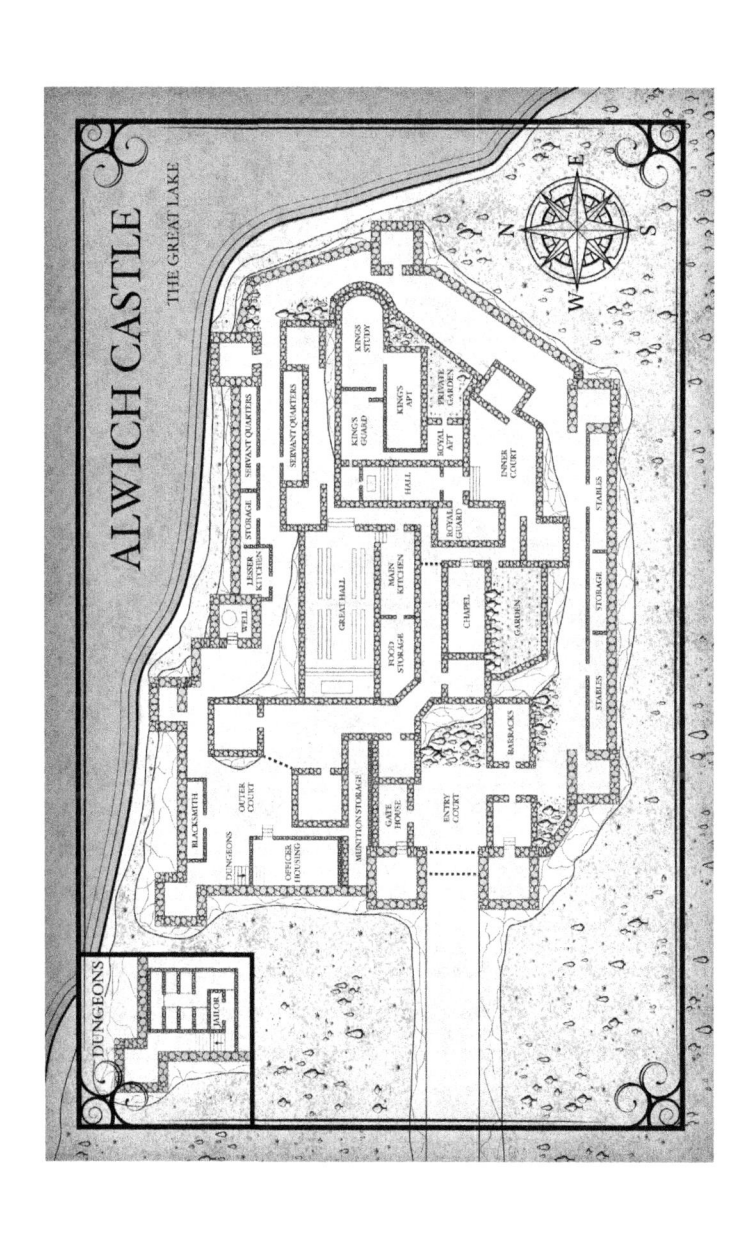

- KING'S STUDY
- KING'S GUARD
- KING'S APT
- SERVANT QUARTERS
- SERVANT QUARTERS
- LESSER KITCHEN
- STORAGE
- WELL
- ROYAL APT
- PRIVATE GARDEN
- HALL
- ROYAL GUARD
- INNER COURT
- GREAT HALL
- MAIN KITCHEN
- FOOD STORAGE
- CHAPEL
- GARDEN
- STABLES
- STORAGE
- STABLES
- BARRACKS
- OUTER COURT
- BLACKSMITH
- DUNGEONS
- OFFICER HOUSING
- MUNITION STORAGE
- GATE HOUSE
- ENTRY COURT

DUNGEONS
- JAILOR

CHAPTER ONE

WASHED ASHORE

Prudence's lungs burned as she coughed up the water she had swallowed. Her skin stung with salt, and the sand underneath her scratched at her wounds. She tried to claw her way up from the surf, but the dead weight of her magickally ruined forearm made her progress agonisingly slow. It had been useless to her ever since she'd agreed to that spell. She lay down on the sand, panting for a moment before lifting her head.

The shoreline was sparse and grey save for the lighthouse that rose up out of the rocks like a stalagmite. She had washed up on Talah, the spit of rock that housed Vaerny's only lighthouse.

A light rain had begun to fall, and the clouds overhead were grey and angry as if Artos himself was preparing to punish her for her mistakes. She crawled further up the sand, throat dry and hoarse from all the water she had swallowed.

Prudence remembered jumping from the gundeck, the icy cold water hitting her in the face, covering her completely until she felt like she was drowning. She remembered Cain's hand gripping hers as they plunged into the ocean. Then it all went black. She couldn't remember them getting separated, but Cain was nowhere in sight along the long stretch of dark sand and stone.

She sucked in a breath as she pushed up to sit. Her ribs, although almost fully healed from her time in prison, still ached from the exertion. In the distance, she could just make out the main mast of *The Bloody Maiden*, sinking below the surface. Her hull was already hidden beneath the waves, wood splintered and broken against the rocks they had sailed into. It was a wreck.

The governor's ships were still hovering just over a mile away. She doubted they could see her from there, but nerves still crept through her like vines up a wall. Prudence assumed they were trying to find a way through the debris of the broken galleon to look for survivors.

Survivors.

Prudence felt a rush of guilt hit her like a tsunami. All those men they sentenced to death. For what? Cain was nowhere to be seen. What if he was still in the water?

Prudence leapt up and forced herself deep into the frigid ocean once again, frantically scanning the wreckage. "Cain!" she yelled. *Shit*. "Where are ye? Cain!" A body floated just a short distance from where she stood. Bracing against the freezing water, she pushed forward, staying afloat as best she could with only one good arm, towards the dead body.

His sandy blond hair filled Prudence with a clawing terror

that infested her throat. She flipped him over and sighed with relief. Charlie's vacant face stared up at her, eyes void and lifeless. She hadn't known him well. He couldn't have been older than twenty-three years old. She closed his eyes and pushed the body away from her. At least it wasn't Cain.

She couldn't get further out towards the ship without being in full view of the governor's men. Reluctantly, she swam back to shore, all the while keeping her eyes peeled for a glimpse of her new husband.

On the beach, Prudence traipsed along the shoreline, her clothes soaked through as the rain beat down harder than ever. She reached the edge of the shore where the sand blended with rough grass and spotted a dark-haired man washed up in the surf, his head face down. Prudence turned him over. Khari.

She tentatively put an ear to his chest but couldn't hear anything. Prudence pounded on his chest in an attempt to get the water out of him. Again and again with no sound. She slapped his face and hit his chest once more, and a surge of water and vomit erupted from his lips onto his face. Prudence helped him sit up while he coughed the sea out of his chest.

His breath came in rough gasps and spurts as he emptied his lungs, and another load of vomit forced its way out of his mouth onto the sand. Khari's arms gave out beneath him, and he collapsed, narrowly missing the puddle of vomit. Prudence watched him silently for a while as he tried to steady his breathing and colour came back to his face.

"How in the hell did ye survive that?" he asked, his voice rough from half drowning. "'Specially in that thing." He glanced down at the drenched dress Prudence was wearing. Her wedding dress. He snorted. "Figures. If anyone was scrappy enough, it'd be ye."

She grabbed his arm. "Ye didn't see what happened to Cain, did ye?"

He crawled to the water's edge and splashed it onto his face, wiping away the vomit. "Lost yer girl so now yer clinging to someone else, eh?" he scoffed.

Prudence growled and pulled him up by his shirt. Of all the people who might have survived the crash, it was an unbelievably cruel god who left her stranded with Khari. The man who'd been a thorn in her side for too long, who'd brought Eleanora back to her death. "Don't push me. Khari. I know full well ye were just the brawn. Avery is dead and I'll happily leave ye here to die, so cut it out. *Did you see him?*"

He sighed. "Peace, *keine*. No, I haven't. I saw the ship begin to break up right in front of my eyes. I bailed as it started to go under. I don't remember anything else." He looked into her eyes. "I'm sorry."

The use of that nickname he'd given her, *little girl*, sent rage coursing through her. Prudence sat back on her heels, pounding the sand with her fists. "He's not dead! He can't be dead. He can't be! We just got married..." She rose to her feet and strode away from him.

"Prudence, wait! Wait up!" Khari stumbled to his feet and followed her, wobbling slightly. "Where the fuck are you going? *Boti*. Prudence, he's not here! What are you going to do? Walk until ye find him?"

"Maybe! Until I can think of something better, yes." She spun on her heel and came face to face with Khari. "What does it matter to you?"

"Ye can only walk so far, *keine*. Look around."

Prudence bit back her anger for a moment and looked at where they were. The tiny crop of rock known as Talah was a stretch of black sand, looking even more hopeless than Prudence felt.

"Ye'd walk into the ocean before ye find him or anyone to help ye. We need to get off here before ye can go gallivanting after yer man like the heroine ye so clearly think ye are."

Prudence looked into his deep brown eyes and narrowed hers. "Well, what do ye suggest? Since ye seem to know everythin'."

It was too far to swim to the main island of Vaerny. The waves and the cold... it was a miracle they'd survived the crash in the first place. They certainly wouldn't make it a second time. They looked around. Debris from the broken ship had begun to wash ashore—splintered, useless scraps of wood, busted crates with nothing in them, a book that must have come from Cain's cabin. Prudence's chest ached. *Cain.*

Khari sighed and bent down to pick up a crate that had been considerably less damaged than the others. "I don't know." He ran a hand through his long hair and huffed. "I don't know, *keine.*"

"We need to collect everything, anythin' that we could use. We need to build a boat, a raft, somethin'. We've just gotta get over there." She pointed to the mainland of Vaerny and his gaze followed her finger. Through the rain and mist, the rocky island of Vaerny could just be seen, rising out of the gloom like a beacon of hope. A hope they currently had no means of reaching.

A chill ran down Prudence's spine, and she rubbed her bad arm in a vain attempt to get some warmth through her skin. "But we need to get warm first. I don't know about ye, but I fear I'll collapse before long if I stay like this." She nodded at the worn lighthouse only a few hundred yards from them. "Come on. There may just be things we can make use of for a raft."

The two left the broken pieces of *The Maiden* and her supplies in a pile on the sand and trudged as quickly as their cold limbs and the sinking sand would allow towards Talah's lighthouse.

Khari jogged ahead, scouting around the lighthouse with a slight bounce in his step that Prudence could only roll her eyes at. His faith did nothing to sway her pessimism. If anything, it just made her angry. The raft may have been her idea, but she couldn't ignore the voice in her head yelling at her that it was a fool's errand and she was an idiot for listening to false hope. *You'll die out here. You'll die cold and starving. You both will.*

A sound danced on the wind towards her. Brushing the instinctual thought of ghosts out of her mind, she paused to listen. There it was again. A muffled, faint groan. Prudence didn't stop to think of her fragile ribs or the ache in her back before she ran as fast as her exhausted legs could carry her to the rocks surrounding the old lighthouse.

Choppy waves pushed up against the rocky edge, cresting and falling once again back into the ocean. Sea spray splattered against her dress as she gripped the rocks and made her way closer to the water below, her feet cautiously moving one step at a time, careful not to slip.

Garrick's soft brown locks, soaked in the spray, hung limply over his closed eyes. Prudence's heart hiccoughed in her chest as she scrambled over the few rocks between them, sheer willpower keeping her from toppling over.

She sank to her knees beside him and pushed the hair away from his face. A shaky breath escaped his lips.

"Shh. Shh. It's all right. I'm here... I'm here. Yer goin' to be fine."

Wearily, Garrick opened his eyes and looked up at her. He smiled briefly before his eyes rolled back in his head and he let out a shallow gasp. Prudence clumsily lifted his head into her lap as best she could with just one hand and stroked his face. The rain beating down dripped from her hair into her eyes, blurring her vision, and she sniffed back a tear.

"Hey, blue eyes."

She started and gripped him a little tighter. "Hey there, sailor." Prudence smiled. "We made it." She sniffed back the tears welling in her eyes.

"If I knew the afterlife was this beautiful, I'd have raced to get here faster." He chuckled then coughed. A glob of blood and spit landed on his chin. Prudence wiped it away.

She scoffed quietly and touched his hair. "*You* are delusional." She shifted but stopped as Garrick winced against her. "Yer going to be fine." She tried to ignore the sound of his ragged breaths. A sound that reminded her of a bag of marbles clacking together.

Garrick glanced down at his lower half and looked back up at her. "I'm not so sure about that, beautiful. These legs are done for, I fear."

A sob threatened to tear through Prudence, but she bit it back. "Nonsense." She smiled, but she could feel that it didn't quite meet her eyes. "I'm going to get us off this rock, somewhere safe. Somewhere I can fix you up." She sniffed again, and he lifted a hand to wipe the rain from her cheek. His touch was weak and shaky. Prudence thought she might be sick.

"I'm not afraid to die."

She closed her eyes and bit her lip to stop it from wobbling. "You are *not* going to die. Do ye hear me?"

His chest rattled as his breaths made it rise and fall. "I don't think I've got much of a choice here."

A tear slipped out of her eye, and she wiped it away furiously. Garrick's gaze softened. "It's all right, blue eyes. At least I'll get to die looking at yer pretty face." He smiled and cupped her cheek as tears filled his own eyes. "It hurts."

A whimper escaped Prudence's lips, and she pressed her forehead against his. He brushed his finger along her jawline and over her lip, his gaze focused on her face. "In another life, you and I would've made some truly beautiful babies." He gasped loudly and his chest quaked. "We... we would've grown old... surrounded by grandchildren." He winced, his eyes closing tight. "I want it to stop hurting."

His breaths came in short, shallow gasps now, his chest barely moving at all. Prudence stroked his hair and murmured to him until his breathing stopped rattling. She let out a sob. "It won't hurt anymore. I promise."

***

She sat like that for what felt like hours. The rain had lessened into a soft mizzling, but Prudence barely noticed. Her good fingers remained curled in Garrick's sopping locks. His face no longer held that pink glow of life but was cold and greying, and she knew she needed to get up. To do something. The governor's soldiers were no longer in view. They had searched the bulk of the wreckage and found no one alive, but that didn't mean she would be safe if they ever got off this wretched rock.

She placed a kiss on Garrick's forehead, lifted his head, and gently placed it on the ground. His head lolled to the side, and she shut her eyes tight, refusing to let any tears leak out. Now wasn't the time to mourn. She needed to get away from here. She needed to find Cain. The governor and his men may have thought they were all dead for the moment, but if they were seen, they'd be done for. Where was he?

She rose wearily and brushed the dirt from her somewhat ruined wedding dress. Her fingers glided over the soft cotton embroidered with flowering buds. *I'm a little rusty on the words, forgive me...* It felt like a lifetime had passed since they'd stood on *The Maiden's* deck promising themselves to one another. Another life. Another person.

The old lighthouse loomed behind her. It had clearly been in disuse for years. The door had splintered and cracked in the cold, its hinges loose, letting it hang open in the slight breeze. The rusted metal creaked ever so quietly as if all had been abandoned just moments before. It set Prudence's teeth on edge. As if the lighthouse and Talah itself was an island of ghosts. Ghosts they had just joined.

The windows of the lighthouse had long since been broken and the walls were covered in barnacles as the edge of the lighthouse stretched out into the sea. Dead seaweed had clung and dried to the stone. The sickly smell of salt water and brine that normally gave Prudence a warm feeling of home suddenly reached her nose, rank and vile.

She wondered if perhaps they might find someone dead once inside. The building felt like a landmark for death. Old, forgotten, just out of reach. It seeped into her mind like a poison, eating away the tiny amount of hope still inside her and replacing it with a sense of dread that she too would die. Old, forgotten, and just out of reach.

Prudence pushed the rotting door open wider and stepped into the gloom. Her feet brushed against the stone floor, sounding far too loud in the deafening silence that enveloped her. Dust kicked up beneath her feet and she coughed, swiping at specks in the shaft of daylight that managed to sneak in despite the colourless sky. The staircase before her was a steep path of uneven stone steps that disappeared far up above her head. Her steps echoed off the surrounding stone as she climbed. Hopefully, Khari had found something useful. Dry clothes, wood, rope, anything.

The first floor of the lighthouse seemed to be a living area. There were remnants of furniture and an old kitchen in the corner. Prudence couldn't help but imagine living there, with only the light at the top, stretching out onto the vast ocean in search of ships. Alone. What had happened to the lighthouse keeper that had left the stone tower in such disrepair? Might he have died of a broken heart?

It reminded her of a tale her father had told her as a child. Of a lighthouse that spread its warm light across the sea in the hopes of saving ships and their men from crashing and dying against the rocks on which it stood. It shined every night, protecting those who spent their lives at sea... but it was lonely. As the years drew on, the lighthouse's melancholy only grew. It wanted to keep ships away for their safety, but it desperately wanted a ship to come near, just once, to see it. The lighthouse keeper tried his best to look after the lighthouse. He would scrape barnacles away from its outer walls, light the whale oil every night. He kept the lighthouse rooms near spotless... but despite his efforts, the lighthouse began to crumble. As waves beat against its rocks and walls, it cracked and groaned. Soon, the lighthouse's bricks began to collapse and fall into the sea, out where the ships would sail, without the warm light of the lighthouse to protect them.

A clatter sounded above her, pulling her out of her haze of memories, and she climbed another load of stairs to find Khari pulling items out of a chest in the corner of the room. "What are ye doing?" she asked, narrowly dodging a boot flung in her direction.

"Looking fer anything we could use. I found some clothes. Here." He threw a balled-up shirt and britches at her. "Ye'll die if ye stay in that ridiculous thing." He glanced at the sopping wedding dress still clinging to her body.

Prudence ran a hand over the bodice. Despite the chill seeping into her bones from the water-soaked fabric, she didn't wish to part with it. It felt like her only link to Cain. In a sudden panic, she remembered the ring Cain had placed on her finger. She looked at her hand. It was still there.

Relief swept through her as she twisted her hand this way and that, looking at it properly for the first time. The silver band had intricate swirls that wound around the entirety of the ring. Little silver leaves held the large red stone in place in the centre. She sighed and put the bundle of clothes down, trying her best to tug the britches on with her one good arm. It was difficult and fiddly, but she managed to hoist the waistband over her hips. Prudence glanced behind her at Khari, who was still rummaging through the chest. She pulled the dress over her head and hastily replaced it with the shirt he'd given her.

By the time Khari had finished looking for whatever he had been trying to find, Prudence was fully dressed in men's clothes and had knotted her hair at the base of her neck. "Look at tha'. With a decent hat, ye could almost pass for a boy." He laughed.

Prudence snorted. "A boy?"

"Aye, just yer damn chest that gives it away." His eyes

dropped from her face to her chest, and she scowled at him.

"Did ye find anything useful? I don't wish to be here with you any longer than I 'av to be."

"Real pleasant." He rolled his eyes. "Not much besides the clothes, but I reckon between the stuff tha's washed ashore an' the bits we've got here, we might be able to fashion somethin' together."

CHAPTER TWO

DEBTS OWED

"How do ye know this'll work? I mean, it's just rope an' wood, in't it? How's that gonna get us to the shore?" Khari kicked the plank of wood at his feet and glanced at Prudence. Despite the determined, almost frenzied look on her face as she lashed another plank to the makeshift raft, he still felt uneasy.

"Wood floats, idiot. I jus' need to make it strong enough to stay together. Come on, help me!" She flung a piece of rope that they had scavenged from the wreck of *The Bloody Maiden* at him. "Tie that plank to the other side. Make sure it's tight."

Khari sank to his knees and began tying a bowline knot. They had managed to scrounge a decent amount of wooden planks from the ship, along with four barrels that hadn't broken up on the rocks. He'd found some rope in Talah's lighthouse to tie it all together. He just hoped Prudence knew what she was doing.

She had said they only needed to get across the short stretch of sea between Talah and Vaerny's shore, and she was right. But Khari knew that the sea was a fiery mistress, and that stretch, whilst small, may very well be the death of them.

The raft was a slightly lopsided rectangle, with one side longer than the other due to the length of the planks. Provided they could make it secure enough, there'd be just enough room for both of them to sit down and use a plank each to paddle towards the shore. The barrels that had survived the wreck had been lashed to the underneath of the wooden raft, one to each corner, that Prudence seemed to feel fairly certain would keep the raft afloat as best they could manage.

"So, what are ye gonna do when we get to shore?" Khari glanced at her furiously fighting with a piece of rope that just wouldn't seem to tie properly. She re-tied it twice before throwing it down in front of her and growling. "Ach, calm, *little girl*." He said it in Aelish this time, with the wrong letters enunciated, and it sounded foreign in his mouth. He liked to keep some Ta'ih in his words; it helped him feel connected to home. "Let me do that," he insisted.

He crawled around the raft on his knees to where Prudence had been sitting and tied the rope. Prudence rose and paced alongside the raft length, up and down, away and back again, over and over until Khari felt like screaming at her. He'd always known she was erratic, but he'd never been around her this long by himself, and every second he felt more and more like killing her just to shut her up.

"Would ye stop that! Fer fuck's sake. If I had my gun still,

I'd be tempted to blow yer head off." He glared at her and she stopped pacing.

"Sometimes I wonder if I shoulda just killed ye when I had the chance. I've not forgotten how ye came back into our lives. Don't forget that," she retorted, not looking at him.

"Ach, nonsense. Yer all talk. If ye had the guts, ye'd have killed me the second I shut my eyes that night." He scoffed at her.

Prudence snarled at him. "Well, next time, I won't hesitate."

Khari watched her for a moment. Wet black hair plastered to her head. Skin that made him think she needed to eat more red meat. The ferocity of a wild animal cornered and ready to attack in her eyes. He laughed. "All right, *keine*. I'll take yer word on that."

They lapsed into silence as Khari continued tying planks of wood to their raft. Prudence simmered down after a short while and got back to work. She was irritating, and he was tempted to tear her throat out, but Khari was also perplexed to find that he felt a kinship with her. He recognised her rage. He *understood* it. Maybe they weren't so different.

It took them over an hour to make the raft secure enough that they both felt confident it wouldn't sink as soon as they got on it. The raft was big enough, fairly tall too, as it sat on the sand waiting to be pushed out to sea. He'd managed to keep his knife tucked into his britches in his swim from the ship, and Khari had used it to shape two planks of wood into the rough shape of a paddle. They were by no means perfect, but they were hopefully sufficient enough to get them across that stretch of water.

There was nothing left to do but put it in the water, but now they were there, they both seemed to pause, nervous and unsure about their voyage. They looked out across the water in the direction of Vaerny's shore and back to one another. There was nothing for it. Only do or die.

He had gotten used to the cold since he'd woken on Talah but still, he winced against the frigid water as it rose against his legs, the urge to cry out filling him as it reached his cock. The raft pushed into the sea easily enough. It took two tries before they learnt to lift it at the front as they pushed to avoid it going under. Once they had it in the water and they were up to their waists, they ungracefully scrambled aboard one at a time. Khari held his breath for a moment, waiting to see if it'd sink. It didn't.

Khari positioned himself at the back, cross-legged, and handed a paddle to Prudence. They started slow, scared they'd fall in, sink it, or that the raft would fall apart altogether. The paddles sank into the water, pushing them further away from Talah, towards the only thread of hope they had left. For Prudence, that thread was Cain. Khari could see in her face that she would do whatever, kill whoever to get back to him, that same fatal loyalty that had bound her to Eleanora prior to her death. For Khari, he wasn't quite sure what that thread was.

They paddled across the calm stretch of ocean and Khari felt his tiny flicker of hope kindle into the possibility of more. They might just make it. What they were making it to, he couldn't be sure, but in that moment, he didn't care.

They had almost reached the shore when a plank began to shift. The raft wobbled underneath them and the planks began to loosen.

"Shit! It's breaking up!" Prudence yelled back to him and began to paddle quicker. They were so close to the shore they could almost touch it. Khari swore and paddled aggressively as the raft shrank beneath them, the planks dropping off the main structure one by one. One of the barrels drifted away and the whole front of the raft sank into the sea. Prudence was flung forward into the water, and she lost her paddle. The rest of the raft followed, and within moments, they were both in the water, the raft sinking below the ripples and out of sight.

"Fuck! Swim! Swim! We can make it. It's not far." He paddled towards her and grabbed her arm. "Come on, *keine*. Swim!" Khari pulled at the upper half of her ruined arm until she began to kick and paddle with the other.

It was bitterly cold, and as the freezing temperature began to feel like it was burning his skin and the chill had crept into his bones, it became harder and harder to keep kicking. It was freezing, so easy to just *stop*. But he kept kicking, kept calling to Prudence to keep going, and by some miracle from the Goddess, they both made it to the shore.

P rudence scrambled up the sand dunes in the direction of Bardur. She reached the top half crawling and scanned the landscape before her. The mining town of Bardur was now just little dots of light in the dimming evening. The houses were nestled in between the two tin mines on either side of the prosperous town. As the sun sank deeper towards the horizon, everyone tucked themselves up indoors, the days so much shorter in this bitter winter than the summer evenings where they could work well past dinnertime.

Prudence squinted, desperate to search every scrap of land in the hopes of sighting Cain. He had to be somewhere near. If he wasn't... she shook her head as if she might physically remove the idea from her mind. She had to find him.

Suddenly, a hand clamped over her mouth, and strong arms dragged her to the floor. A muffled scream forced its way out of her throat, and she felt lips against her ear.

"Shh! Shh, *keine*. It's just me." Khari loosened his grip on her ever so slightly and she turned her face to look at him with questioning eyes. He kept a hand over her mouth but jerked his chin to the west away from town, just a short distance beyond the sand dunes.

A group of soldiers, visible only by the few lanterns they had to hand were grappling with someone, preparing to depart in their wagon. A flash of blond hair in amongst the blue coats made Prudence start. Cain was bucking and kicking out against the soldiers that held him in place, shackles binding his wrists. Prudence tried to leap up, but Khari held her down.

"Don't be stupid!" he hissed. "You'll be caught and hung right alongside him. There's nothing you can do for him now."

She strained against Khari's strong hold, but he refused to let her go. A soldier, barely discernible in the dark, slugged Cain across the face, cutting his cheek, and Prudence shrieked. No one seemed to notice Khari or Prudence so close. They were too consumed with laughing and congratulating themselves. They had caught the crown's biggest enemy and would no doubt be rewarded by their sadistic governor. Prudence had seen just how desperate he was to gain favour with the king during their last meeting. Tears sprang to her eyes at the thought of what they might do to Cain. He would be lucky if they just killed him.

The soldiers took Cain roughly by the arms and threw him into the back of their prison wagon, slamming the barred door behind him. He sat up, his face peering out into the night. The soldiers climbed onto the wagon and the driver clicked at the horses to move. The wagon's wheels started turning as Cain caught sight of her. Their gazes locked on each other as he was taken further away until he was finally out of sight.

Khari released Prudence, and she crumpled to the floor and sobbed. "I'm sorry, Prudence. I really am."

Khari placed a hand on her shoulder before standing and heading towards Bardur. For a moment, Prudence considered simply staying where she was, to either die from cold or let people find her and kill her. She wasn't sure she cared which. But despite her best efforts to merely give up, the niggling voice of Eleanora in her head telling her to just *get up, get up, get up* would not stop.

She sighed, begrudgingly pushed herself to stand, and hurried to catch up with Khari.

"Knew you'd follow. Just surprised it happened so quick. Thought for sure you'd whinge for a good while longer first." Khari spoke to her without turning around.

Prudence rolled her eyes and shoved him. "What are ye going to do when ye get to Bardur?"

"Honestly... I don't know."

The wagon's wheels creaked and groaned over every lump and into every hole along the road as they headed to port. Cain winced as they hit another dip, his tailbone bearing the brunt of most of the lurching. He could still see Prudence's face, looking at him with wide eyes through the gloom as he was shoved into the back of the wagon. His relief that she was alive outweighed the pain that he would never see her face again.

Another lurch sent his head back, knocking it against the wagon wall.

"Son of a bitch!" Cain rubbed his head. They had been travelling for a while; they must be reaching port soon. He'd heard one of the bastards that nabbed him say that the governor would be meeting them there. A rider had gone ahead to him with the news that Captain Morris was now apprehended. Cain could picture his smug old face already.

The shackles that held his wrists together chafed against his skin, but at least they permitted him to shuffle to the edge of the wagon to see where they were. They were on the main road towards Malaine and the port. He had travelled down this road with Prudence, off on a wild adventure, gallivanting and stealing as they pleased. It looked much bleaker now.

He could see the ocean in the distance. Soon enough, he would be chucked into the bowels of a ship bound for Aelin, for the castle dungeon, for the noose... Cain had no regrets though. He knew in his gut it would end like this sooner or later. He had been on this path, leading to this end, since he was a child; the moment he and his sister found themselves on a royal ship, sold into a life of servitude. His fate had been preordained since before he was born. His childhood had been a brief spark of light in a world otherwise plunged into darkness. Until Prudence.

It was all worth it. Vengeance for his sister. Meeting Prudence. He could die content knowing it was worth it. His wife was alive and safe now he was in the governor's clutches. Atkey wouldn't waste time and resources searching for her anymore. She could get away from Vaerny and start a new life somewhere. His wife... It still felt so surreal.

They reached the outskirts of Malaine, and the road beneath the wagon changed into cobbles. The soldiers' laughter floated back to Cain from their seat at the front of the wagon. One of the men gestured cupping big breasts in front of him as he started to grind against nothing. "*Fu*ck. It's been too long since I've been inside a tight cunt."

His colleagues laughed and the dark-haired one next to him shoved him hard enough that he almost fell off the seat. "What good is a wife if ye can't eat from the honeypot whenever ye wish?"

The soldier scoffed and shook his head. "She's too fat with that baby in her stomach. Doesn't want me near 'er and I don't wanna be. Get me some of that redhead wench from Madame Francine's. *Mmm*. Ripe 'n' juicy like a peach."

"Yer punching well above yer weight there, Fawcett." The blond one chuckled. "That's premium snatch right there."

"Good fucking thing I pay fer it then, ya fat bastard."

The cobbles of Malaine changed to loose stones as they reached the edge of town and the port.

Khari marched across the heathland in the direction of the nearest houses, with Prudence trying to keep up with his giant paces just behind. She huffed quietly to herself, her ribs ached something fierce, and walking so fast only made it worse. She didn't know what Khari planned to do, but he looked awfully determined, or maybe it was desperation to not sleep outside after being in the freezing ocean.

"Do ye have any money on ye, *keine*?" he asked without turning around.

"Oh, sure. I'll jus' check me bag, shall I? No. I don't have any fucking money. We were in a shipwreck. These aren't even my clothes!" Prudence yelled, flinging her arms up in a rather dramatic fashion.

"Peace. It was a simple question. Ye may have had some in ye pockets earlier. Worth askin', don't ya think?" He shrugged. "Well, we can't sleep outside. Winter fever'll set in faster than a blink, if it hasn't already. We could trade that ring o' yours for a couple a beds." He pointed at Cain's ring on her finger.

"I'd sooner freeze to death!" She clasped the ring tightly against her chest.

"How... how sentimental and *bloody stupid* of ye," Khari scoffed and folded his arms angrily. "Tha' may happen sooner than ye'd wish, then."

Prudence gestured to the horses nearby. "We could find a barn. No one'll be checking their animals once it gets completely dark. We'll be fine until mornin'."

Khari frowned for several moments before nodding reluctantly and heading towards the buildings with a grunt. Prudence followed, making a mental note to keep a close eye on her wedding ring.

"I still think yer fucking stupid," he grumbled.

They stalked through a few rows of buildings, doing their best to stay out of the light, with silent footsteps. Back on Llynne, plenty of homes had small barns, but in this mining town, they were few and far between. Eventually, they came across a modest farm that must have provided crops to much of Bardur's tiny population.

The farmers seemed to have gone to bed for the night. Most

of the lights inside had been put out, leaving only embers in their hearths. Prudence poked her head up to peer into a window. She could see no one moving around in the main room. She watched quietly for a few moments before gesturing for Khari to follow as she made her way around the homestead to the barn and slipped through the door.

The barn was piled high with hay and straw, and a pair of goats stood in the corner, munching on straw and oats. They bleated quietly at the sight of Prudence and Khari but otherwise ignored them. Up in the hayloft, it was surprisingly warm from all of the hay and the animals' body heat. It would make for a decent night's sleep, Prudence thought. She lugged a bale from the edge of the loft to create a makeshift bed and settled down on top of it.

"Well, don't ye look comfortable? I guess this barn idea wasn't such a bad suggestion," Khari mumbled. He kept talking, but Prudence's eyes began to drift shut and his voice faded into the background of her mind almost instantly. The exhaustion of the ship going down, Garrick, losing Cain, and fighting to survive had finally caught up with her. It was hard to believe so much could happen in one day.

The early morning sun began to rise and Prudence blinked, throwing her hand up as a barrier from the bright light. She took a breath and shut her eyes once more before bolting upright. She leapt up from the hay bale and shook Khari.

"Khari! Shit, Khari! Wake up! We slept too long!" She yanked at the lapel of his jacket, trying to hoist him up. The winter sun was decidedly slow at waking and they had fallen prey to relying on her to rouse them from their sleep. Now, they risked being seen.

"What? Ach, fuck." He launched up and grabbed his boots, throwing them on to head straight down the ladder and out the door. They left the safety of the barn hesitantly, as silently as they could manage, peering around every corner looking for sight of the farmer or his wife. But the outside world was calm and quiet. A low mist hung around the hills, no sounds yet coming from the mines. Most of the houses lay still, not yet stirring for the new day.

"So..." Prudence said, "what are we goin' to do now?" She was unused to handing over control, but she was a boat being knocked about by giant waves, unable to change course.

"I'm gonna find a ship to get me off this rock and head to the Northern Border. I 'av no idea what you're gonna do, but tha' ain't my problem." Khari turned away from Prudence and began walking.

She watched him striding away from her. His towering form, dark scowl, and long hair. He was a menacing sight. Since the events of yesterday, she'd almost forgotten her aversion to the man. Their history as enemies at worst, begrudging and hostile colleagues at best. She'd somehow lapsed into acting as if they were friends. She'd almost forgotten *everything* he'd done.

"Ye owe me!" she called.

Khari paused but didn't turn. "If ye'd not taken Elea hostage, she'd still be alive right now."

Prudence ignored the twinge in her gut at her dead friend's name, the knowledge and guilt that really... Eleanora dying was on her and her alone. "Please," she begged. "Ye're all I've got."

Khari sighed slowly and turned around. "I'm not promising shit... but what exactly is it ye seem to think I owe?" A scowl remained on his dark features, hands crammed into his coat pockets, shoulders hitched up around his ears to protect from the cold. He was formidable, with his well-muscled arms and scars evident of many fights. He didn't look the least bit helpful or trustworthy, but he was Prudence's only option. And better the devil you know.

"I need to get to Cain." She took a step towards him, eyes pleading. "I have to save 'im." She wasn't great at begging. In fact, she'd made a point of never begging for anything, from anyone. She was above that. But she was desperate, and Cain's life meant more than any pride. Her pride meant nothing in a world without Cain. She'd already lost her best friend; she wasn't about to lose her husband too.

Khari let out a raucous laugh. "Get to 'im? Yer delusional if ye think *you* can save him. He is bound straight for Aelin and the king's dungeon. Odds are the gov'nor 'as already shipped your beloved captain off with the royal fleet. Ye won't ever see 'im again, *keine*."

Prudence's gaze darkened. "Yer going to the Northern Border! Aelin is on the way! Just get me to Aelin. Please jus' get me that far. I can't do it on my own. Vaerny's the farthest I've ever been." She grasped his arm. "Please. Yer going that way anyway."

Khari stared at her long and hard before scoffing. "Fine!" he yelled. "But tha's my sole part in it. I'm not helping in a jailbreak, and I'm not about to save ye from dying. Got it?"

His brows were lowered so far over his eyes she could barely see them. She might have thought her glare was enough to reduce people to ash, but it had nothing on Khari's. But even so, she didn't feel any malice behind it.

Prudence locked eyes with him. "Deal." Khari began to move away, but she tugged at his arm. "I- I must thank ye fer doin' this. I really, really appreciate it." She held out her hand to shake Khari's.

"All right. I've told ye I'll help, now stop seeming so agreeable. It's unnerving. Go back to being yer obnoxious, aggressive self."

Despite herself, Prudence chuckled. Maybe they'd be able to reach Aelin without killing each other, but it would be a very long journey. Only time would tell. She felt her chest clench as her mind drifted to Cain. Where was he? In the brig of some royal ship, chained like an animal? Were they hurting him? Did he know she was trying to get back to him? The pain swept over her like a wave of nausea before she pushed it down deep, locking it away.

An unfamiliar sense of calm settled over them as they made their way in search of somewhere they could get something warm to eat and decide what they should do next. Aelin was on the far side of The Tides. She didn't know how many ships sailed that far, but she couldn't imagine there were many.

They made their way out of the tiny town of Bardur heading further south. The twin mines that stood at either side of the miner's homes shrank slowly in the distance as they walked in the direction of Dagmaēr. It was even further away from the port in Malaine than Bardur, but they wouldn't get far on empty stomachs. The first priority was food, and whilst Dagmaēr was one of the smaller towns of Vaerny, it was at least busy enough to warrant an inn, according to Khari. His travels selling stolen goods had taken him all over the island many times and much further afield.

Dagmaēr was surprisingly bustling when Khari and Prudence arrived in the little town. Women were busying about down the street, heading in and out of buildings. The butchers were so busy their door remained open as people ducked in and out, buying meat for their dinners.

Chickens clucked in unison as they pecked the dusty road in search of insects. A cart creaked as it moved down the road. Its left wheel lurched into a hole and splashed muddy rainwater all over a man's trousers. Prudence bit back a smile as he yelled obscenities at the driver.

"Right. Food this way." Khari gestured down the road, and soon Prudence could smell freshly baked bread and meat cooking over a fire. Her mouth watered. There had been many times in her life when she'd gone without any food, and it became easy to forget about it with plenty else on her mind, but the smells brought the intense hunger back immediately.

The inn came into view as they rounded the corner. Smoke wafted slowly out of the chimney. A dog tied up out front lay happily in the sun, warming his belly. A fly buzzed around his head, and after a moment, the dog gnashed his teeth at the tiny disturbance.

Prudence gave a wide berth as she headed for the door.

"Don't tell me yer scared of a little pup." Khari laughed, a deep sound that erupted from his belly.

Prudence shot him a glare. "Not scared. Jus' wary, tha's all." At Khari's amused smirk, she sighed. "All those sharp teeth," she mumbled.

Khari snorted, trying to bite back his chuckles.

Inside, the inn was mostly empty. An old man, clearly familiar with drunken stupors, sat or rather slumped at the bar in the corner as the barkeep kept himself busy wiping the already clean tables. The pair took two seats at a table and Prudence called the barkeep over.

He was a tall, spindly fellow with crumbs of the Gods only knew what in his beard, and the stench of mead radiated off of him. He looked as if he lived solely off of the alcohol behind his bar. Prudence wondered if he was responsible for the food they served. She hoped not. The man dumped two meads in front of them and cleared his throat.

"Will ye be wantin' sommin to eat? The cook's got some meat fresh in the pot," he asked.

Prudence silently said a prayer of thanks and nodded earnestly. Soon, they were stuffing their faces. Their plates were piled high with beef, pork, and hunks of bread. Khari tore into a chunk of veal with his teeth, and the juices dripped down his chin. Prudence's stomach cramped from the sudden onslaught of food, but she ignored it, eating as much as she could manage. She wiped her mouth with a sleeve and reached for her drink.

The door swung open as two men walked in.

Prudence's drink clanked to the floor and her mouth hung open in surprise as they looked at each other. Gabe and Thomas rushed to the table, and Prudence was overwhelmed with arms pulling her in for hugs.

"Wh-what are ye doing 'ere? I... I thought ye were dead." Prudence smiled weakly, still taking in the sight of them in front of her.

"'Tis a blessin' to see ye, mistress. I fear most 'o the crew were not so fortuitous. We barely made it out alive. She sank so fast." Thomas's mournful face brought tears to Prudence's eyes.

"Is...?"

"Rupe is alive," said Thomas, and Prudence breathed a sigh of relief. "His leg's pretty badly wrecked. Can't walk on it. Not sure if he ever will again. We left him to rest while we came to get some food. We're all starved."

"How are ye even here? Khari and I walked from Bardur after... well, after a hell of a journey. We barely made it," said Prudence. She couldn't imagine what happened to everyone after she and Cain had jumped from *The Maiden's* deck.

Gabe grabbed a seat next to Khari and pinched some bread from his plate. "I don't even know what happened. She started taking on water. Next thing I knew, I was waking up on a beach. The Gods only know how much sea water I vomited up. I started walking and came across Thomas here trying to set Rupert's leg. Bigger piece o' luck than I could ever have imagined."

"Rupe pulled me from the surf," said Thomas. "No fucking clue how he managed with his mangled leg, but he did. Don't know what I did to deserve him." Thomas smiled softly. Prudence offered the seat beside her and he took it.

"It's good to see ye, lads. I've been stuck with the new Mrs, 'ere. Not the easiest of persons, ye know." Khari cast his eyes at Prudence before tucking back into his food.

Prudence glared at him and the men chuckled. Gabe turned to Prudence. "But, the captain? He-"

"He's alive!" Prudence cut in. "He was taken by soldiers. He's probably on a ship bound for Aelin already." She couldn't keep her voice from trembling slightly at the end, despite her best attempts.

"Bollocks!" Thomas slammed his hand down on the table. "What a terrible way to go for such a tremendous man." He sighed and raised his glass in Cain's honour. A deep silence fell over the group.

So many lives. So much loss they had all experienced. How many of the crew had survived? Just this lucky five and Cain? Their friends, their family...

"This is not his end!" Prudence cried, her voice so loud she startled the drunk at the bar. "I am not leaving him to rot. He is my husband and a good man. Ye would abandon yer captain to the noose because of some difficulty?"

She eyed the men in front of her. Thomas reluctantly met her eye, the apologies clear on his face as Gabe stared hard at the table. Prudence felt her stomach drop. They weren't going to help. She was on her own. May the Gods look out for Cain if she was his only chance. She'd need all the luck they could bestow as well.

"I'm sorry, Prudence. I have to think about Rupert. I have to think about my love, just as you must yours. I wish the captain was here with us right now, I truly do." Thomas placed a hand on hers and squeezed gently. "I'm sorry."

Prudence nodded with reluctant acceptance. "I understand, Thom. I don't like it, but I understand. Gabe?"

The young man wouldn't look up from the table. "I can't go through it again," he mumbled.

"What?" Prudence snipped.

"There've been too many. I won't watch any other friends die. I spent years following Captain Morris. Years. I won't do it anymore. I'm tired of mourning people."

"So, ye'll allow Cain to walk to his death?"

"Isn't that what you did with Miss Elea?" Gabe retorted,

finally meeting her eye.

The words were like a gut punch. A sharp jab to her ribs that immediately disabled her. She rose from the table and stalked out of the inn without another word. Let them do what they will. She would save Cain alone. The Gods would meter out their punishment at death's door. The worst of which was saved for traitors.

CHAPTER THREE

NO TURNING BACK

The ship swayed aggressively to and fro as the waters outside grew rougher. Each jostle tugged at the shackle around Cain's neck. His skin felt raw after hours of aggravation. At least it was quiet now. The sole other prisoner on the ship bound for Aelin had finally shut up and fallen asleep. His constant panicking and mindless chattering caused Cain's mind to envision a myriad of ways to silence him for good.

He was unsure how long they had already been at sea, stuck down in the brig unable to see the sky, but at a guess, they had left port half a day ago. He tried his best to ignore the familiar yet painful memories that threatened to fill his mind. The old days of servitude to the Royal Fleet that so severely changed the shape of his life forever.

Everything around him sent his mind back to that place. The sounds of men working up on deck. The smells of animals, of straw and filth. The evidence of rats around the room. The odd piece of shit, teeth marks in sacks spilling supplies out onto the floor.

"Full fucking circle," Cain muttered to himself. He'd always known he'd be back, that he'd end up right here, journeying to his death. He'd accepted it, embraced it at one point, in fact. Avenging Florence's death had been worth it. Worth his life and anything else he'd had to give. But since meeting Prudence... for a moment, he thought he'd outrun his past for good. That they'd start a new life together, without any more pain for either of them. For a moment.

He wondered what Prudence was doing then. He hoped she was safe. The anguish in her eyes when they saw each other had left a knot in his stomach. He would never see those piercing blue eyes again. Cain closed his eyes, trying to keep the memory of Prudence's face at the forefront of his mind for as long as possible.

Her dark brows furrowed in anger. The moonlight reflecting off her pale skin. Her wild unruly black hair blowing around her face. She was a sight to behold. How lucky he'd been to be hers. At least she could stop running now.

The ship lurched to the left, suddenly yanking the shackle around his neck, making him cough. The prisoner beside him woke with a start, banging his head on the wall.

"Ow, shit!" He rubbed his head and looked at Cain. "How long was I asleep?" He looked slightly younger than Cain, with a rough smattering of stubble across his jaw.

"Does it matter?" asked Cain. "Minutes or hours, we still

have months until we reach the noose."

The young man shuddered and brought his knees up to his chest. "Well, yer a fuckin' pleasure, aren't ye? Gods, going to be a bloody miserable few months before I die stuck 'ere with *you*."

"No point beating around the bush. We're dead men. Best square all your troubles away with your Gods." Cain leant back against the wall, expression blank. He was here by his own actions, and for that, he would accept his fate.

"I 'spose ye want to die, do ya?" the man scoffed.

"What's your name?" asked Cain.

"Jed."

"Well, Jed... I've done things that have led me right here to this very spot, as I'm sure you have. There's no changing the past, and I don't really believe in wishing on stars, so there isn't anything else to do is there? Naught but think back on the luck I've had."

"Luck?" cried Jed. "Yer chained up in the bowels of a royal ship bein' shipped off to die as the king watches. Hardly seems like luck."

Cain shifted until he was facing Jed. "I can die a happy man. I had years of freedom with my men. I got to meet the most... incredible woman. Got to know her, be with her, love her. And if I've got a little luck left, once I'm gone, I'll get to see my sister again. That's a lot of luck as far as I'm concerned. More than one man might deserve."

The younger man fell silent for a moment, taking in what the captain had said, and Cain settled back down in the comfortable quiet.

"I still think yer fuckin' insane," Jed quipped.

Cain laughed.

Prudence pulled her jacket tighter around her shoulders against the chill. She'd been sitting in the same position for a few hours by now, and her legs had long since gone numb, but she refused to head back to the inn. If they wouldn't help Cain, she had no use for them.

She nudged the stones at her feet with the toe of her boot. She didn't want to think about how difficult this would all be alone. She couldn't. Not when Cain needed her. The sound of boots crunched behind her and she turned to see Khari.

"What?" she asked sharply. "Ye think I was too harsh?"

Khari scoffed. "I've never felt loyalty like you do to yer captain and I don't intend to. Ye can be as harsh as ye like. I couldn't care less, *keine*." He sat down next to her. "Besides, seems we're in luck. The gents know of a ship. A ship we can hopefully barter passage on."

"What? Where? The only port is in Malaine. That's about a fortnight's walk away." She couldn't wait that long, but what other choice was there? There was no other way off this hunk of rock. Gods, if she could swim the length of The Tides to get to Cain, she would. Every moment he got further out of her reach. A swell of nausea rose up her throat, and her pulse quickened in panic. She wasn't going to get there. He was going to die alone, wondering what happened to her, why she wasn't there. Prudence tasted bile in her mouth and spat it out on the ground.

"Fuckin' hell. Ye need to calm down. We don't need to get to Malaine. Nothing to panic about, *shit*. Not all ships dock in a port." At her confused expression, Khari cast a wink at her. "Not those looking to hide." He brushed his nose smugly.

Prudence couldn't help the smile that began to spread across her face as realisation dawned. Maybe there was hope, even if it was just a little. "So what's the plan?" she asked.

"I will go and speak to the captain, see if we can't strike up a deal." He picked at the dirt under his fingernails absentmindedly.

"Why wouldn't I go with ye?"

"Well…" Khari trailed off.

"Well, what?!" Prudence's voice rose rapidly as she waited to hear what he was going to say. She couldn't imagine what acceptable answer could come after 'well'.

"Well… yer not exactly the kind of person they're used to dealing with. Ye may have had yer way amongst *The Maiden's* crew, but come on, Prudence. You know that's not the way it works out 'ere. Ye might be a force to be reckoned with, but ye must know the dangers of getting too comfortable acting like a man. They've killed women fer less, ye know." His voice was uncharacteristically soft, as if the fact pained him.

Prudence chuckled lightly. "Ye sound like ye care what happens to me, Khari."

"I may not like ye, *keine*, but I don't relish the thought o' someone stringin' ye up, or worse. My mama didn't raise me that way."

"Yer ma? I've never heard you mention her. Where is she now?" Prudence asked.

"Back home, across the ocean. I was born on The Eastern Shores to the Ta'ih. My mother is the matriarch of our people. She decides where and when we move our homes across the sand. She protects us, guides us, teaches us." Khari stared ahead as if lost in his memories.

Prudence wondered what it must have been like. To grow up like that, as someone important, in a tight-knit community. It seemed so staunchly different from her own upbringing. She was almost jealous. "It sounds wonderful," she said. "Why would ye leave?"

"It wasn't by choice, believe me."

They fell silent for a moment, Prudence giving him room. Khari eventually turned to look at her. "So, ye'll let me go speak to this Captain Beckett alone?" he asked.

Prudence pursed her lips. "I can't not go!"

Khari rolled his eyes. "Fer fuck's sake, *keine*. Don't be so bloody obstinate! I'm not trying to screw ye over, I'm trying to fuckin' help ye, despite my instincts tellin' me to do otherwise." He paced in front of her. "I can still leave ye sat 'ere in the dirt. Maybe I damn well should."

"I'm not gonna just sit and wait, do ye hear me?!" Prudence yelled, her glare cast right at Khari. "I am coming. Whether ye fuckin' like it or not. Do you understand?" She lowered her voice, the final sentence coming out with a measured calm.

Khari breathed through his nose sharply. "Fine! But if this turns bad, I'm leaving ye to die in the sand where ye fall." He stalked over to her to stare down at her. "Do. You. Understand?" He towered over her, almost twice her height.

Prudence felt her body instinctively start to recoil, but she stopped herself. She wasn't going to let him intimidate her. She was very familiar with men getting too close, and she was fucking done with it. "Understood."

The town square was bustling with people despite the dark clouds that threatened a torrent of rain. Khari and Prudence weaved in between baskets and small children as they made their way down the road towards food. Today, they would meet with the smuggler Thomas had told him about. Today, they'd secure a way off this godsforsaken spit of land... Khari hoped.

They made their way towards the middle of town, back to the inn where they had met Gabe and Thomas the day before. It didn't feel like a day had passed. It felt like mere moments and yet years all at once. Khari supposed that it was what people meant by time standing still. That he was so close and still so far from leaving this place. Time was tormenting him.

The walk to the inn was busier than expected, with dozens of people making their way in the same direction as the pair. Prudence barely seemed to register them, her thoughts on food and Cain no doubt, but Khari frowned and grunted as a small woman shoved past, stepping on his foot. *Bloody cow.* He resisted the momentary temptation to yell at her and followed Prudence on her hunt for breakfast.

Khari had been to Dagmaēr several times over the years. It wasn't a particularly large town, and he and Avery hadn't had that many clients that bought their smuggled goods, but there was a brothel madame and a local lord who had greatly benefitted from their services. They had had a knack for sourcing items not available in this part of the world. Items that proved very popular with the gentry, especially at parties.

He felt a twinge of... not quite grief, but sadness, thinking about Avery. They hadn't been overly familial with one another, but they had worked alongside each other for a few years. It was still a loss he was not completely used to yet. Avery hadn't been a nice man, but someone should miss him, even if it was only a little.

A crowd had begun to form as they neared the centre of the square. Khari and Prudence pushed through a few people at the edge of the large group, heading for the inn. Khari's height allowed him to peer over most heads, and he could just make out some men in the middle, drawing the crowd. There were three of them, yelling into the audience excitedly as one of them held out an old cap for coins. Another held onto a thick rope that was attached to some kind of animal. It was filthy and stilted in its movements like it was lame or perhaps injured. He couldn't help but pity the poor thing.

People paid the men to get closer to inspect the beast, poking and prodding it, jeering and shrieking when it reacted. A child hurled a tomato at it, hitting it square in the head. The tomato juice dripped down its body. It recoiled slightly as if it felt the hit but couldn't retreat.

"I'm hungry. C'mon, let's get something to eat," Prudence muttered, her demeanour sullen and her face not trying to hide it.

"All right, all right. Give me a moment." Khari brushed her off, wanting to see what all the fuss was about. "Look, why don't ye go into the inn and I'll catch up with ye." He watched as she stalked off, slamming open the door of the inn. Once she was out of sight, his attention turned back to the men and their animal. He couldn't work out what it was. It wasn't like anything he had seen before. Some deformed monster they'd found who knows where. But it was then he noticed it. It wasn't walking on all fours. Two legs... and two arms.

It was human.

Within moments, Khari had pushed his way to the front of the crowd, both fascinated and revolted. What happened to it? To... her? Khari thought it was a young woman. She was much shorter than he with a very different build. He tried to get a look at her face but her gaze remained downcast, unfocused, unalive. Her skin was sagging and grey, as if it didn't sit right on her body. The stench was overpowering, and he couldn't breathe through his nose without it making his eyes water.

The more he looked, the more he noticed how *wrong* it all was. The drooping features. The gaping holes in her skin. The jerky way she moved. Underneath all the filth, her hair was a fiery red. It made Khari's blood run cold. It wasn't possible. It shouldn't be possible. But he couldn't deny what his eyes were seeing. He tugged at her, forcing her head up. Red hair. Brown eyes. Still *her* despite the glaze and deathly pallor. A bullet hole in her chest, now ragged and black from decay.

He shook her softly, but her eyes still wouldn't meet his. There was no recognition there. She might have been crouched in front of him, but she was dead.

It made him want to vomit. Clearly, Prudence's arm hadn't been ruined for naught. *Prudence*. She couldn't know about this. She'd turn it into a pointless crusade that would achieve nothing. The girl was dead. Khari didn't feel joy about it, but there was nothing to be done. Except maybe to dispatch the poor thing. To put her out of her misery. If she could even feel anything. He couldn't tell. There was no light behind her eyes. No words on her tongue. Seemingly no thoughts in her brain. She was a shell.

No, he would ensure Prudence would never find out. Better for them both. They had plans he wasn't willing to risk.

He left the square as swiftly as possible and entered the inn. He found Prudence already halfway through a plate of eggs, meat, and bread. Khari's stomach rumbled, but he wilfully ignored it, the stench of death still thick in his nostrils.

"We should make haste. Time has gotten away from us. It isn't long before we need to meet the captain." He ushered her out of her seat, trying to appear as normal as possible. Prudence swiped one last hunk of cheese from her plate and allowed Khari to push her out the door.

"All right. Fuck, Khari. I'm moving! We'll get there soon enough. Sometimes, you are the strangest man, I swear." She rolled her eyes but did as he bid.

Despite the crowd still filling up the town square, Khari managed to steer Prudence away and down the road. Back towards the shore and their meeting, and away from her past.

The roar of the waves was almost deafening as they walked along the shore edge towards the cove. It was completely hidden from sight from their view at the beach. This, Prudence supposed, was what made it the perfect place for smugglers to hide out. They followed the path of rocky outcrop until it finally came into view.

The cove was small, its cliff walls unbelievably high. The crumbling edges made Prudence uneasy, looking as if they might collapse at any moment. The water was a bright blue, so clear you could see far below the surface. It must have been deep, as their ship had anchored not far away, but Prudence felt like she'd be able to wade in and touch the ocean floor.

She caught sight of the group of men on the other side of the cove. There were five of them, deep in conversation that slowly petered out as they noticed Prudence and Khari approaching. Heads swivelled in their direction and focused on Prudence in a way not dissimilar to wild dogs spotting a rabbit. She gulped quietly, preparing herself to come face to face with them. Khari put an arm out in front of her, stopping her in her tracks.

"Right. Ye've come along. Now I'm gonna talk to Beckett alone." He strode off before she could answer.

"Fuckin' prick," she grumbled and shoved her hands in the pockets of her britches. She watched Khari greet Captain Beckett. The captain glanced over at her, his expression unreadable. The minutes ticked by as Prudence grew more and more bored.

Eventually, Khari returned to her.

"So? Will they give us passage?" she asked.

"They will... for a price."

"But we don't have anything," sighed Prudence. They had a few pennies. Certainly not enough for a journey.

"Not nothin'." Khari looked pointedly at Prudence's ring finger. "Look, do ye truly ever wish to see yer husband again? Or would ye rather cling on to some piece a' jewellery?" he asked.

Prudence hated the idea, but she knew Khari had a point. She didn't care for the ring because it was valuable, and she'd do anything to get Cain back. What good was a ring if she never got to see him again? She didn't care more about this symbol than her husband.

She held out her hand to Khari so he could slide the ring off.

Her left hand was considerably lighter without it. It had left a mark round her finger just below the knuckle. The ghost of her wedding ring. She clenched her fist to stop the shaking.

"It will be worth it, *keine*. 'Tis only a bit o' metal," said Khari.

He gave her a brief nod before returning to the crew. She watched him talk to Captain Beckett for another moment. They both cast a glance back at Prudence and she rankled. What were they talking about? And what did it have to do with her? Khari handed the ring over and shook Beckett's hand.

Acceptable payment. It seemed they would be travelling to Aelin on board *The Wayward Damned*. Prudence tightened her knot of hair and made her way over to the men. Now they'd agreed, it was time for introductions.

The Wayward Damned departed from their hidden cove just two days later. The crew of *The Wayward* had swiftly offloaded the items they had smuggled to Vaerny when they first arrived, and after restocking for their voyage, they were ready to make way.

Prudence was both surprised and delighted to find that she wasn't the only woman aboard. An elegant woman by the name of Vivienne, paramour of the captain's brother, resided on the ship with the men. And whilst she clearly wasn't treated as one of the crew, she appeared to hold the men's respect. Prudence soon saw why. Vivienne carried herself with the poise of royalty and acted as such. She glided across the deck, far more graceful than even the most seaworthy legs.

She was tall in comparison to Prudence. Her ash brown hair was wavy and fell way beyond her hips. Her steely eyes were surrounded by thick, long lashes. Her face was sharp with high cheekbones and sunken cheeks. The words *ethereal* and *haunting* came to Prudence's mind.

She was... different. She rarely let her gaze meet anyone else's, eyes often cast at the sky as she drifted about the deck humming to herself. No one ever spoke directly to Vivienne, despite the many eyes always staring at her. Prudence got the distinct impression that this was because of Julian.

She had only met the captain's brother once briefly so far, but he had certainly made an impression. He was broad-shouldered with a slim waist and a mop of black hair that hung over his eyes, obscuring them from view. Something about him unsettled Prudence.

Where his brother was particularly formal and calm, Julian was erratic and almost predatory. He stalked over to them when called, his gaze overly intense. He had held Prudence's eye far longer than normal. She found herself, numerous times, catching sight of him chuckling or smirking to himself, unaware of what was so amusing. He was fond of flicking his knife into whatever wood was nearby as if he were hunting.

The only time he seemed genuine and kind was when he spoke to Vivienne. He called her his 'little dove,' and Prudence noticed he often murmured sweet words to her and was always her rapt audience. Despite his intimidating exterior, he was undoubtedly in love with Vivienne and she with him.

Prudence and Khari had been permitted two hammocks at the far end of the sleeping quarters. They had agreed to work as part of the crew for the few months it would take to reach Aelin. She didn't have any belongings, as nothing had survived *The*

Maiden's crash except for the men's long coat she had stolen, and the clothes on her back, so there was nothing to unpack.

Khari had dumped his boots on the floor and was currently snoring obnoxiously loud after spending the day working with the riggers. Prudence had found herself assisting Penn, the sailing master. He was a kind man, she guessed between thirty-five and forty years old. He had hair cropped so close to his head that the scars underneath were visible. Prudence had learned that he'd been part of the crew for almost ten years now and was very well respected amongst the men. He'd quickly made Prudence feel at ease and helped her get the lay of the land sailing with a new crew.

According to Penn, it was a fairly good group. Most had grown up on the sea and were either born into this life or took to it as young men with nowhere else to go. They worked in moving stolen goods, much like Khari did when Prudence had first known him, travelling all over The Western Tides. On the way to Aelin, they had a schedule to stop off in Napor and Pirn, to move wares and stock up for the next leg of the voyage.

It would soon be a new moon, indicating the start of a new month. A few months to get to Aelin Isle. Another, at least, to cross the country to get to the castle and where Cain would be sent to wait for trial.

Prudence felt an overwhelming apprehension at how long it would take, but she took comfort in the knowledge that they weren't far behind the ship taking Cain. She could do this. She would do this. With her conviction renewed, she turned over in the creaking hammock and tried to sleep.

She spent most of her days at sea helping out wherever she was instructed. It was a peculiar experience; the only life she'd known at sea had been on *The Maiden*. Everything was different on this ship. The crew were all unfamiliar. The ship wasn't the same. She missed the laughter and jokes of Mr. Lowell, the less-than-stellar cooking of Mr. Duarte, the smell of old books in Cain's cabin. And despite how silly it sounded, she missed the creak and yaw of the rigging. She could've sworn it sounded different on this ship.

Abraham, the quartermaster, had put her to work down below, cleaning up after Mr. Hare, the ship's carpenter. Prudence found the work strangely satisfying. It kept her busy and stopped her mind from wandering to the darker thoughts that kept inching their way in.

Mr. Hare was relatively nice. A man of few words and more grunts. He didn't seem to expect too much from Prudence and she was quite content with that.

They worked side by side until the dinner bell rang and they followed the smell of food. Sigurd, the ship's cook, dumped a large pan of some kind of stew in the middle of the table and everyone dug in. The meat was a tad chewy, but Prudence didn't mind at all. She'd worked up quite an appetite and couldn't shovel the food in quickly enough. She washed it down with a tankard of rum and rose from the table.

"Where ya going?" asked Julian in a slow drawl. His eyes were pinned on her from under his brows.

Prudence felt a little like a rabbit that knows it's in the sights of a hunter. "I fancy getting some fresh air before heading to bed. It's been a long day," she said slowly. She hoped that he wouldn't take that as an invitation to join her. She glanced at Vivienne watching them intently, although not with jealousy, more like... amusement.

"Don't catch a chill," Julian sang mockingly. "Wouldn't want you getting ill, would we?"

Vivienne giggled quietly and licked some stew off her finger. She waved to Prudence as she ascended the stairs to the deck somewhat hurriedly in an attempt to get away from them.

Prudence rolled her eyes. She didn't understand those two. Whenever they spoke to people it was like they had some joke no one else was privy to. She wondered if they actually joked at the others' expense or if that in itself was the joke. That you'd never know.

The air had cooled considerably as the sun had started to go down, its glow now only a half circle over the horizon, bathing everything in a pale orange light. She loved the view from out at sea. Only the soft waves, the horizon, and the occasional gull in sight. No land for miles. It made the world feel very big.

Prudence liked that idea. A big world meant lots of places. Lands nothing like she had known. Infinite towns and landscapes to explore. Where might she end up? That was the beauty of it—she didn't know. She and Cain could travel far and wide to find their perfect home and they wouldn't settle. No, they'd keep searching until they found somewhere just for them. Somewhere they could just be. To say farewell to The Western Tides completely and make their way to the other side of the world. Where no one knew them and they could finally find some peace.

The winter air was fresh and sharp against her face. It felt good. She had always preferred the colder months, even when it made things harder. The village of Llynne may have always despised the lashing rain and freezing cold, but it gave Prudence hope. She longed to see flecks of white coat the ground.

Whilst it never happened often—being by the sea meant it mostly rained and stormed—she had seen snow a few times in her life and it always filled her with wonder. It was so beautiful. Sheer white covering the entire landscape, hiding the browns and reds of heathland. It made the world look better. Quieter too. Being surrounded by snow made Prudence feel like she could be the only person in the world. It was serene.

She hoped to see it again one day. She'd never return to Llynne, but perhaps wherever they went could be cold. They could live somewhere that saw snow all the time. It made Prudence think of fires in the hearth, warm bread, and stew to eat as they curled up inside for warmth.

Snow would fall softly through the windows and they could spend the day tucked up inside, telling stories and singing songs. Cain would tell stories of his adventures at sea. Prudence would listen intently, imagining Cain and his men fighting soldiers, exploring far mountains, trekking across vast sandy beaches. It would be perfect.

She looked up at the greying clouds above *The Wayward* and smiled. They would see that life one day. She knew it. A few raindrops began to fall. They wet her cheeks and hair. She blinked as one landed in her eye, but she didn't look away. The rain was cleansing. It was washing away her worry. Washing away the disasters of recent days, making way for that bright future.

The more time that passed on *The Wayward Damned*, the more frustrated Prudence got with her arm. The magical rot that had spread up her forearm hadn't progressed any further since Cain had taken her out of that hut, but it wasn't healing either. It looked like grey tree bark. It was hard, far harder than skin, a mottled grey that snaked up from her fingers to her elbow. Her veins had turned black and swollen, permanently raised off the skin as if bulging. It was basically dead.

She felt nothing, not cold, nor heat nor pain. She couldn't move her fingers at all. It was as if she were carrying around a log. A weight holding her back even with everyday things. She fucking hated it. She had mutilated herself for nothing.

"Couldn't ye try to find another witch to fix it?" asked Khari, suddenly appearing at her side, making her jump.

She looked at him blankly.

"Don't think I haven't noticed yer silent stewing, *keine*. I know it's driving ye mad." He nudged her ruined arm and gave her a slight smile. "Besides... could be worse."

Prudence grunted. "I fail to see how."

"It could have carried on up yer arm all over ye 'til ye were nothin' but a living statue. It might have killed ye, but we can't know for sure."

She looked down at her arm again, in all its ugly glory. Taunting her. As if it were saying *you're broken now. Just give up.* It was revolting. Most of the crew had been painfully polite, looking anywhere but her rotten arm. It just made her feel more like a freak. After all this time, it seemed she was going to be stuck like this forever. Unless...

"Cut it off," Prudence demanded.

"Excuse me?"

"I cannot live with this anymore. I'm losing my mind! We must remove it."

Khari's glance told Prudence that he wasn't sure if she was serious or if she had indeed lost her mind. Maybe she had. They stared at one another for a long time. Finally, he looked away and sighed. "Fine. If yer serious, then I'll fetch Mr. Hare. But I think yer making a mistake. Good luck saving yer beloved captain when yer dead."

Prudence opened her mouth to speak, but he was already striding away from her. No matter. She did not care for his concerns. He did not have this burden attached to him. Soon, it would no longer be attached to her either.

Surprisingly, Mr. Hare shared Prudence's thoughts without hesitation. Whilst the rot hadn't spread at all, he expressed his concern about what it might be doing inside Prudence. He and Captain Beckett agreed that, considering its potential impact on her, it was best to remove it as soon as possible.

Before she knew it, Prudence was lying on a table they had set up in the infirmary as Mr. Hare tightened a ligature above her elbow. She barely felt it. Her heart was hammering so hard she couldn't focus on anything else. She wanted it gone, but she couldn't control the fear snaking up her spine at the sight of the saw.

It was as if she could already feel it cutting through the bone, the teeth sawing back and forth until the inevitable *crack* of her arm being removed from her body. She could do this. She had to do this. She thought she might be sick.

Captain Beckett had instructed Khari, Cyrus the carpenter's mate, Elliott and Tor, two sailors Prudence had not met previously, and Carter the cabin boy to assist in the surgery. To hold her down so she couldn't move too much as Mr. Hare removed her arm. It struck her then how young Carter was. He couldn't have been more than twelve, and he looked as frightened as she felt. He reminded her of Taj. Sweet Taj who had just wanted to be part of a ship. She deserved the pain she was about to endure. She deserved everything that had happened to her.

Khari shoved a drink into her hand and she drank it immediately. "Is that it? Surely ye have more I can drink?"

"I'm afraid not, Miss." Mr. Hare turned to face her, momentarily pausing his preparation of an array of tools. "Too much and ye may bleed out before we've even removed it. Tha's all ye get until after."

Prudence scowled, her anger giving her a small amount of bravado. She clenched her teeth. "Let's get started."

Once Mr. Hare had prepared all of his tools, he instructed the men to each take hold of Prudence. Two of them braced at her shoulders, two at her legs, and Cyrus at Mr. Hare's side to assist him. They had given her a block of wood to bite down on and it sat wedged in her mouth as she anxiously awaited the first cut.

A sharp point entered her skin and she bit down hard, a whistle of a scream dying in her throat. It was going to get much worse than this.

"Cyrus, lad, a bucket if ye will," called Mr. Hare, and Cyrus placed a wooden bucket underneath Prudence's arm. The drip drip drip of her blood became faster and more frequent as he cut into the flesh, peeling away the skin and muscle underneath to get to the bone.

Sweat began to bead on her forehead and her jaw ached tremendously from biting as she tried to keep her whimpers to a minimum. With every new cut, she would twitch, and the men put more pressure on to hold her still. It felt like eternity when Mr. Hare finally put the knife down. He wiped his hands on a cloth and Prudence breathed a momentary sigh of exhaustion, tiredness hitting her like a great wave with the absence of new pain.

"Pass the catlin, lad."

Cyrus handed his master a wicked blade with double edges, so sharp and thin it was almost rounded. "Men, hold her tight."

As Mr. Hare used the catlin to cut into her arm, what felt like scraping at the bone, she couldn't hold it in anymore and let out an inhuman wail. She bucked and kicked against the table, but the men held firm, pushing down at her shoulders and thighs so she could not move. Mr. Hare peeled away what looked like very thin skin, like a threadbare sheet, almost see-through. It was then that Prudence's vision went hazy and she promptly vomited over the edge of the table at Tor's feet.

Time passed incoherently then. Prudence's mind must have given up at points because, in one moment, she was vomiting on the floor, the next, her blurry gaze was watching Mr. Hare bearing down on her, saw in hand, carving back and forth through the bone. She screamed again, tears streaking her face, and then as if outside her own body, she heard herself sobbing like a child.

She woke again to the blazing sensation of her arm on fire and she let out an unholy shriek like a banshee, thrashing against her captors, trying to get away from the danger.

"Peace. Peace, *keine*," stressed Khari as he forced her still. She fought against him with all her might until the burning began to subside. She found she was quite weak and soon could not fight him at all. "Mr. Hare here just had to cauterise the wound. Yer arm is gone, Pru. 'Tis almost done, I promise ye."

Her breaths came in short, sharp bursts, panting like a dog. She couldn't get any air into her lungs. It took her a moment to fully understand what he had said. Finally, she cast a glance down at her limb... half of which was now no longer attached but sitting in a bucket of water on the floor. She stared at it for a long moment, with the odd sensation that that was somebody else's arm. It couldn't possibly be hers. Her vision swam again and the faces of the men were lost in darkness.

When she regained consciousness once more, a flap of skin had been stitched over the cauterised stump and a bandage wrapped around the entirety. Elliott remained seated on a stool beside the table, his eyes flickering slightly as he dozed.

"What time is it?" she asked, her voice croaky and throat dry.

Elliott's eyes opened immediately and he shot up from his slumped position. "Oh, uh... it's evening, Miss. Supper has already passed, but I'm sure cook would be able to bring you somethin'."

Prudence shook her head slowly. "N-no. A drink?" She felt unbelievably thirsty.

Elliott nodded and handed her one.

"And Mr. Hare?"

"I'll fetch him for ye." He dashed out the door to find the carpenter.

As she waited, Prudence found herself staring at what was left of her arm. She touched the edge of the bandage gingerly. It ached sharply, the distinct pain of cut flesh, but much worse than she had ever experienced before. A tear slipped out the corner of her eye and she sniffed. She had done it. It had been death twice over, but she had survived. She was fine, and once she had healed, she would learn to manage with only one hand at her service.

What would Cain think? Would he be proud of her? "Cain, I'm coming. I swear it," she whispered, her eyes squeezed tight in promise.

When Mr. Hare returned to the room, she startled, quickly regaining her composure. He assessed the stump of her arm for a moment, checking the bandaging and the surrounding skin before looking at her face. "Well, you've got a healthy colour, considering. Provided you rest for now, you should heal up just fine." He helped her to sit up very slowly and handed her another drink.

"How long?"

"How long?" asked Mr. Hare.

"How long until I'm well again?"

"A month or so," he mused, admiring his work once more. "We'll change this," he gestured to the bandage, "in a few days. Check how the skin is doing. Make sure it's not dying. Ye'll need to rest completely for that time, then we'll see how we go. But it won't be a swift process."

CHAPTER FOUR

AN UNEXPECTED REVELATION

Prudence found herself falling into a comfortable routine as time passed on *The Wayward Damned*. Now that her arm had mostly healed and only needed to be checked every so often, she spent most of her waking hours working alongside Penn as well as helping Mr. Hare when he needed it.

The ship had been making great progress. With the wind in her favour, they soon found themselves nearing Pirn. It was a relatively small island according to the captain, but it was far bigger than Vaerny. To Prudence, it felt like a huge country.

The Wayward made berth along Pirn's southern coast, a short ways from the port, but well hidden from any passing royal ships, and the crew took to unloading dozens of boxes for their latest patron, a local governor, who was apparently not ashamed to look the other way if a few crates of The Southern Border's best wines found their way into his cellar each month, along with his favourite cigars.

They finished unloading the crates onto a pony and trap, and Captain Beckett headed off to the governor's estate, with a few men just to be safe. That left Prudence and the rest of the crew free to do as they wished until the morning.

Prudence followed a few of the men up a rocky path that led to the nearest town. She could already see roofs and chimneys in the distance. It was a fine place, far richer than she had ever known. As she made her way down the path, she could see smoke streaming up into the sky and hear the sounds of people in the street. She rounded the corner and gasped.

The town was incredible to behold. Tall, stone buildings lined every street. Colourful banners draped across the walkways from one house to another. The streets were full of people gathering, talking loudly, eating food from stalls set up on every corner selling a variety of delicious treats. She could hear music coming from somewhere, and after a moment, she spotted some kind of band, cheerily wandering down streets, playing as they drank and sang at the top of their lungs. It was magnificent.

Prudence tapped someone on the arm. "Excuse me?" The older lady turned to look at her. "What's going on?"

The woman grinned. "It's Lumiladh, of course! Here!" She shoved a drink into Prudence's hand and dragged her into the fray of people. The band moved towards them, and the sound of their drums filled her ears. A horn of some kind sounded a merry tune, and the player nodded frantically at the people around him, encouraging them to dance. Prudence smiled. It was so unlike where she had grown up or in the towns of Vaerny. This town, whatever its name was, was bright and colourful, full of laughter and smiling drunk people. She couldn't help but join in the dance that was forming around her.

The hours flew by as Prudence drank, ate, and laughed with strangers. They didn't seem to care that she was a stranger. They opened their arms wide and welcomed her without a second thought. She was dragged enthusiastically from one tavern to another, drinks flowing in every one as people followed the band around town. People gave gifts to one another; some live chickens, dried fish, beautiful wicker baskets, and hats that had clearly been made with love.

"So-" Prudence burped and wiped her mouth with the back of her hand. "So... what exactly is Lumiladh?" She drank another slog of mead and hiccoughed. Her new friends laughed.

An older woman by the name of Mildred clapped a hand on Prudence's shoulder. "It's the coming of the light! The darkest days are done, and now the warmth is on its way, our crops will grow. Artos be merciful, we shall have a prosperous year." She raised her hands in the air and murmured a thanks. The other people at their table copied Mildred's gesture.

"Aye, a year of light, warmth, good crops, and healthy livestock it shall be!" A man named Fred slammed his drink down in agreement, sending the drink sloshing out over the wood.

Prudence smiled. They were nice people. She hoped the Gods would be kind and provide them with a truly bountiful year ahead. In many ways, it had slipped her mind how fast the previous year had gone. She hadn't given much thought to weeks and months passing ever since she left The Wanderer's Inn. There had been no desire to wish away time anymore. She'd been relishing it.

Now a new year had come so swiftly, and with it the promise of new life. It felt hopeful.

Prudence downed the last of her drink and rose from the table. "Well, it's been grand. Thank ye for welcoming me so kindly into yer town. I fancy taking a gander around before I must be headin' back."

"May your fortunes only rise, miss." Agatha, a lady who looked as old as time itself, gripped her arm in farewell.

Prudence walked out of the inn in good spirits, taking the time to glance at every cart, stall, and seller that she passed.

A baker shoved a pastry into her hand, grinning. "Blessed Lumiladh!"

"How much?" Prudence asked.

"Nay, no price. 'Tis a gift! We're celebratin', after all." He chuckled jovially and carried on down the street, handing out treats to every person he could.

Prudence bit into it and warm honey seeped out down her cheek. It was sweet and soft. Gods' teeth, it was divine. She almost turned back to chase him down for another one. She swallowed the last bite and wiped her chin, making her way back to the path that led to *The Wayward Damned*.

Back aboard *The Wayward*, Prudence busied herself with tidying up the galley. They would be departing in a few days and she could barely keep herself distracted. A few days, then they would be on the move again, heading for Aelin. She cleaned, tucking the pots in the crook of her amputated arm, and wiping them down as Sigurd pottered about preparing food for later. It smelt... edible, just about.

Definitely not comparable to the food she had enjoyed earlier in town. She warily glanced at the food, hardtack, bread, and salted pork that Sigurd was going to take ashore to cook up with some vegetables and bone broth into a stew. Her nose wrinkled instinctively. Maybe she wasn't interested in dinner.

After wiping the table for the third time, Sigurd sent her out, declaring her now to be a nuisance rather than a help.

Prudence went to her bunk. She didn't know what to do but soon found herself yawning and decided to take a nap. The men wouldn't be back for a while and they didn't have much preparing to do until they returned with supplies. A short sleep would be good. She really needed it. All of a sudden, her limbs felt achy, her head felt cloudy, and all she wanted to do was shut her eyes.

It was dark. An encroaching dark that filled the air and threatened to suffocate her. Prudence couldn't see anything, and she reached out her hand in the nothingness. It was all-encompassing, surrounding her from every angle. She didn't know where she was, nor where she was going, but she knew she was looking for something.

For someone.

She kept blinking in an attempt to clear her vision, but it was to no avail. The dark wasn't her sight but substantive, right in front of her, like smoke but thicker. If only she could find a way through it. She took a few steps and mercifully didn't fall despite her lack of sight. They were tentative and wobbling like that of a calf learning to walk for the first time, but she knew she had to keep going. To keep pushing on.

In the distance, she could hear voices. Too far off to understand and no way to establish who was speaking. It sounded like someone was calling her name. Someone she knew, someone she cared for. Desperation and urgency surged inside her. She needed to find her way out of the darkness *now* and find them. She had to find them. It was life or death.

She woke to the unpleasant surprise of vomiting all over the floor.

It shocked Prudence back to reality instantly and she grabbed the edge of her hammock to keep from falling out. She retched a few times until the only thing coming up was bile. It stung her throat and burned her eyes. Once the final wave of nausea passed, she took a deep breath and tried to stand.

After breathing heavily for a moment, gripping the hammock to ensure she didn't fall over or worse, vomit again, she cleaned herself and the floor up. She grabbed a brush and a rag to mop up, sweeping the chunks of vomit into a pile that she could then scoop into a bucket. Once the worst of it was off the floor, she scrubbed.

The smell still lingered in the sleeping quarters, and no doubt she'd get hell for it later, but there was nothing more she could do. She could still taste it in her mouth and down her throat, remaining no matter how many times she spit. It filled her nostrils and made her gag. She wasn't squeamish but the smell was certainly gross. She hacked some phlegm and bile out of her throat and spat once more. It must have been something she ate. It was definitely most likely to be Sigurd's cooking rather than the delicacies she'd had in town, not that she ever planned on telling him that. Not if she wanted to continue living.

She had to get away from that smell. She climbed the stairs, one step at a time, still a little uneasy on her feet until she was out in the open air on deck. The wind in her face helped somewhat. It got rid of the smell mostly and allowed her to breathe properly again. Fresh air in her lungs made the nausea ebb.

Prudence leant against the side, allowing her body to rest as she watched the men make some final preparations before their departure. Two of the sailors, Mr. Wilson and Mr. Davis, carried some boxes of supplies up the gangplank and down to the lower deck. The riggers, Eli and Mr. Anders, and the twins, Lekan and Imari, were up in the rigging, checking the sails. She watched them for a while but had to stop. The constant gazing upward made her nausea return. The swaying of the men, at the whim of the rope under their feet with nothing else to secure them as the wind made it creak to and fro was enough to make her head spin. Better to look at the floor, or at least stick to watching the men with feet on the solid deck.

The waves were still that evening. The sun had just begun to hide beyond the horizon. They were to leave Pirn at first light. Penn had been making preparations whilst the captain was away. Newly filled crates of food had been stashed below along with a few barrels of rum. Some pigs had been well salted and stored for the first leg of the journey. They were ready to depart. All that was needed was to wait for the morning light.

Prudence was ready. One step closer to Aelin. One league closer to Cain. Khari had assured her that there was no chance the royal ship had reached Aelin yet, but she still felt that nag of unease. Even if they hadn't yet, they would. *The Wayward* was behind; no one really knew by how far. The soldiers and Cain as their prisoner would reach Aelin first and be welcomed into the royal port, where they would transfer Cain to the palace dungeon. She just had to get there before anything else happened. Before he was put to death.

She couldn't allow that to happen. She wouldn't. She was going to save her love no matter what came into her path. If it was the last thing she did. If she had to see him freed as she lay dying, that would be acceptable. So long as Cain was free.

Her stomach felt absolutely fine now, no longer roiling with bile, and she knew the chill air was helping some. She would probably skip dinner, though, just to be safe. She touched her stump gently, the ghost of her lost limb still there as if it had never been cut off. An image of Cain floated into her mind, seeing her for the first time since they were separated. Would he mind her arm? Would he be shocked it was gone? There had been no saving it, Prudence knew. There was no messing with magick; she knew that now.

She'd need to re-learn how to fight. To re-learn a lot of things. She had been wise to wear men's clothes for all this time, Gods knew how she would manage a corset when she didn't have two hands to tie it. At least it had been her weaker hand. The one she used less. That made the harsh reality of being incapable slightly more palatable. She wasn't useless. No, she'd make do. She always did.

Prudence stood on the deck of *The Wayward Damned*, staring up at the night sky. She couldn't sleep. Her mind was stormy, away with Cain, wherever he was at that moment. Was he chained in the bowels of a royal ship? She hoped wherever he was, he wasn't suffering too much. It felt like her heart was torn in two without him. The pain of losing Elea had come back fresh and raw since her hand had slipped out of Cain's. She wouldn't settle until he was back in front of her.

Wayward's crew had gone below deck to sleep a few hours ago, but still, one of them, Lorcán she thought his name was, sat up in the crow's nest, half dozing. The deck was still and silent aside from the gentle lapping of the ocean against the ship's sides. A giggle startled Prudence, and she spun around. Beckett's brother, Julian, waltzed up the gangplank with Vivienne in his arms. She giggled again as he nibbled at her neck. He grazed his teeth along her jaw, making her purr like a kitten.

They pulled apart for a moment and caught sight of Prudence watching them quietly. "Didn't see you there, missy. Bit late to be out alone, isn't it?" Julian murmured, his eyes drifting back to Vivienne before he'd even finished his sentence.

"Mm, wouldn't want you getting hurt now, would we?" Vivienne smiled wide. She ran a hand down Julian's arm, entwining her fingers with his. Julian played with his pistol in his free hand, twirling the gun round on a finger before catching it again and again.

It was then that Prudence noticed the splatter of dried blood on his hand. "What have you two been doing so late?" Her fingers twitched to grab the knife sheathed at her waist, but Julian's eyes bored into hers as if he was just waiting for her to move.

Julian watched her silently for a moment before cocking his head to look at his lover. "Oh, we've just been having a little fun, haven't we, darling?"

Vivienne was humming to herself, her thumb stroking

Julian's hand softly as she broke out in a wicked grin. "So much fun." She giggled and pulled another pistol from its holster at her side. "Want to play?" Vivienne opened the barrel of the gun and put just one shot inside. The flintlock glinted in the moonlight, wicked and deadly. "Do you believe in fate, *pretty one*? Are you meant to see the dawn? What do we think, love?" She turned to Julian with her last question.

Julian's eyes were alight, gleeful. "Let's find out, shall we?"

Prudence paled and raised a hand in surrender. "I don't think tha's the best idea."

Vivienne laughed, her teeth flashing white like fangs in the moonlight. She looked positively murderous. "What is life without a little risk? It's how you know you're alive!" She handed the gun to Julian, who walked ten paces away from her.

He blew her a kiss before pointing the gun, aiming right for her chest. Julian's finger squeezed the trigger as Prudence screamed 'no!', but her scream fell on deaf ears. The shot fired, embedding itself in the deck only a few steps from Vivienne's feet. She giggled and reached for the gun. She put another shot in and cocked the hammer.

Prudence breathed as if all the air had just been crushed from her lungs.

Vivienne smiled wide like a cat when it yowls. "Your turn!"

"This is madness!" Prudence cried, covering her head with her arms and looking around wildly for someone to intervene.

"This is chaos." Vivienne locked eyes with her.

"Chaos is king," Julian murmured and planted a kiss against Vivienne's hair.

She smiled at him and echoed, "Chaos is king." Vivienne pulled the trigger just as Prudence dropped to the floor, landing uncomfortably. The bullet landed in the trunk of the mast, splintering the wood. Right where Prudence's head had been. Vivienne pouted.

"Maybe next time, darling. Besides, be a shame to waste such a pretty face." He stroked her face and Vivienne giggled, once again acting the spoilt child with a favourite toy.

"What the *fuck* is wrong with you?!" Prudence screamed, shattering the calm that had enveloped the ship before.

"Now, now. It's all in the name of fun. You look like you could do with a bit of fun." His eyebrow raised with his smirk, stretching the scar that cut through his brow and making it even more obvious. His eyes fell to Prudence's hips and seemed to settle there, unnervingly comfortable.

Vivienne's hand snaked up his arm, up his collarbone, and into his shirt, her feline grin making Prudence's stomach churn. "What do you think, my love? Could she keep up?"

"Mm... I think she might, little dove. She's got that gleam. Don't you see it? There's a little chaos in her, I'm sure." He murmured into her hair, their hands far too entwined in one another. Prudence could almost see them melding into one. They cast their glances in her direction once more, a shared lustful glance. Prudence resented the blush that rushed to her cheeks.

"I'm not so sure, my love. Seems a little timid to me." She ran her tongue up his jaw to his ear. "Bring her or don't, but if you're not in that bed soon, I'll have to start without you." Vivienne cast a wink at Prudence and brushed past her as she headed to their bedroom.

"You're both *insane*."

"It keeps life interesting, little one." He moved swiftly across the deck and was before her in an instant. "Don't you want life to be entertaining?"

"Ye'll end up dead. Did ye think of that? Do ye want to die?"

He tapped a finger against his chin, pretending to think. "To go out in a blaze of glory with her by my side?" He looked towards the cabin where Vivienne was undoubtedly waiting for him, naked and playing with knives. "What bliss that would be." He ran his finger across her lips, making her freeze. "Well, little one, sleep tight." He blew a kiss at her and drifted away. Gone as quickly as he had arrived.

The sway of a ship on a choppy sea was something Cain was well accustomed to, but experiencing it chained to the floor in a cramped brig was not. At least it hadn't been for a long time. The sores on his neck and around his wrists were red and angry, the chains biting into his skin with every push and pull of the ocean. A sailor had informed the two prisoners that they had been travelling now for a couple of months. Cain didn't know whether it had felt like years or just one day. Time seemed to stand still. Lifetimes could have passed by. His might well have done.

It might have been wise to pay as little attention to time passing as possible. What was coming was only bad. He should hold onto the happier moments of his past for the final period of his life. It didn't matter whether he lived another year or whether he were to die tomorrow. He would cherish his time with Prudence, cradle his memories of his sister Florence, and be at peace when he took his last breath.

The ship rocked suddenly and he was thrown against the

wall, the hard wood slamming into his back making him cough. Once again, he was back on board *The Drake*, at ten years old, holding his little sister's hand as she sniffled and cradled her bleeding knee. She had dropped powder; the tin had rolled across the deck, spreading it everywhere. The quartermaster had shoved her to the floor and made her scrub until she couldn't hold herself up anymore.

Florence had only been seven at the time. A sweet, innocent little child who didn't have a bad bone in her body. She wouldn't even speak bad words about the sailors who tormented them during their indenture. He hugged her closer to him, her blonde ringlets tickling his face, but he dared not move them. His only concern in that moment was the shuddering sobs wracking her tiny frame.

Cain had wanted to fight. He had wanted to beat the quartermaster with his own cat o' nine tails, but he knew it would just make it worse for Florence. He had learnt from experience. All he could do was hold her and whisper comforting lies in the dark.

Cain shook himself out of his memories, a lone tear escaping before he locked it all back away in his mind. He sniffed once and shifted, trying to find a somewhat comfortable angle.

"Are ye okay?" Jed asked quietly, almost embarrassed to intrude. His eyes were downcast as if he were too shy to meet Cain's glance.

"Yes." He cleared his throat. "I'm fine. Or at least I will be. It's bringing back some memories."

"Good ones, I hope?"

"Some," Cain answered quietly. "Some, but mostly not. But I need to remember. It's good for me to remember."

"Why the fuck would you want to remember bad shit?"

snorted Jed. "That sounds like a terrible idea. Bad shit is what got me in this mess. Do I wanna remember that my girl... well, I thought she was my girl, but she was nothin' but a lyin', schemin'... anyway, that don't matter. Why would I wanna remember that I'm about to swing for stealin' all because a pair of pretty eyes and great tits got me thinkin' it was an easy score? Then a' course, soon as I'm clapped in irons, the little bitch fucks me cousin." His expression turned from indignation to aggression as he began mumbling angrily about the girl.

Cain chuckled lightly. "Perhaps it's best to not remember that. Me, though... I need to remember why I'm here. What brought me this far."

"What do you mean?"

"Everything in my life has led up to this point. I am where I'm meant to be. When I committed the crimes I did, I knew I'd end up at the noose, and I did so willingly. The price was worth it, so now I welcome the reminders so I can be content and grateful rather than bitter and miserable about all that I will miss that is still to come."

"Shit, that's deep." There was a long pause then Jed laughed. "Fuckin' glad I'm not you. That's depressing as fuck."

Cain almost laughed with him. He may have been ready for his grave, but Jed sure wasn't, and for that, he was almost glad. The poor lad didn't deserve this fate, not like he did. Maybe it was better for Jed to live out the last of his days delusional in bitterness rather than focusing on the truth of the matter that no matter what brought him here, he would be dead at the end of this journey.

K hari finished up his shift with the riggers just as the sun disappeared from view. Imari and Lekan were nice lads. Young for their positions, but good, reliable men who knew the ropes better than their own hands. Khari enjoyed working with them.

"Come on then, lads. Shall we head to the galley, fetch some grub?" asked Khari.

"I could do wi' a drink, that's for sure," replied Imari.

"Aye. Am drier than an old whore." Lekan slapped him on the shoulder in agreement and led the way downstairs.

The smell of pork wafted into Khari's nose, making his stomach rumble. After being in the sun for that long, working up a sweat, he could have eaten a horse, but salted pig would have to do. He plonked down opposite Prudence and grabbed a plateful of food. He practically inhaled it, eating at such a pace that if his mother had been there, she would have boxed his ears and scolded his lack of manners.

When he was on his third plate, he looked up just long enough to notice that Prudence had barely touched her food, pushing it around the plate with a fork. She stared at the wall, eyes looking through people in a vacant gaze.

"Not hungry, *keine*?" he asked.

She came back to herself at the sound of his voice, blinking away the daze, and looked at her plate. "Oh, uh, no. I'm not feelin' it." She pushed a lump of pork around before putting it in her mouth. It was clear from the way she chewed that she didn't like it.

She blanched slightly and rose to her feet, heading up the steps to the main deck. She swayed as she walked, grabbing the wall for support for a moment before pressing on. Khari watched her go silently. She didn't look well.

"Man, I don't care what the captain said. The things I would do to her."

Khari's head spun and his eyes landed on Harris, the boatswain's mate, and Eoin, the master gunner, chuckling as they gestured lewdly. In one swift motion, he'd crossed the room and thrust his fist into Harris's face. The man fell backward onto the floor, clutching his nose.

"My nose! Ye broke my fuckin' nose!" The shock quickly made way for anger, and he lurched up, hurling himself at Khari. Another sharp jab in the face sent him sprawling on the floor again.

"I hear ye talkin' about her again and I'll rip yer tongue out and feed it to ya. Are we clear?"

The room had fallen silent, all eyes on the two men. Blood gushed out of Harris's nose and he slowly nodded.

Khari sat back down in his seat and continued eating. After a while, people began speaking again and all resumed as before.

He'd surprised himself with his fierce reaction. He'd heard many a man speak like that before, and whilst he thought it a tad juvenile, he'd paid it little mind. Perhaps he cared for the stubborn woman just a little, despite how frustrating she could be. He couldn't say he liked her, but he didn't wish to see her come to more harm. He owed her more than that.

In a way, she reminded him of his grandmother. They both had that wild, untameable air about them. An iron will that could crush men and wither the hardiest plant. She couldn't be told what to do by anyone. That had been his grandmother in her time. An immovable force, beholden to none.

Once he'd finished, he went in search of Prudence. He found her in the brig, hunched over on an old barrel.

"Do ye think he's going to be all right?" she asked, and Khari knew she was speaking of Cain. "I wonder if they're feeding 'im... if they're hurting him." It was more like she was speaking to the empty brig than to Khari, but he felt the need to answer anyway.

"He's going to be all right. They want him alive for the trial and sentencing."

"Oddly, that doesn't make me feel better." She gave a sardonic laugh. "I wish I could take his place."

"No, ye don't, *keine,* and he wouldn't want ye to either," he said quietly.

She stared aimlessly at the wall, a grim expression on her face. She didn't deserve this, neither of them did. It was uncomfortable seeing her so vulnerable. There was a time when he didn't even think she had that side to her. "Ye definitely don't look well."

Her face was positively green as she sat there clutching her stomach. She took a breath, then promptly vomited on the floor.

"Oh, fuckin' misery." He pulled a face, retreating a few steps at the smell.

Prudence held her hair out of the way as she vomited a second time, hunched over as chunks of food and bile came out of her. She retched once more then spat, attempting to remove the taste from her mouth. "I'm fine. It must have been somethin' I ate."

"No. It fuckin' isn't. I watched ye not eat all evenin'. Saw how faint ye were, and don't think I didn't notice ye'd puked in the bunks the other day." He walked over to her and took a seat.

"Ye've widened too."

Her eyes flicked up to meet his. "No," she whispered. "No, I can't be… it's not possible."

Khari laughed. "Ye can't seriously think I'm to believe that you and yer beloved captain haven't fucked each other senseless as many times as possible."

Her head whipped up, eyes boring into him. "That isn't what I meant."

He sighed and pinched the bridge of his nose. "When was yer last bleed?"

"That's none of yer fuckin' business," she spat through gritted teeth.

"Oh, come on. Don't pretend to be too proud. 'Tis a simple question."

He watched as her brows creased, thinking. A lot had happened in the last few months. It would be easy to forget. She counted on her fingers wearily as realisation dawned on her face.

"Yer with child, *keine*."

CHAPTER FIVE

DEEP WATER

"What the fuck is going on here?" roared Captain Beckett, shoving his way through the throng to see the commotion. The crew was piling around the mast and Prudence rose up on her toes to look between their heads. Julian was at the centre of all the attention. He had a man pinned against the mast by the neck, a wicked grin plastered on his face.

"It seems, dear brother," said Julian, "that our prize master here has been skimming off the top. Taking an extra share just for himself."

A few angry jeers erupted from the watching crowd. The prize master struggled for breath as Julian's hand tightened around his throat. His black fringe fell over his face, but

Prudence didn't miss the gleam in his eye. The bloodlust.

"Well, Mr. Peck," said the captain. "Do you have anything to say for yourself?" He strode closer and Mr. Peck visibly paled.

"I didn't do anything!" yelled Mr. Peck, his voice raising in panic with every word.

Julian slammed his head backwards against the mast. "Let's try that again, shall we?" He moved his face close against the prize master's, his gaze so unflinching he didn't even blink. Julian stared at the man for a long moment. It even made Prudence feel uncomfortable.

"I- er... I'm sorry, Captain! I was a fool! I didn't think. Please," he begged, choking as Julian tightened his grip once more. "Please take it out of me wages," he croaked out.

"Perhaps," Captain Beckett mused, pacing in front of him as if in contemplation. "Or, maybe I should just give you to my brother to do as he pleases."

Mr. Peck's eyes bulged out of his head as Julian loomed in his face.

"Betraying the crew is a capital offence, lad."

"Mm, and betrayal of the most heinous kind deserves a most severe punishment," Julian crooned, running his knife across Mr. Peck's cheek. "Abraham, Mr. Fisher, if you would please."

The quartermaster and boatswain brought rope and bound Mr. Peck's hands and feet, as he thrashed wildly against Julian's hold. Their faces were set in a grim line, sealing the fate of a brother. The unspoken rules were clear. This life was a democracy, a band of equals. They stole from merchants and lawmakers but to steal from each other was to sign a death wish. Despite the sadness in some of the crew's eyes, everyone stayed silent. They weren't prepared to meet the same fate.

Prudence watched as they hoisted Mr. Peck into the air. He

hung over the side of *The Wayward* over ten feet above the deck. The look of feral panic in his eyes made Prudence shiver. "What are they doing?" she whispered to Vivienne, who had appeared at her side.

Vivienne's eyes darkened hungrily; it could have almost been lust. "Ever heard of a keelhaul?" At Prudence's headshake, she grinned. "Keep watching." Her eyes moved to Julian, watching every move of his arms, her look of hunger mirrored in his own. They were a perfect match, each as deranged as the other.

Julian grabbed the rope attached to Mr. Peck and pulled. It had been hooked up to pulleys and as Mr. Peck was dragged lower, realisation dawned on Prudence. Mr. Peck was inching, feet first, closer to the ocean's surface. He let out a high-pitched shriek. His legs sank into the water, then his waist, and soon, his head went under. He thrashed at his bonds but the rope was tight against the ship. The world was silent save for the sound of Mr. Peck's body being dragged under *The Wayward*. The scraping sounds turned Prudence's stomach.

After what felt like hours, Mr. Peck came out of the water on the other side of the ship. Julian kept pulling on the ropes until he was level with the hard surface. Abraham and Mr. Fisher grabbed him by the arms and dragged him onto the deck. Blood pooled on the wood underneath him. His back was in ribbons, the skin hanging off, some parts so deep you could see the muscle.

The silence was overwhelming until Mr. Peck sucked in a ragged breath, his whole body shaking with the force. He looked broken, but Julian wasn't done with him.

"Haul him up! We're sending him over again," he yelled.

"Do ye really think that's necessary, man?" Abraham spoke up.

"Are you questioning me?" Julian's eyes darkened, his focus shifting to the quartermaster.

Abraham swiftly closed his mouth, taking a step back. It was baffling to Prudence. On *The Maiden*, or indeed any ship, there was only one person above the quartermaster—the captain, and yet the entire crew made way for Julian. Despite his lack of a rank and sheer psychopathy, he was free to do as he wished. He was Captain Beckett's guard dog, but Prudence wondered how long it would be before the rabid dog would have to be put down.

Vivienne giggled beside her and clutched Prudence's arm. The men tossed Mr. Peck back over the side and soon the dragging of his flesh against the barnacled keel could be heard again.

The second time his body was hoisted above the water's surface, Prudence had thought he might be dead. It would have been better. It would have been an end to the pain. But then he breathed once more.

"Again," commanded Julian, and once more Mr. Peck's head was pulled beneath the soft waves. He was barely recognisable now. His face had been battered so much it had swelled to twice its size, his eyes forced shut with large gashes of skin torn. Everyone waited with bated breath as Mr. Fisher checked him over.

"He's dead."

A universal sigh spread across the deck as Mr. Fisher moved to untie his bonds.

"No! We are not done! I say when we're done!" spat Julian, hurling himself at Mr. Peck, his fists pummelling his already broken face. Blow after blow, Julian kept hitting. Prudence winced at the audible crack of Mr. Peck's skull, but Julian made no signs of stopping, his hands bloody with both Mr. Peck's and his own as he caved the man's face in. He took the man's head in both hands, smashing it against the deck over and over again.

"He's dead, brother. You've done your job." Captain Beckett was eerily calm as he strode over to Julian and placed a hand on his shoulder.

Prudence expected Julian to explode at his touch, but he merely froze in place, his body radiating rage. He slowly rose at his brother's gesture and then Vivienne was upon him, cradling him. They locked eyes as she took his fingers to her lips and sucked the blood off. His hand wound into her hair and gripped tight, pulling her in for a kiss. If looks held any power, they might set the world alight with their gazes. The rest of them no longer existed for the pair.

Vivienne coaxed him away to their cabin and almost immediately the crew began to disperse, leaving the broken body of Mr. Peck laying there. It was as if they had all forgotten him already.

The cabin boy, Marcus, came down the steps to the brig, food tray in hand. Jed looked up excitedly, like a puppy being permitted scraps.

"Here," mumbled Marcus, in the monotonous dead tone that Cain had grown accustomed to.

He reached through the bars and took the tray. Hardtack and salted pork again.

"Oh, man, what I wouldn't give for some cheese," groaned

Jed, stuffing three biscuits into his mouth at once.

"Careful you don't choke to death," said Cain dryly. He had never known a man eat as much as Jed. Despite what his scrawny frame might suggest, he could eat enough for ten men. His legs must have been hollow.

"Oh, sure. Would be an absolute travesty if I were to die before they could kill me." Jed spoke with his mouth full, spitting bits of food everywhere.

Cain glanced up at the cabin boy. He was a young lad of around fourteen, slightly short for his age with fluffy brown hair that curled at the nape of his neck. He was sporting a new bruise on his jaw, fresh by the look of it. No doubt it would be larger and darker tomorrow.

"What happened?" Cain asked quietly.

"Got in the way again," he grumbled. "Made Mister Hornby drop gunpowder everywhere."

"Oh. That's not good." Cain had learnt to speak softly to the young boy. He was a twitchy little thing who scared easily if you weren't careful. "You'll need to put a damp cloth on that. It'll soothe it some." The young boy reminded him of himself before, not yet numb to the pain. His face still held confusion and anger. Cain didn't know whether he wanted the boy to lose himself, to save himself from the hurt, or to keep his head up and refuse to be cowed... as if it were as simple as choosing one or the other.

"Aye, sir. I will."

"Good lad." Cain smiled and reached up with shackled hands to ruffle the kid's hair. Marcus brightened ever so slightly and stood a little taller. "Just remember to take care, yes? Be helpful and try not to get in anybody's way."

"I'll try, sir." He beamed at Cain before scampering back up the steps to the main deck.

"You are the only person I know who could be in chains and yet still called sir." Jed eyed Cain, an amused expression on his face.

Cain's serious facade cracked for a brief moment, and he smirked. "Well you see, people like me." He winked. "I command respect." He enjoyed teasing Jed. It lifted his spirits and helped both of them forget, at least for a moment. Having a friend made the time pass a little quicker. Just a little.

"Let's see how far that gets you come yer trial, *sir*." Jed flashed a cheeky grin at him, knowing he was pushing it.

"Oh, it shan't help at all." He chuckled. "We're both dead men."

Jed snorted unexpectedly. "Fuck, ye know how to bring down a mood, don't ya?"

"Where's the fun in dying if you don't laugh on the way?"

Jed laughed and tore off a chunk of pork, chewing slowly. "Yer an odd guy, Cain. An odd guy." He burped before eating more of the pork. "But I like ye. I can imagine worse people to be locked up with."

Cain grinned. "Why, thank you so much," he said dryly. "You're not too bad yourself." He reached forward and plucked some hardtack off the tray Jed was hoarding. It was stale and tasted no better than the wood under their feet, but his stomach grumbled appreciatively all the same.

The nausea had finally dulled to the point where Prudence was, for the most part, able to eat as she normally did. And so she did. She willingly tucked into any food she was provided with, even going so far as to joyfully consume Sigurd's stew, despite its unusual smell. This pleased Sigurd greatly and he frequently tried to offer her more, piling her bowl well beyond what she could manage.

She soon found her belly to be showing, the rounded little bump of something growing inside her. Mercifully, it was small and easy to conceal under her shirt. She didn't wish for the crew to know what ailed her. Whilst she may have been relatively safe with them thanks to the payment for travel and the menacing threat of Khari by her side, she didn't feel secure in allowing this secret out into the open.

Not to mention that she herself felt much better when she could pretend all was well, that her belly did not protrude obviously as she looked at herself, and that nothing had changed. This delusion of deniability could not withstand the ache in her lower back, however. It was a regular reminder that, for now, her body was not her own, that there was a significant weight pulling her down from her midriff. It could have as easily been a stranger's body.

She assisted Penn with his duties, taking the noon sighting as they neared Napor, one of the biggest islands in The Tides, housing some of *The Wayward's* best trade contacts. He had shown her how to hold the sextant up against the line of the horizon to establish a dead reckoning longitude. She took it a few times to ensure that her readings were suitably accurate before noting it down.

She liked working with Penn. It had become more and more difficult for her to do anything that required heavy lifting, and whilst she had not revealed that she was with child to the crew, Khari had encouraged more work with the sailing master. Penn seemed very grateful for the extra help. He had had a mate to assist in the duties of navigation, but the boy had been killed the previous year and the crew were loath to take on strangers. Prudence filled the position nicely, plotting their course, taking regular sightings and doing anything Penn asked of her.

They reached Napor with unexpected speed, the wind on their side for almost the entire journey. The crew had an impressive cargo of silks, spices, and tobacco to deliver to their numerous clientele. Gulliver, the spotsman, in charge of directing the ship to shore, took over from Penn as they approached the Aldington coast under the cover of darkness.

All lanterns were doused, minimising how visible they were to any patrolling officers manning the beach. *The Wayward's* black hull and dark sails made them almost invisible to anyone on land. Gulliver raised a pistol above his head, missing its barrel, and pulled the trigger. The sharp pop of the hammer was deafening in the silent dark, and it sparked a bright blue light.

A hush fell over the crew, and Prudence looked around. They all watched the shore earnestly until, after a few moments, a light appeared in the distance somewhere high up, way above the beach.

"Now that..." A shiver ran down Prudence's spine as Julian whispered close against her ear. "That is our cue."

Gulliver brought *The Wayward* as close to shore as possible before dropping anchor as quietly as the crew could manage. Before long, Prudence could hear the gentle lapping of water and she looked out towards the land. Little row boats were making their way towards the ship, all rowing in darkness, manned by only two men each.

"The tubsmen," murmured Julian, noticing her curiosity. "They'll take the cargo to shore for us. Move it inland and store it until they can sell it."

She looked up at him, intrigued. His dark eyes sparkled with excitement, the promise of lawlessness and danger bringing him to life.

"Beckett will go with them. He has sums to settle with the man on the 'ill, probably bring a couple men with him. *Wayward* will dock at Aldon and he'll return to us tomorrow."

"Who is the man on the hill?" asked Prudence, raising an eyebrow.

"None of us know, aside from Beckett, that is. He deals with him. Alls I know is he pays for the goods. He's got contacts all over Napor to sell it. Although, the stories would have you believe he is not of this world." Julian waggled his eyebrows, amused.

"Oh?" Prudence loved a ghost story, but if her life had taught her anything, it was that this world was not as it seemed. If people believed he were not quite human... there could be some truth to that. Her heart thrummed with excitement and trepidation.

"The man on the hill is a demon!" piped up Carter. "He's an evil, wicked being who preys on mortal vices."

"Oh, silence, man. What, are you soft in the head? He's a man. No more, no less. With, I imagine, his hands in numerous men's ambitions across the county and further. He's not any more supernatural than I am." Penn rolled his eyes and slapped Carter on the arm. "It's just a bunch of ghost stories meant to scare the locals."

"'Tis not! Captain brought me with him last time, don't you remember? I stood outside that 'ouse for over an hour while the captain spoke to him. I felt that chill. It weren't natural. I saw things, I tell ya! Heard things too." Harris leant forward to share his take and shuddered.

"You mustn't mind them, little one. A superstitious bunch to be sure." Julian slung an arm around Prudence's shoulders and leaned into her. "I'll keep you safe from any ghosts hanging about," he murmured.

Prudence shrugged out of his grip and scowled at him. The tubmen worked in unison with the crew of *The Wayward Damned*, passing down crates and barrels of stolen goods from deck to dinghy until they had handed over everything.

Captain Beckett climbed down and took a seat in the last boat, bringing Mr. Fisher and Mr. Wilson with him. Prudence watched as they rowed to shore and disappeared into the mouth of a cave, lighting lanterns to guide their way once inside, safe from any watchful eyes.

They departed Napor soon after, the bulk of their journey now behind them as they pressed on to Aelin. They were now just over two hundred leagues from the Isle, the crown jewel of The Western Tides, Cain's place of birth and the location he was returning to to die. Their arrival couldn't come soon enough. With every league, her chest tightened and a sense of overwhelming dread enveloped her.

They were so close she could almost taste him, and the idea that she might not make it in time, that he could die, made her want to vomit. Not when they were so close. Not when she had come this far.

Khari appeared by her side and put a hand on her shoulder. "It'll be all right, *keine*. Any doubt I may have had that ye would be getting back to yer beloved captain is certainly gone. Ye've already done far more than I ever expected. He's a lucky man."

Prudence sighed and shut her eyes. "I hope so." Her hands found her belly automatically, cradling the bump that held their child.

The ship made good time, her hull cutting through the choppy waves like a knife. If they kept this pace, they would reach Aelin in no time at all. Whilst her shores were not yet visible, Prudence could swear she could feel it out there, just beyond the horizon, almost within reach.

The weather held relatively well, only being marred by a soft drizzle from such pale grey clouds they could have almost been white. The waves remained, rising and falling as the wind stirred up their resistance, but *The Wayward Damned* was unimpeded. Despite the distance they still had to go, Prudence remained on deck, staring out over the open ocean.

Lorcán yelled something unintelligible from the crow's nest, and Prudence and a number of the crew looked up at him. He yelled again, the wind taking most of his words. All that could be made out was *'starboard'*. They all looked starboard at his urgent pointing. The ocean was a deep blue, its waves topped with foamy white caps. All seemed calm. There were no ships in sight, nothing floating in the water, no men had gone overboard.

Something caught Prudence's attention out of the corner of her eye. Her head whipped around to identify what she had seen, but she could make out nothing except the sea.

Lorcán yelled once more and descended the rigging as swiftly as his feet would carry him. The crew by now were all running for the side, staring out into the ocean, squinting to see whatever it was.

A wave broke, a fin slicing up through the surface a few hundred yards from *The Wayward*, and a chill ran up Prudence's spine. She had never seen a fin like that before. It was the size of a rowboat and just as wide. Its dark blue hue blended in with the surrounding waves, making the rest of the beast almost invisible to them on deck. The fin itself was covered in white, jagged scars. A rough open wound, revealing the pink flesh beneath, ran along the very edge. A previous battle. Something told Prudence that the beast had won.

"Morgawr!" screamed Lekan from the rigging, and he and his brother descended the ropes at speed.

The ship lurched suddenly as the beast knocked against its side, throwing Prudence across the deck. She landed sharply on her hip and let out a cry. Despite his usually sure footing, Imari slipped from the rigging above her, falling twenty feet onto the hard deck. He landed with a sickening thud, unmoving. Prudence watched as Lekan raced to his twin brother, struggling to breathe with the wind knocked out of him. His leg was twisted at an awful angle, most unnatural as his calf bent out to the left sharply.

Prudence's attention was drawn away by the screams and yells coming from the rest of the crew. Carnage scattered *The Wayward Damned*. Wood splintered from the foremast as it crashed down. Water soaked the deck, a wave ricocheting off the morgawr's unimaginable back, twice as long as *The Wayward* was from bow to stern.

Prudence staggered to a stand, her hand clutching the gunwale. The ship jerked once more and the loud sounds of the hull breaking down below sent the crew into a frenzy. She stumbled backwards, her head bouncing off the main mast. The men dashed about tightening the halyards, grabbing buckets to bail out the water and cloth to plug the holes in the keel. Prudence's ears rang, her head pounding in pain as she cradled her belly.

CHAPTER SIX

NECESSARY MEASURES

"Haul on the mainbrace!" yelled Captain Beckett from the helm, straining to keep *The Wayward* on course against the ongoing attack. "We must put as much distance between us and this beast as possible!"

"Captain, it's no use! She's too fast for us!" cried Mr. Fisher, his face a mix of stout resoluteness and sadness. He saw the end. There was no running. No fighting. This was it. The ship lurched wildly and a keening crack sounded from below deck. The crew ran about in a panic, trying to garner more speed and loading the cannons with gunpowder.

The Wayward juddered again, and Captain Beckett was

thrown against the gunwale. His head made a sickening thud against the wood and he dropped like a stone, eyes closed as he lay slumped on the deck.

Prudence moved slowly, trying to get to him on unsteady feet. She reached a hand up to the back of her head and it came away sticky and red. Beckett's head lolled forward onto the soaking wood, unconscious. Prudence knelt down beside him and put a finger to his neck. He was alive, but he was no use to them now.

Julian appeared at her side, a hand on her shoulder, and she turned to him. "Ye need to take the helm. We have to fight."

His usual smirk was gone, replaced by a seriousness that made him look like his brother. "What's your plan, little one?"

"Take the helm. I have to find Khari." She stood and swayed lightly, and Julian reached out to steady her. After taking a deep breath she took off towards the stairs, ignoring the pounding in her ears. There would be time to recover later, once they had survived. She took the steps two at a time, allowing the momentum to carry her forward. She found Khari with a number of the crew, trying to fill the holes the morgawr had created.

"Khari!"

He straightened immediately. "What is it?"

"I need you. Grab all the whale oil we have!"

He nodded sagely. "Elliott! Carter! Mr. Wilson! Assist me. We need to bring the barrels of oil up on deck. Now!"

At his yelling, the men rushed into action. They quickly brought three barrels up behind Prudence.

The deck was a wreck. Water sloshed across the floor. The foremast was mostly whole and leaning heavily against the main. The rigging was holding for now, at least.

Prudence raced across the deck, dodging crewmen and trying

to stay on her feet. She ran past Julian at the helm, straining to steer as the morgawr thrashed, turning the ocean into a raging sea. The ship jerked wildly, and she grabbed hold of the captain's door frame to keep from falling over.

Tucked against the wall and a shelf, she spotted the gleam of brass. The flintlock blunderbuss was a heavy gun, almost as tall as her, with a thick stock and muzzle. She grabbed it and loaded the gun swiftly. It wasn't much of a chance, but it was the best they had.

Prudence hastened to the gunwale, where Khari now instructed the men to place the barrels of oil.

"What now, *keine*?" he asked, ready to do whatever she needed.

"We're going to dump it. We need to get them into the water as far away from *The Wayward* as possible."

Khari's eyes glinted, understanding her plan. "Come on, lads. Do as she says. Hoist them over with as much strength as you can muster!"

The men lifted the barrels, and with effort, threw them into the water a few yards away from the ship.

"Now what?" asked Carter.

Prudence handed Khari a lit lamp. "When I say... throw it."

He nodded.

Prudence looked for the beast. It was off the port side, near *Wayward's* stern. She raised the blunderbuss, propping it up on the gunwale to steady it, where her arm could not. Her finger sat on the trigger and the muzzle tucked under what was left of her arm. She fired a shot at the first barrel. She braced for the recoil, but it still forced her backwards a little. Oil leaked slowly out of the hole and she shot a second. The water began to shimmer a beautiful array of colours as the oil leaked.

She needed the morgawr to get closer. It needed to be right beside the barrels. She gestured to the men. "Ye need to make noise, lots of it. Draw it over here."

A few of the crew nodded and began yelling at the top of their lungs. Mr. Wilson grabbed his sword and used the hilt to strike a cannon over and over again. The clang of metal cried out across the water.

"Come on, ye bastard," Prudence muttered, willing the beast closer. The noise had begun to work. She saw its tail twitch as it changed course, heading towards her and the men near the helm. "Come on..."

It knocked against the side of *The Wayward* again and Prudence heard a yell as one of the sailors, Tor, was knocked overboard. He screamed as he fell, his body hitting the water, and within moments, the morgawr had turned, her maw closing down on the man. They heard a sickening crunch and then the yelling ceased.

"It's not working," Prudence mumbled. Her plan wouldn't work unless it got close enough. She raised the gun once more and lined it up.

"Come on, that's it. Come closer." She took a deep breath. She needed to make this shot count. She pulled the trigger as she breathed out. The large lead shot fired, hitting the beast square in the eye. A howl of pain erupted from its jaws and it set its sights on *The Wayward* once more, coming straight for them.

"That's it. Hold..." she warned Khari. "Not yet." She watched the beast swim closer. The oil sat on top of the rippling waves as it moved. One fin brushed the slick substance, then another. "Just a little more..." Prudence muttered. "Khari, now!"

Khari threw the oil lamp into the water, and as soon as the

little flame met the spill, it all went up. Flames spread across the water in an instant. She had never seen anything like it. The fire touched the beast, climbing up its fins, up over its back, and over its head. It roared with agony and thrashed desperately, attempting to be rid of the flames. After a moment, it dived down deep, the fire extinguishing on its body once submerged.

Prudence sighed in relief and she heard a number of the men cheer. A hand clapped her on the back.

"Ye did good, kid." Khari grinned at her and she felt herself grin back. "Julian!" Khari called to him, still at the helm. "Get us away from these flames, man."

Even with the foremast down and a number of leaks, *The Wayward* sailed away from the blaze that now raged, the only evidence of their attack.

A few of the crew picked Beckett up and carried him back to his cabin at his brother's instruction. He was semi-conscious, still in and out of sense. He should be fine, they surmised, but they would leave him to rest. They could cope without him.

T he men managed to sufficiently plug the holes that punctured *The Wayward's* hull, and they continued to make relatively good time. The foremast was more difficult. Once Beckett had rested up for a night, he had needed twenty of the men to assist in its mending. They first had to untangle its rigging from that of the main mast. As they crashed together, they had gotten stuck. It took them an entire day to get it standing upright again.

By the time evening came around and the sun sank below the waves, everyone had gone rather quiet, exhausted from the day's tasks. Prudence, of course, hadn't been able to assist in mending anything that required heavy lifting, but she had made herself useful.

Now she sat in between Khari and Penn, drink in hand.

"I can't believe ye did that! It was incredible!" Penn shoved her shoulder excitedly. "We were sunk! I thought for sure we were dead. I mean, when the captain got knocked out, fuck. Yer my hero now." He grinned at Prudence, more drunk on the elation of surviving than on the drink in his hand.

Prudence laughed. "I 'av no intentions of dying. Not yet at least."

"Ye know what ye've gotta do now?" He leant into her, eyes sparkling.

"What?" Her brow furrowed, confused.

"Every sailor worth his salt has the tattoos to prove it and you, my dear, have certainly earned the ink." He smirked and pulled up a sleeve. "Know what this one's for?"

Prudence shook her head. A swallow in flight had been tattooed across his bicep.

"This one's for sailing 5,000 nautical miles. Got a matching one on the other arm." He winked at her. "And this one here..." An almost naked woman with rather large breasts had been tattooed on his inner forearm. "Now, this one is for Maria." He waggled his eyebrows at Prudence, smirking again. "The prettiest angel I ever did see. No offence, a' course."

Prudence chuckled. It was sweet, if a little... exaggerated.

"If she's the prettiest girl you've ever seen, Penn, then why the fuck would she be interested in you?" Captain Beckett sat down at the table across from them, laughing.

Penn's smirk fell into a scowl, and he narrowed his eyes at his captain. "And when was the last time ye had yerself a girl, Captain?"

"Every time we set foot on land, old friend. Every. Single. Time." Captain Beckett's eyes told tales of delicious sinfulness, and Prudence almost choked on her drink laughing at Penn's face.

For a moment, it was almost easy to forget where she was, to imagine she was back on *The Maiden*. Laughing with Gabe and Shuu, hearing Mr. Lowell play, teasing Garrick… it made her heart feel heavy.

"So, what kind of tattoo am I meant to be getting then?" she asked Penn.

"Ah ha!" He tapped his nose and grabbed her hand, dragging her up to the top deck with Khari and a few of the men on their heels. He sat Prudence down. "There's better light out here." He ran back down the stairs for a moment and re-emerged holding a wooden block, a pot of ink, and a needle. Prudence eyed it warily.

"Now this…" He squatted down beside Prudence and showed her the block. An image had been carved into the centre of it—a blooming rose with a dagger piercing its centre.

"What does it mean?" she asked.

"This tattoo is reserved for those of us who show great bravery and a willingness to battle anything. I don't think I've ever tattooed anyone who deserved it more."

Prudence flushed. The use of 'us' hadn't escaped her notice, and she felt a rush of warmth for Penn and this crew. A tear welled in her eye, and she sniffed it back.

"Don't go soft on us now." Penn nudged her, smiling. "Where do you want it?"

Prudence thought for a moment. She pulled down her sleeve just enough to expose her shoulder. "Here." She tapped the back of her right shoulder. She shifted so that her back was turned to him and took a deep breath. Penn coated the carved block in ink and pressed it firmly against her skin for a moment to make sure the design transferred.

"All right, this will hurt a little," Penn warned her before pressing the needle into her skin.

At the first puncture of her skin, she hissed sharply and bit her lip. It was uncomfortable and sharp, but in comparison to all of the pain she had experienced throughout her life, it was undeniably manageable. Nothing more than a nuisance, like a fly buzzing near her ear. She kept as still as possible as Penn pushed the needle in over and over again, forcing the ink deep into her skin.

"How's it looking?" she asked, turning her head slightly but not so much as to move her shoulder.

"It's looking good, young miss. Makes ye look tough." Mr. Wilson grinned, winking at her.

Prudence chuckled. "Well, that is good news." She closed her eyes and tried to picture the design being stabbed into her skin. The petals of the rose, curled and slowly unfolding around the blade of the dagger as it plunged through the centre. It was both beautiful and fierce.

After what felt like the longest time—so much so that a number of the men had gotten bored of watching and returned to other activities—Penn straightened behind her and put the needle down.

Prudence breathed in. "Is it done?" she asked, hopeful.

"Aye. Looks good too." Penn smiled, smug at his work. "Suits ye very well."

Prudence turned her head, but she couldn't see the tattoo that now inked her shoulder blade.

"Stay still a minute. I'll fetch a mirror." Penn rose from his seat and disappeared into one of the cabins. After a moment, he returned, holding a little mirror, and handed it to Prudence. The mirror itself was worn with time, and the handle was heavy, silver with filigree on the stem. It was lovely. She held it up at an angle to the right of her shoulder so she could look at her back.

The tattoo was tinged red at the edges where her skin was sore and angry at the irritation, but the ink itself... she couldn't quite believe it. The thick lines outlined the design, stark against her pale skin, visible even from a distance. It stood out beautifully from the white. Penn had coloured in the centre of the tattoo; red for the rose petals, of course, a small sample of green at the bottom for the stem, the dagger was naturally a dark grey, and he had put swirls and stars along the hilt. The ink itself was more of a yellow, but as part of the artwork it glowed like gold.

Prudence wanted to reach out and touch it, to run her hand along it and feel the ridges under her fingers. She looked up at Penn and smiled. "Thank ye, truly. It's beautiful." She couldn't help but look at it again in the mirror, turning the handle this way and that so she could admire it from every angle.

"Ye earned it, saving us from that beastie. We'd have been sunk and claimed by Barinthus if it weren't for yer quick thinking." Penn held out a hand for her and pulled her up. "Yer one of us now. Don't forget it."

Prudence felt her eyes get misty once more, and she shook her head to rid herself of the tears. This child was making her far more emotional than she felt comfortable with.

Soon enough, they were nearing Aelin, and her shores could be seen very vaguely in the distance. They were approaching the country from the south near Falryn, and they needed to sail up past the cape and head east a short ways. Before the port at Eastcliff would become visible, Captain Beckett had reported that there was a little-known bay tucked away from view or access on foot that they used whenever they made berth in King's Country.

It would only be a few more hours until they were there, and so Prudence headed down to the sleeping quarters, to her bunk to collect her few things. It wouldn't be long until she was saying goodbye to Khari and the crew of *The Wayward Damned*, heading off into unknown land, alone, in search of her husband.

Captain Beckett had been kind enough to provide her with a few coins in exchange for her ring, alongside the passage they had bartered it for, and she had purchased a number of items in their stops to Napor and Pirn. A bag to carry everything, a thin coat that would help against the cold when night fell, and a small but sharp blade she could conceal in her sleeve if need be.

She hoisted the bag over her shoulder and went to the galley where Sigurd had wrapped some hardtack, some dried, salted pork, and a small flask of brandy in some cloth for her. She took it gratefully.

"Thank ye, Sigurd. I shall never forget yer kindness to me." She looked up at the big, gruff man with a feeling of warmth. She might even miss him on her travels.

"No need to thank me, girl. 'Tis nothin'." He rebuffed her thanks gruffly, but she could see the hint of a smile that tried to reach his eyes.

She shoved the cloth full of goods into the top of her bag and took the steps back up to the main deck. It was bustling with crewmen as they prepared to make berth. She caught sight of Julian and Vivienne, clutching one another at the gunwale, looking out across the glittering waves towards Aelin, their eyes gleaming. A shiver instinctively ran down her spine at the sight of them. She didn't want to know what they had planned once they reached shore.

Julian paused and spun his head to look at her as if he could tell she had been watching him. His catlike grin spread wide, showing lots of teeth, and he nodded at her. She definitely wouldn't miss him or his uncomfortable glances.

She forced herself to look away, breaking the eye contact first, and headed up to where Mr. Hare was speaking to the quartermaster. She took in both men, one tall and slim with a shock of reddish hair that stood to attention on his head, the other shorter, rounder, and slightly older but still just as formidable. They both set eyes on her.

"All ready to depart I see, are ye, Miss?" Mr. Hare nodded at the bag slung over her shoulder.

She shifted the bag slightly as she stood. "Yes, I believe so. I've got a long walk ahead of me. I need to get started as soon as we reach shore."

Mr. Hare grunted softly. "And how is the arm holding up?" He took her arm in his hand firmly and lifted it, assessing the stump. It had healed very well for the most part. No doubt it would take a considerable while longer before it looked just like skin, and it would certainly never look 'normal' again. The stitches had held up very well and the stump was no longer red or sore. The large scar across the base of her elbow had started to turn white, and the skin at the edge puckered ever so slightly, a jagged edge that signified the loss of her right forearm.

"It feels good," she answered. "It certainly doesn't hurt anymore. I have to thank ye. I don't know what I would have done if ye hadn't removed it for me."

"Yer welcome, Miss, but it is my job as ship's carpenter, don't forget." He smiled softly. "Make sure to continue taking good care of it once ye leave us."

She nodded. "I will." She cast a quick smile at Abraham too.

The Wayward Damned rounded the shore edge at Falryn and sailed straight past the port, heading for the hidden bay. It wouldn't be long before they were weighing anchor and lowering the rowboats, the crew taking it in turns to disembark from the great galleon and then... Prudence would be taking off on foot either towards Falryn or Merton; she hadn't quite decided yet. She would need a place to stay, and whilst the smaller town of Falryn was closer, the bigger town of Merton was in the direction of Alwich Castle and Cain.

Cain tried his best to keep his eyes closed, willing himself to drift off into an uneasy sleep. No matter how terrible sleep was chained up in the bowels of this ship, it was better than staying conscious. They had been at sea for so long now without the opportunity to stand and stretch, or even to speak to anyone besides Jed and occasionally Marcus. It was slowly driving him mad.

He had resigned himself to his fate, to his death, but it was taking too long to arrive. The sheer pain of waiting, wasting away, being left with nothing but his thoughts and regrets... it was worse than torture.

At the sound of footsteps on the stairs, he cracked open one eye half-heartedly. One of the sailors, just a deckhand as far as Cain could tell, descended the creaky stairs and came to a standstill at the door of the brig. "We'll be making berth tomorra'," he stated. "We'll reach port, and once all of the supplies and goods have been unloaded, you'll be handed over to the royal guard. From there, you'll travel by cart to the dungeons. Got it?" He half scowled at Jed before turning his eyes to Cain.

"Got it," Cain grumbled.

"Then you'll be the jailor's problem." The sailor was spindly, not a lick of muscle along his arms or across his back. His legs reminded Cain of twigs. He imagined briefly how good it would feel to break free of these chains, kick down the metal gate and choke the life out of this weak excuse for a sailor with his bare hands. He shifted slightly, clenching and unclenching his hands. He was restless, and it would feel so good to move properly again, even if it wasn't for long.

Prudence appeared like a flash in his mind, her eyes wild as she choked the life out of her landlady. She was gone too quickly and he closed his eyes again, trying to conjure up her image. He chuckled softly. She knew this feeling that stirred in him. She understood it. He wondered how many times she had felt it since he last laid eyes on her.

"Fuck are ye smiling at?" Jed nudged him with a foot.

Cain looked up and hummed softly. "Nothing."

"Thinking 'bout yer girl, huh?"

Cain nodded briefly. "Aye. I hope she's safe. I don't know what happened to her after they clapped me in irons."

Jed let out a rushed breath and ran a hand through his hair. "Fuck. Sorry…"

"She's tough." Cain spoke as if he was reminding himself as much as informing Jed. "She's smart, capable. She'll have cleared out and found somewhere to recoup." His mind drifted off to Prudence again, picturing her face as she reached for him, a scream visible in her eyes even though he couldn't hear it. "She'll be fine," he murmured as if to himself.

"She sounds like an impressive woman," Jed said.

"That she is." His mind swam with images of her. Prudence singing in The Wanderer's Inn after the fight was over, bodies littering the floor; Prudence gripping a sword, steely gaze in her eye ready to swing at him; Prudence sat on the floor of his cabin, nose scrunched up in concentration as she learnt to read; Prudence's ivory skin squeezed under his fingertips as her chest rose and fell in desperate pants; Prudence clutching his hand as they said their vows; Prudence's hand slipping out of his grip amid choppy waves, her head dipping under the surface and out of his view…

He huffed out a pained breath, trying to dislodge the ache in his chest. It wouldn't do to dwell on what might have been. He was never going to be able to touch her again, to look into her bright eyes. Would never hear her laugh or the feeling that sucked all the air out of his lungs whenever she looked at him with that adoring expression.

He would treasure the memories they had created until his last moment. He sighed and leant his head back against the wall, knocking it steadily. The regular thump, thump, thump of his head against the wood helped somewhat. It helped to drag his thoughts from his wife's thick hair, or the scent of her. The slight pain was welcome, and Cain rhythmically threw his head back repeatedly, quickening in pace and intensity.

"Shit, Cain. Take it easy, man," Jed said, a concerned tone lacing his normally sarcastic voice.

Cain couldn't hear him. His chest rose and fell rapidly with haggard breaths. Sweat formed on his brow and his hands grew clammy. An invisible force held a tight grip on his chest. "I- I-" He tried to speak but no words came.

His eyes fluttered open and closed involuntarily, fragments of images flashing in his mind. Prudence's soft eyes, her hand slipping away... her head going under the waves... Prudence's body lying lifeless... blood pooling on her chest.

"Cain!" Jed's hand met Cain's face, snapping his head back sharply.

Cain sucked in a rough breath, his body faltering for a moment, allowing him to surface from the chaos.

"Sorry, man. I didn't know what else to do. Are ye all right?"

It took a long moment, but finally, Cain started to compose himself, allowing the tension to ease from his shoulders. He unclenched his hands and winced. Little crescents of blood lined his palms where his nails had dug in.

"Sailor, are ye in there?" Jed half-joked, the worry still clear on his face.

"I don't know what that was..." Cain muttered, staring blankly at his hands.

"My mother used to get like that sometimes," Jed said grimly. "She'd bloody her hands and scream and cry, and no amount o' talking'd calm her down. She was all right, though. Ye will be too."

Cain appreciated the boy's blind optimism, choosing not to point out that they'd both be dead soon enough anyway. "Well, I'm sure she'd appreciate you trying to help her," he said softly. He couldn't take his eyes off his hands, still quaking slightly as he held them out in front of him. The lack of control was unnerving. A foreign experience he had no desire to repeat.

Khari watched as Prudence made her way around members of the crew of *The Wayward*. It amazed him even now that, despite her standoffish behaviour and overall unpleasant demeanour, she still managed to befriend people. Perhaps she wasn't fit for common society, unbearable at the best of times and downright monstrous at others, but on the edge with the other misfits and outliers, she seemed to have found her place.

The Wayward Damned was now anchored in a little bay off Eastcliff, its whereabouts hidden from view unless someone happened to take the very long, steep, and unforgiving path down the cliff face through a thick smattering of trees. They had disembarked by seniority, Captain Beckett, his quartermaster, and his boatswain leading the charge in the first dinghy to shore. They had built a small fire on the pebbles and were now drinking, laughing, and relaxing on the rocky beach.

Khari strode over to Captain Beckett and shook his hand. This was where they would part ways. "Thank ye, truly."

The captain nodded at him. "Well, I didn't do it out of the good o' my heart now, did I?"

Khari nodded. "Right, right." He shrugged, shoving a hand

deep into his pocket. He cast a furtive glance at Prudence as she laughed with the sailing master. "I should uh- I should be goin'." He nodded at the captain once more and turned on his heel, heading for the path up and out of the bay.

The rocks became bigger, the path uneven as he climbed. Despite how fit he was, it still left him panting for breath, a little twinge in his side. Once he reached the top, he stretched, forcing his back as straight as possible, and he let out a little moan. He stood assessing the view for a moment, allowing his breathing to return to normal, the twinge fading from his side.

He turned, the sound of rushing footsteps behind him. Prudence stood there, bent over clutching her waist, panting.

"Khari, wait up!" she huffed loudly, trying to force her breathing to steady long before she was ready to. "I didn't- I didn't get to say," she wheezed again, her face contorted in a scowl. "I didn't get to say thank ye."

He stood silently, staring at her while she pulled herself together. It took a long time, but eventually, she stood upright and faced him.

"I need to thank ye for everything ye did. For getting me here. For helping me. I-" she paused and Khari could see from her face that she was struggling to say whatever came next. That it felt unnatural to her. "I greatly appreciate it."

Her face twisted in displeasure as she said the words, and he couldn't help but smirk slightly. High praise indeed from the argumentative shrew.

"Where will ye go now?" she asked, looking up at him.

"I don't know. I thought I might head to the port, catch a ship somewhere far away from here."

Prudence nodded. "Aye... well, good luck." She didn't even cringe that time as she spoke to him with something akin to warmth. "Be safe."

He nodded and cast a look over her. Her cheeks were still flushed from the climb, a bag was slung over her shoulder, and she still wore the britches and men's jacket they had found in the lighthouse on Talah. Her belly, with the child, had just started to show a little if you looked too hard at her stomach. "What's yer plan, *keine*?"

"I'm going to find Cain," she stated plainly.

He rolled his eyes. "Yes, I know that much. How do you intend to do that?"

Prudence pursed her lips. "Well, right now, I'm going to walk until I get to the next town and hopefully find a place to stay before dark. Then I'm going to make my way to the castle, get to Cain, and find a way to get him out somehow."

Her plan was feeble, if not non-existent, and they both knew it. It would have been hard enough to rescue the captain with resources and a solid plan... with Prudence alone with nothing and no one, the man was going to hang without ever seeing her again.

Khari sighed and slowly met her eyes. "Ugh, fine."

"Pardon?" She cocked her head at him, confused.

"I'll come with ye, *keine*. We'll rescue yer man, and then I'm going to find a very quiet place to live somewhere far away from you."

Prudence didn't even try to hide the grin that broke out across her face. "Really?"

Khari rolled his eyes again and took her bag from her. "Don't make me say it again or I might change my mind." He took off walking in front of her, his strides so much larger than her own that it was already difficult for Prudence to catch up. "I'm not slowing down for ye. Don't talk constantly, I don't care for it, and so help me Gods, if ye get too irritating, I will turn around and leave."

He continued his tirade of rules as they walked, but Prudence didn't mind. She was too grateful for his accompanying her to make a retort or consider tripping him.

Soon after, he fell into silence and they walked side by side, one sombre and one beaming, poised to take on the world to achieve her goals. Eventually, just as the sky started to turn an inky black, no longer a deep blue still illuminated by the sun even after it dipped below the horizon, they reached Merton and stepped into the first inn they came across.

With a small number of the coins Prudence had, she purchased two rooms and two meals, large bowls of stew that filled their stomachs so completely it could have kept them warm until morning. They soon retired and fell into dreamless, deep sleeps, ready to face the morrow.

CHAPTER SEVEN

HOMELAND

After a long few days of travelling on foot, the pair stopped in Holmston. It was agonisingly slow progress as far as Prudence was concerned, but the child in her belly had riddled her back and ankles with pain, and she had to keep stopping for rest.

The little town was nestled in a thick woodland that stretched far and wide. Sycamores and ash lined the path that led into town; a beautiful canopy of green was beginning to grow above them as the season made way for warmer weather. It seemed idyllic. The pathway was pebbled, a neatly carved walkway amongst the forest that looked like it had been created with a loving hand.

They followed the winding path around many turns until finally, the edges of Holmston came into view. Cottages lined the main road; dogs, chickens, and other livestock roamed freely outside as people busied about with their daily lives. Numerous faces looked up and smiled at them as they passed. It was almost unsettling, the sense of friendliness around them. It wasn't something Prudence was used to.

In the centre of Holmston sat the sole inn. A tall building with wonky walls and slanted roofs. It was made up of multiple sections that didn't quite fit together, as if they had been built on after, without any real thought to how the rooms would function. It sat in the middle of everything, surrounded by a bustling marketplace full of stalls, small shops, and sellers walking about with their wares, enticing people to try.

Prudence pushed down the initial feeling of panic at being around so many people. They had spent so much time running, keeping a low profile and hiding away, it still felt natural for her to shrink under many gazes. To make herself seem as innocuous as possible.

She followed Khari through the stream of stalls and into the inn. Like outside, it was bustling with people. Many patrons sat eating and drinking, a fire roared in a corner of this one hall, and a fiddler played music beside it, a woman accompanying him with her singing. It was a stark contrast to The Wanderer's Inn and Prudence wasn't sure how she felt about it.

Khari strode up to the man behind the bar as she hovered in the doorway. She cast a glance around the room, taking in all the faces before her. A wide range of people lived here, it seemed. A number of more well-dressed merchants enjoyed a drink after a day of trading. Some, what she assumed to be farmers, sat around a table by the far wall discussing their livestock and crop yield projections for the year ahead.

A ball rolled in through the door, stopping as it hit Prudence's ankles. She bent down and picked it up, turning around to see where it had come from. Three children ran headfirst at full pelt, eyes on the floor, straight at Prudence. They looked up and saw her just before it was too late and screeched to a halt. The tallest, a girl with scraped knees and mud all over, even speckled on her face, met Prudence's eye.

"That's our ball," she said plainly.

Prudence's lip quirked. "I can see that."

"We need it back."

Prudence looked over at the other two, two boys of around nine years old. Scruffy and dirty just like the girl. They shuffled nervously on gangly legs a few steps behind the girl. "Yer lookin' awfully muddy for jus' playing in the street."

"We *were* playin' in the woods, but these chickens got scared." The little girl rolled her eyes at Prudence, clearly frustrated with her companions.

"Oh, really?"

"We weren't scared, Tilly!" yelled the dark-haired boy.

Tilly scoffed. "Oh, yeah? Then why'd ye look like ye might piss yer pants when I told you I wanted to go in the cave!"

The poor boy blushed and grumbled, kicking at the stones at his feet.

Prudence couldn't help but bite back a smile. She crouched down to Tilly's level and dropped her voice to a whisper. "Ye can't blame them. Some of us girls are jus' braver than boys." She winked at the girl as she broke into a grin.

Prudence passed her the ball, Tilly's grubby little fingers grabbing it out of her hand before running off. The boys followed suit, chasing after their leader with a 'thanks, Miss' yelled over their shoulders.

The ship docked in the port at Kilead, and soon enough, rough hands dragged Cain and Jed out of the brig, hauling them out into the fresh air. The light was blinding after so long below deck. Cain squinted, unable to shield his eyes with his hands bound as he was forced down the gangplank and onto dry land. They were passed from sailors to soldiers and shoved into the back of a prison wagon that was already waiting for them.

It was just the same as the one before. Hard wood under their feet, shackles around their wrists and ankles, a troop of obnoxious soldiers talking loudly from their seats at the front of the wagon. The journey was made only slightly better this time by the company of Jed and the much-improved road conditions. No jerking bumps as they travelled, only the occasional jolt as the wagon lurched forward after a stop.

The closer they got to Alwich Castle, the paler Jed seemed to become. His normally ruddy complexion had taken on a meek pallor, his gestures becoming jittery and skittish. Cain felt a pang of sympathy for the boy, the anticipation only making his panic worsen. He tried his best to comfort him.

"You know, it's not so bad," he spoke softly. "You'll be fed far better than we have been these last few months, and whilst it certainly isn't comfortable sleeping in a cell, it's easier than chained in a brig." Jed didn't bother to look up or acknowledge he had even spoken. "And when the time comes... yes, it will be scary, but it will also be over soon."

He wasn't completely lying. Odds were the boy's neck would break immediately. It, of course, was in the realm of possibility that it wouldn't and then his suffering would be extended somewhat... but even then only by minutes. Cain felt a little stab of guilt in his gut but he pushed it down. Better for Jed to be buoyed up with false courage than to be dragged to the block struggling and weeping for his mother.

Jed finally looked up at him then. "Ye promise?" His voice wavered, uncertain.

The stabbing pain came back with a sharp vengeance and Cain grit his teeth. "I promise," he forced out. It was better this way.

Jed stopped quaking mostly and nodded, his eyes downcast to the floor. "All right."

They rode on, the wagon's wheels creaking with every turn, and when they passed through the main square of Kilead, a harsh throng of voices rose around them.

"Thieves!"

"Criminals!"

"Let them hang!"

Cain saw Jed attempt to look out the bars of the wagon and pulled him back. "Don't look. lad. 'Tis better to not give them a glance." A rotten vegetable of some kind—it looked a little like cabbage to Cain—smacked against the bars and broke upon impact, sending parts in all directions both inside the wagon and across the road. The smell was vile, stinking of vomit. Cain plugged his nose with his fingers and forced himself to breathe through his mouth.

It took them a while to collect all of the little pieces and throw them out the bars of the wagon, but once they had, the smell lessened somewhat. The wagon wheels continued turning, bringing them closer to their final resting place.

As they pulled out of the square, the buildings began to spread out, becoming larger with more land in between. People paid less attention to them here, their focus instead on their work or eyes glued to the road as they walked with purpose in the direction the wagon had just come. They rounded a corner and the smell of baked goods hit their noses, pushing out the final smells of rot from the back of the wagon and sending Cain spiralling into a memory.

The smell of freshly baked bread wafted out of the tumblestone house all the way to the little boy's nose. It drifted into his nostrils and filled his head with images of warm nights curled up with his family in front of their small hearth to fight away the winter chill. Any moment, his mother would yell for him, cutting his game far too short, but he would be rewarded with hot bread and melting butter to fill his belly.

The wind tousled his blond locks against his cheeks and his sister giggled at him. "You look like a girl with hair that long, Cain." He huffed, and air blew out of his nose like a bull when it locked eyes on a target.

Cain shoved his little sister in the side, knocking her to the floor. "Shut up!" Despite being three years her elder, Cain was only slightly taller than his scrawny sister, Florence. He puffed his chest out as far as possible as he towered over her. She was always teasing him. "Shut up, Florrie. What do you know? You're just a kid."

"You're just a kid, stupid."

"No, I'm not. Not really. Papa said he'd take me with him hunting soon, so there." He hated how easily his sister got under his skin. He wasn't a kid. He was ten. He could go hunting soon;

Papa had said so. What did Florrie know? All she did was help Ma with the cooking and play with her little friends.

Florence picked a daisy and tucked it behind her ear. "Still a kid," she sang, the grin on her face widening as Cain's expression became more and more thunderous. "Why would you want to grow up anyway? Grown-ups don't get to play. All they do is chores. Being a kid is much more fun." She kicked her shoes off and ran to play with the other children in the valley.

Cain watched as she launched herself at one of them, sending them all toppling into a heap on the floor. He could hear their laughter from where he stood, face still as dark as night. He didn't want to play all day. He had more important things to do, like catching dinner with Papa. That would be much more fun.

He looked at the stone in his hand he had so diligently been hacking into a point and threw it as far as he could. Stupid Florrie. He wasn't a kid.

"Cain! Florence! Inside, now!"

Their mother was hurrying about the house when Cain entered, kicking off his muddy boots at the door. He grabbed a fresh roll and shoved it into his mouth, taking a bite too big to chew.

"Get yourselves ready; we've got to head to town." She bundled items into a wicker basket, not meeting their eyes.

"Why, Ma?"

"Just hurry up so we don't miss Mr. Denny's wagon, lad." Cain rolled his eyes but pulled his jacket on regardless and helped his sister find hers.

The ride out of the village was bumpy and long. Torrin Down lay at the edge of a deep valley that led into the mountain range that spread across Aelin Isle like a gash. Cain watched his cottage grow smaller and smaller as the little wagon and pony climbed the rough path out of the valley in the direction of the closest town.

It took a few hours to reach the town that sat at the edge of the Great Lake. The town was bustling with people, and their mother clung tight to his wrist, pulling him and his sister along through the crowd.

She stopped suddenly, and Cain bashed into her back. "Now, you two wait right here, all right? I won't be long."

Florrie's mouth opened to ask why, but their mother was already too far away to hear. She pulled on Cain's sleeve. "What's going on? Mama never takes us to town."

Cain's brow furrowed, but he didn't answer, his eyes trying to track his mother through the hordes of people.

They waited there, leaning on one another for support for quite some time. Cain had given up looking for their mother returning when a man in uniform stepped in front of them. He looked up into the tall man's face. A bushy moustache covered his top lip like a caterpillar, and his eyes were dark and hard.

"You two. You're coming with me."

"We're waiting for our mama, Sir," Florrie muttered with a quiet voice. She leant close into Cain's side and his arm moved around her shoulders protectively.

"No. We're waiting for our mother, Sir. Good day."

"No, you're not, lad. Not anymore." The man shifted his weight and tugged at his shirt awkwardly. "You're property of the royal fleet now. You need to come with me."

Prudence and Khari left Holmston, heading north, taking the longer route to avoid the mountains. If it weren't for Cain, Prudence would have been tempted to stay in the quaint little village. She was almost sad to leave. They took off on foot, following the stone path out of Holmston through the forest.

Her belly was now showing to the point where it could not be hidden under britches, and the innkeeper's wife had been kind enough to provide her with some skirts that would hopefully be more comfortable for the journey.

Khari had insisted on carrying most of the supplies, so her pack was rather empty save for some cheese and a skein of wine.

"If we can keep this pace, we'll make good time," said Khari, slightly ahead of her. "We'll take a short break only when absolutely necessary and make camp at nightfall. All right?"

Prudence mumbled a noise of agreement. She didn't wish to admit that she was a little out of breath. If she did, he might stop, and it would take even longer to get to Cain. She leant backwards as far as possible without tumbling over, hands pressed firmly into her lower back. It helped a little. She felt a click in her spine and sighed with relief.

"Ye all right there, *keine*?" Khari had paused his long strides and was watching her intently.

"Yes, fine." Prudence scurried to catch up with him. "Come on. Let's get a move on." She felt rather than saw him pull a face beside her, but he didn't argue. He knew how important this was.

"Ye know ye'll be no good to 'im if ye push yerself too hard."

Prudence rolled her eyes. "I'm not. But it'll be no good if we get to him too late either."

"It's not just *you*, though. Not anymore." He gave Prudence a pointed look.

She grumbled. "I didn't ask for this."

"I know ye didn't."

"Not exactly the best timing," she huffed, her hand still cradling her bump even while she complained.

"Ye know, if ye don't want it-"

"I didn't say that!" Prudence snapped. "I just... it makes things harder." She trailed off, not sure what else to say. She hadn't ever pictured herself having a child. She hadn't expected to live this long. But did she want it?

Yes.

Yes, she did. She wanted her child. Cain's child. But only if Cain could be there. The idea of doing it all alone... it didn't bear thinking about.

"I didn't mean anything by it, *keine*. Only that ye don't have to do anything ye don't want to," Khari said softly.

Prudence said nothing in response and they lapsed into a tense silence. She hadn't given the child growing in her belly much thought over the last few months. She hadn't allowed herself to. Every possible path forward was a scary one. She wasn't ready to be a mother. Taking care of something so small and helpless... what if she did it wrong? What if she couldn't protect it?

She didn't have time to focus on a child. Cain needed her. They were running out of time each day to get to him. Prudence didn't even know where he was.

A pang of grief swept through her at the thought of what he might be dealing with. She hoped he was still fighting, still pushing to survive, but how long would that last when there was no hope? He didn't know she was coming for him.

Prudence stroked her stomach, lost in thought. "Hold on, Cain. I'm coming," she whispered to herself.

Despite her ever-growing belly impeding progress, they travelled a good distance during the day, settling down for the night only when it became too dark to see at all. They took shelter under a large oak, the ground mercifully soft with moss and lichen. Khari lit a small fire while Prudence set a snare a little ways away. The weather had begun to warm even more over recent days, leaving a pleasant breeze on the air. The sky was free of clouds, allowing the moon to beam down on the little glen.

The harsh days of winter were long behind them now the world had made way for the drizzling, sunny days of spring. New growth emerged in every woodland and meadow, new life birthed in the fields and rivers. A bird landed in the tree above them, settling into its nest for the night.

Prudence felt a flutter of movement in her belly as she leant back and gasped. She put a hand hesitantly over the spot and felt the movement again. There was life in there. Life she and Cain had made.

"It's really something, isn't it?" Khari spoke up from his spot across the fire.

Prudence found her eyes had become misty. "It really is. Ye've felt something like this before?"

Khari nodded. "Many a time, back in my village. I used to assist my mother with the births."

"I thought yer mother was the leader of yer people?"

"She is."

"Then why does she aid in childbirth?" asked Prudence.

"Birth is a sacred rite. Who better to watch over them than our leader? Mother to us all." Khari said it so plainly, as if the entire world worked this way. Prudence wondered why it didn't.

Prudence left Khari sleeping where he lay and took off further into the woods in search of food she could forage. She walked away from their makeshift camp, keeping her eyes peeled for deciduous trees and streams.

The woods were beautiful at this time of year. The sun was shining a soft light through the trunks, not yet high enough to reach the canopy. The air was still relatively damp, dew dripping off every blade of grass, every cobweb glistening, and a faint mist clung in corners.

She trudged through the undergrowth. The rustle and creak of things underfoot startled a deer just a few feet away, and its head flung up, nostrils flaring, smelling her before it ran off.

Underneath a large beech tree, Prudence spotted a few morels and sank to her knees to harvest them. She dug the stems out of the dirt and carefully stashed them in her skirt pocket. Alone, they wouldn't satisfy, but it was a start.

She continued to search for a while. She had found some sorrel growing and near a quiet little stream, some butterbur leaves. It wasn't much, but if they could catch a rabbit or two, it would make for a very decent meal.

Prudence turned back in the direction she had come, making her way back to Khari. The trees all looked the same, but she followed the sun back east; she just had to keep heading straight. A stick cracked somewhere behind her, and she froze. A long silence followed, broken only by birdsong.

"Must have been a deer," she said to herself, shaking her head at her paranoia. "Don't be stupid, Pru. It's nothing. Don't lose yer nerve now." She picked up her pace slightly, her hand instinctively going to cradle her bump.

Prudence found herself straining for any sound to indicate she was no longer alone as she walked, but nothing. The crack from behind her did not repeat, nor did she hear anything else and yet... it felt like eyes were on her, watching her every move. She couldn't help but turn her head to check behind her every few seconds.

Prudence turned back to flaming eyes and a thick, bedraggled mane. The gytrash was as black as night and clearly wild. It snorted at her, a puff of breath billowing like smoke in the cool morning air. Eyes locked with her own, far more human and knowing than they should be.

Prudence stilled, wary it would charge her. "Whoa, there. Easy, boy." She spoke softly, making her voice lower. "It's all right, I won't hurt ye. In fact, I'd quite like to leave. Yer just blocking my way," she murmured to the horse, her hands raised as if in surrender.

The creature that resembled a monstrous horse watched her curiously. Its gaze never wavered from her own. She stepped to the side slowly. If she could inch around to the left, she might be able to get past it without alarming it. She took another cautious step, but the horse didn't move; it just watched her intently.

Prudence inched around the animal, maintaining the distance between them until she was parallel to its flank. "All right, good boy," she crooned. "I'm just gonna head this way now..." She turned and took a step away.

Immediately, the horse's eyes blazed, and it lunged around, blocking her path once more. A threatening scream made Prudence step back. "Fuck! Sorry, sorry." She held her hands up again in submission. She glanced in the direction of her exit.

The horse moved towards her swiftly. It made her gasp. "Guess ye don't want me to go that way, huh?" Prudence huffed.

What was she meant to do now? She looked around the woods. The feel of eyes on her still hung around, and it wasn't coming from the horse. It made the hair on the back of her neck stand up.

"Will ye let me go this way?" She cocked her head to the right. When the horse didn't move, she took a hesitant step forward. Still, it didn't move. "All right. Yer fine, aren't ye?" she murmured as she moved forward again.

It seemed to settle once she stopped trying to pass it. She walked a short way in completely the wrong direction. Her shoulders remained tight with her back now fully turned to the horse. It was too close, too open. If it charged her now, she wouldn't be able to move away in time.

It didn't charge but Prudence could hear it move towards her. She couldn't help but watch it. It moved gracefully, almost unnaturally, through the woods, its hooves not making a sound. Its black coat changed and shifted in the light, looking like a deep green as it moved through the brush, blending in with its surroundings.

Prudence was certain now. Whatever it was, it definitely wasn't a horse. Even more need to do as it bid and not make it angry. Although if it were some malevolent spirit, it might have been luring her to her death.

She cast a quick glance at the creature. It was most definitely an intimidating sight. Bigger than most farm horses she had seen, with hooves the size of her head and a long, thick crest. His head was held high with ears pointed directly to her, eyes the colour of fire that blazed in their sockets like the real thing. But despite its appearance it didn't feel like a threat, not now that she was doing what it wanted.

Another crack of breaking sticks sounded and Prudence's head flung round. That had definitely come from somewhere near their camp. Her pulse quickened in worry.

"Khari," she whispered. Prudence locked eyes with the horse again. "Yer going to need to let me pass now, ye hear? That sound? I have a friend over there and I think he might need me. I need ye to let me pass."

She tried to retrace her steps, but the horse whinnied nervously and stamped its front hoof. "Look, I'm sorry. I don't know what yer trying to tell me, but I can't jus' leave my friend, not now." She managed to scurry a few yards, but the horse got more and more agitated. It surged forward, trotting around her in circles to keep her in place.

"I don't know what ye want from me!" she yelled, exasperated.

Another crack and a yell.

"Khari!" she called. Prudence saw a gap and made a break for it, running right past the horse. It screeched, chasing after her, but before it could reach her, she stopped short.

A man emerged from the treeline. "I told Barty there was a girl out 'ere somewhere." He smirked. "I saw the panicked look in yer friend's eye when we started searchin'. Ain't no man gettin' that worried over anything but snatch." His smirk morphed into a grin showing all his yellow teeth. His eyes swept down over Prudence's body and landed on her stomach. "Well, shit. Looks like someone got there first. Was it yer tall friend over there? Oh, well; I didn't want a brat anyway. Don't worry," he murmured. "Yer baby'll be fine." He inched towards her. The horse lunged in front of Prudence, getting between them. The man flinched.

"Fuckin' beast," he muttered and tried to sidestep the horse, but it lunged again, sinking its teeth into the man's arm. He cried out, and Prudence heard a crunch as blood began to drip down his arm.

"Jer?" another male voice called, and a second man appeared at Prudence's left. "Oh, shit!" He raised a gun in a shaky hand and fired at the horse. The shot flew and sank into the flesh on its shoulder, or at least Prudence thought it did.

She watched in fascination as the wound expelled the lead ball, the shot dropping to the ground. As soon as the metal had left its body, the wound sealed itself back up.

The horse spun and kicked out at Jer, kicking him in the gut before running to the west. With a quick look at Prudence, it nickered as if telling her to follow. She didn't hesitate and ran after the horse. Whatever it was, it seemed to want to protect her.

She did her best to follow it through the trees, but its shifting colour made it hard to spot. She lost it momentarily, and her heart pounded as she turned in circles, searching. "Not now," she muttered quietly. "Help me just a little more." She looked around wildly and finally caught a glimpse of it through the trees. She surged towards it only for strong arms to wrap around her middle, trapping her.

"Not so fast there. Come on now..." She felt hot breath in her ear. "Don't run. Ye've still got to meet my friends."

CHAPTER EIGHT

REPERCUSSIONS

F irm hands gripped Khari's arms as he thrashed against them. They had come while he slept, already ransacking most of their camp before he woke. They had hauled him to his feet as they tore into everything available. It had taken three of them to hold him. Khari had looked around wildly, relieved when Prudence was nowhere to be seen.

"Now, now." A man as tall as Khari with dirty blond hair and stubble peppering his jaw sauntered up to Khari. Presumably the leader of this little group by the way he spoke. "Let's all take a breath here. We're calm, aren't we? Let's be friends." He smirked.

Khari thrashed against their hold, trying to rip his arms free to no avail.

"A tough one, aren't you?" The man squared up to Khari, locking eyes with him, amused. "You can stop fighting. My boys here have you; you'll only wear yourself out. We won't be long. Once we've accepted your... generous donation..." He looked around at his men taking their possessions. "...We'll be out of your hair."

Khari's heart hammered in his chest. Where was Prudence? He hoped they left before she came back. Just then, a jeer sounded through the trees. Two other men joined the group before Khari, one of which had Prudence slung over his shoulder.

Khari fought against his captors and wrenched free of them, only to be brought to his knees by a pistol slamming into the back of his head. He tried to stand, but his vision swam, his head pounding, and he sank to the earth once more.

Prudence kicked out at the man holding her, her fist pummelling his back. The other man already looked a little worse for wear. His left arm was coated thick with blood and it hung limply at his side. He walked with a limp, the other hand cradling his stomach gently.

"Gods' teeth, what the fuck happened to Jeremiah?!" the leader yelled.

"There's somethin' freaky out there, Mr. Gordon. S'not fuckin' natural." Jeremiah quaked. He looked unbelievably pale, more from fear than blood loss.

"He lost a fight with a horse," the other man chimed in, leaving everyone including Khari perplexed. Prudence gave him a swift kick in the crotch, and he growled, tightening his grip on her. "Fuckin' bitch. Cut it out before I gut you."

"It was a demon horse, Barty!" Jeremiah argued.

"I dunno 'bout demons, but it certainly wasn't normal, tha's for sure," the other man, Barty, agreed.

Khari watched Prudence warily. She didn't seem hurt, only incredibly pissed off as she kicked and hurled insults so filthy they almost made Khari blush. It filled him with an amusing sense of pride. They'd bitten off more than they could chew with that woman.

"Enough!" Mr. Gordon yelled, and he pinched the bridge of his nose as if to stave off a headache. "Jeremiah, help Jonah and Mr. Burke load the stuff. Fuck me!" He took a closer look at Jeremiah's arm as he walked past and recoiled. "Get that thing wrapped up. It's disgusting."

Mr. Gordon grimaced. It was a ghastly wound. Whatever the 'demon horse' had been, it had torn the flesh all along the man's forearm, chunks of skin left barely hanging on. The blood no longer poured but had begun to clot and congeal in the teeth marks. A horse bite could be bad, but this looked even worse.

"Let the girl go," Khari hissed at Barty, who only laughed in response.

"Why should I? I caught the whore. She's mine now." He smiled, showing off a mouth full of holes. "Don't worry, I might share 'er. Not with you, mind, so I guess there is cause to worry." He laughed again, a deep chortle from his belly.

"Put her down, Bartholomew," Mr. Gordon sighed. "Are you really so desperate for a fuck that you'd rape a pregnant whore?"

Barty huffed and let go of Prudence, dropping her on the ground hard.

"Ye fuckin' cunt! I'll fuckin' kill ye! Ye slimy, skeevy, old fuckin-" Prudence's obscene rant was cut off by a sharp slap to the face.

"You watch your mouth, bitch." Mr. Gordan's voice was a

quiet threat, and it was clear he was to be taken deadly seriously. Prudence clamped her mouth shut.

Khari's blood seethed with rage, but he didn't move to help her, he had a feeling it would only make matters worse. Prudence looked up, hand still covering her cheek, and met his eyes. This was a volatile situation and they both knew it.

Mr. Gordon instructed a tall, slim man with short-cropped hair by the name of Mr. Sinclair to tie Khari and Prudence up. They sat, tied together, leaning against the big oak as the band of thieves got organised.

"I say we camp here for the night boys. This is a pretty decent spot these two found." Mr. Gordan grinned and patted Khari on the head patronisingly, earning a feral growl from Prudence.

The dank cell that Cain now resided in was empty of any other prisoners. He knew that it could not simply be a matter of luck to be left to his own devices, rather that something worse must be coming down the line.

The cell was relatively dark, with no light coming in aside from the lanterns that lit the hallway outside his bars. The dungeon itself was under the grounds of the castle, under the floors walked on by many feet day in, day out, hiding the screams and horrors that its prisoners endured.

Jed had been tossed into a cell a few down from Cain, amongst a band of what could only be murderers, thieves, and other lowlifes. The poor lad had looked positively terrified, but Cain had done his best to appear reassuring and confident despite the uncertainty in his mind that he would ever see his friend again.

They had shoved him further down the corridor once the barred door had been slammed shut behind Jed, blocking him from view, and opened up this bare cell. Just for him.

No doubt his peace would be destroyed by untold terrors eventually but for now, he leant back against the cold stone wall and shut his eyes, grateful for some semblance of quiet. Visions of his black-haired wife, wild and carefree in her element, drifted into his mind and kept him company until he felt the merciful embrace of sleep.

He woke to the soft caress of her fingers on his cheek and groped for her blindly in the dark, keeping his eyes closed to preserve the illusion. He could feel her gentle touch against his skin, the brush of his beard as her fingers moved through it, and if he concentrated hard, the weight of her presence right beside him.

She leant into him as she knelt at his side, thigh pressed against thigh, arm against arm, breath mingling. He breathed her in as if she were oxygen. He longed to hear her voice, ears straining as if he might be able to hear her now even from this distance. Soft moans at his touch, whimpers yearning for more. The sound of flesh meeting flesh sounding ever louder in the quiet of the night.

His hand found its way into his britches, tugging the buttons open, but it was her hand he felt on his cock. The soft skin of her delicate fingers wrapped around him, thumb brushing against the head as it twitched. A grunt fell from his lips as he gripped tighter, and he swore he could smell her, her long dark hair falling into his face, the whisper of his name from her mouth.

"Pru..." Her name was murmured like a prayer. A fragment

of salvation in a sea of grief. The divinity of the temple in which he worshipped.

His blood roared in his veins, pulsing through his ears until it was all he could hear. His eyes screwed up tight in desperation as he held the image of her in his mind.

A groan shuddered through him as he found his release, so short-lived as reality came crashing down. There was no Prudence. No hand touching him save for his own. His wife was not kneeling in front of him, lips parted like a temptation. He didn't even know where she was.

The sudden high was met with a deep low full of longing. He pulled his hand back out of his trousers and slumped heavily against the wall. Where was she now? Was she safe? Cain had never been one for gods or belief, but in that moment, he found himself questioning, vowing that if they did exist, if they were listening, that they would protect her where he no longer could.

"So, what are we to do with them?" the man who had been identified as Mr. Burke asked. He was of average height, at least a head shorter than Cain, with curly brown hair and dark brown eyes. His beard was short, almost stubbled, and covered his jawline up to his ears.

"Yeah, what's gonna happen to the li'l bitch?" asked Jeremiah, his arm now wrapped badly in a worn shirt. He stood next to the youngest of the group, Jonah they had called him, who was surprisingly quiet, his eyes on something in his hands. He looked to Prudence no more than a boy. Young and nervous, and less than keen to join in with the suggestions of what to do with the pair.

"She ruined my fucking arm!" Jeremiah complained loudly, his fiery gaze on Prudence, knife in hand at the ready.

"Lower your fucking voice, you imbecile. We don't want more company and we're not too far from the main road." Mr. Gordon rolled his eyes at Jeremiah from his perch on their wagon. He pulled an apple from one of the sacks and bit into it. "You'll get your chance for revenge, but not tonight. Let's get some sleep and deal with her *friend* in the morning, then you can do as you please with the little miss."

A wave of nausea rolled through Prudence and bile worked its way up her throat into her mouth. She turned her head to look at Khari but couldn't quite catch his eye from the way they were tied to the tree next to one another. They needed to get away. They needed to get out of these ties.

There were numerous grumbles from the other men, but they didn't argue with their leader. A few looks were cast at Prudence as they prepared to settle down for the night; looks that made her skin crawl. Eyes attempting to undress her.

She resisted the urge to shift positions under their uncomfortable gazes and instead put on a look of sheer indignation, jutting her chin out determinedly. They may have had every desire to see her worn down, to see her shamed and naked, stripped bare for the world to see both physically and emotionally, but she wouldn't give them that. Whatever else they might do to her, they wouldn't take her dignity.

Barty leant in close, his breath wrapping around her face like rancid tendrils. "See you on the morrow, Miss." His eyes gleamed and he cast his gaze unashamedly down her dress to her bosom.

Prudence gave him a swift kick to the shin.

"Ow, you stupid bitch." He grabbed her by the hair, tugging her closer to him. His grip on her scalp was so tight Prudence thought it might rip some hair out. "I'm going to make you fucking pay for that on your knees."

"Bartholomew!" Mr. Gordon barked, and the odious man released her head with a harsh swing, forcing it against the tree trunk.

Prudence watched with venom pulsing through her as 'Barty' sat himself down around their fire and took a swig of their ale. Mr. Gordan stood off to the side, his position as head of this little group emanating from him even with the way he stood.

Prudence watched as he leant over to Jonah still sitting on the wagon, fiddling with whatever he was holding. The poor boy looked positively riddled with nerves, his fingers spinning around, his leg jiggling up and down. He looked up when Mr. Gordon spoke to him. It was clear that he respected the man; he might have even liked him from the way he opened himself up in conversation.

They were deeply focused on something, their heads bowed together as they spoke, Jonah seemingly becoming more and more confident in himself as the conversation went on. Every now and then, one of them would turn to look at Prudence, accidentally making eye contact with her as she watched them.

Mr. Gordon's face twitched and he seemed to speak more harshly to the boy, but to his credit, Jonah didn't back down. His face was nervous but determined. Resolute. He locked eyes with Prudence once more and she felt a sense of calm control from him.

Eventually, Mr. Gordon sighed and nodded before leaving Jonah to his own devices. He left the wagon and joined the rest of the men around the fire. He was closer now and Prudence could just make out what he was saying.

"No one touches the girl."

Roars of complaints and arguing erupted from the rest of them.

"No one," Mr. Gordon spoke slowly, his voice quiet but commanding, "touches the girl. Do you understand me?"

It was a long time before anyone spoke. The men shared looks of shock, disbelief, anger, and more as they tried to understand why their leader was saying such a thing. Prudence tore her gaze away for a moment and found Jonah watching her intently. She didn't know exactly what had been discussed between the young boy and his mentor. She certainly didn't understand the dynamic or the power that Jonah seemed to be able to wield over the hulking, terrifying man... but Prudence knew in that moment that she probably owed him her life, and by extension, her child's.

There was no doubt that the tension within the group of thieves was not the norm for them, but instead brought on by the presence of Prudence and the consequent restrictions placed on them regarding her. They were pissed. Prudence could see it in every hungry glance thrown her way, every venomous retort when they spoke. When a fight broke out, it was anything but surprising.

It started simply, as most conflicts do. Barty was in a foul mood, hoarding more than his fair share of the food they had prepared that morning. A few of the men had complained but when Mr. Burke leant forward and snatched the last of the rabbit out of his hands, tearing into it, he erupted.

Barty leapt up and lunged for the stoic Mr. Burke, knocking him off his seat, on a fallen tree, to the ground. The rabbit leg flew upwards as it slipped out of his hand at great speed and landed on the grass beside the two grappling men.

Mr. Burke landed a solid punch to Barty's head, his chin snapping backwards sharply, and Prudence thought she heard a crack. She could tell it must have hurt but it seemed to only make Barty angrier. He threw himself on top of the other man, both striving to get a hold on the other.

Jeremiah piped up, yelling but not engaging as he held his torn arm protectively. "Fuckin' get him, Barty! Make it hurt!"

Mr. Sinclair promptly smacked him upside the head, hard, and the two of them got sucked right into the ridiculous fight. Prudence watched with amusement as they went for each other. All logic and thought had gone and they were brought down to their basic primal urges as they whaled on each other.

Mr. Sinclair tried to offer Mr. Burke a hand as he managed to take control of his own battle, only to be punched in the gut by the raging bull that was Bartholomew. Prudence sniggered; she couldn't help it. Underneath the bravado and scare tactics, they were simple men and most stupid if she did say so herself.

She watched them for a long time, taking in the entertainment as if it were a play put on just for her. She felt Khari watching her and bit back a grin.

"Yer lovin' this, don't lie."

"And what if I am? Is it so bad that I'm amused that our captors are preoccupied beating the shit out of each other?" she replied plainly, trying to hide the laugh in her throat.

Mr. Sinclair grabbed Barty by the hair and tugged, hard, a clump of his hair coming out in his hand. The man was already balding, and Prudence snorted. Barty's eyes flashed.

"Ye fuckin' prick!" Barty was now cradling the patch that was missing some hair. "Yer dead, ye hear me? I'm gonna fuckin' kill ye and cook ya."

Mr. Burke suddenly appeared behind him, knife in hand and thumped him on the head with the hilt sending him sprawling to the floor instantly. Prudence wondered for a moment if he were unconscious but then the hideous beast breathed and his eyelids fluttered. No such luck.

"Definitely not bad, *keine*, I would agree. It is most amusing. In fact..." he leant into her, dropping his voice to a whisper, "it might be to our advantage."

She looked up at him. He smirked, his eyes dancing with mischief. Realisation dawned on her, and she grinned. Turning back to the brawl in front of them, Prudence watched with a more focused attention this time around.

She paid attention to the way Mr. Burke seemed to favour his right side; how Barty struggled more and more each time he had to get off the ground, his knees struggling with his weight and age; Jeremiah was already injured—that was useful—and Jonah kept himself away from the fray, watching with nervous eyes.

This was what they needed. To merely wait for the right moment, the right instigating comment, and they'd be able to use the carnage to their advantage. She wasn't sure how it would all come about, nor how they would use it, but she knew they could. These men were too focused on bickering and trying to kill each other that they paid Prudence and Khari no mind at all. If they were to vanish in a puff of smoke, she wouldn't have been surprised if not a single one of them noticed.

Finally Mr. Gordon stalked into the mess of men and grabbed Barty and Mr. Burke by the collars, hauling them up either side of him. His face was set like rock. Prudence couldn't decide whether he looked more furious or disappointed. She hoped it was disappointment. She hoped he would kick the both of them out of their little group, leaving them to either succeed in killing the other or survive on their own. Either way, a victory in Prudence's eyes.

"Are you done?" Mr. Gordon's voice was low and menacing as he spoke, far too calm considering the situation.

Both men were panting, still reeling from their rage and the exertion of fighting. Their faces were bright red and their chests heaved as they stood like naughty children being chastised by a parent.

"I said... are you fucking done?" he growled and gave each of their shirt collars a tug.

"Yes."

"Aye, Mr. Gordon. Am done."

He released both of their shirts, rendering each with a sharp slap to the back of the head. "Fucking idiots," he grumbled, walking away from them. "Swear it'd be fucking easier to train a pig."

The pair was solemn, licking the wounds from the verbal lashing, but Prudence didn't mistake the look of malice in Barty's eye as he stared at Mr. Gordon. Something was brewing there. Discourse, insurrection. This band of brothers might not stay together for too much longer.

The door to Cain's cell flew open, and in strode two guards, hands on their sword hilts as if expecting Cain to fight despite being in chains. And then in walked the face Cain had been expecting ever since he arrived.

He was a slim man with a head of copper hair that matched his neatly trimmed beard, piercing green eyes, and a sure stance. Frederick III, King of Aelin, Ruler of The Western Tides.

He turned to the guards. "Leave us." The king strode around the cell, hands clasped behind his back as if examining the quality of housekeeping. After a few minutes, he turned to face Cain.

"Mr. Morris." His eyes met Cain's. Not cold as he suspected, but a firm resoluteness in them. "You've been a hard man to find."

His tone was formal and indifferent, as if he were addressing anyone in the world.

"Your Majesty." Cain looked up at King Frederick from the floor.

"We've never met before, and yet I feel as though I know you."

"Is that so?" asked Cain. He was curious. He had been expecting this visit, but it was certainly nothing like he had imagined so far. He had been anticipating anger, rage... He had anticipated torture, not this sense of calm.

"Yes. I have spent a lot of time thinking about this moment. I've spent many moments over the years envisioning what it would be like. To meet you. Speak with you. Watch you die. I know a lot about you already. Aelish born, served in the fleet as a child-"

"Sold," said Cain bluntly. "I was sold to the fleet as a child."

King Frederick did not reply but a slight nod indicated he had heard and conceded. "The ship you were... contracted to," he continued. "Was set upon by mermaids and lost almost half its crew. It wasn't long after that that you abandoned your post. You disappeared for a number of years before re-emerging in adulthood as a criminal. Earning quite a name for yourself if I do say so." A small smirk appeared on the king's face as if he were actually amused by that fact.

He took a lap around the cell once again, before turning back to Cain, all amusement gone, an icy glare in its place. "Then a few years later, your name came across my desk once again... after the murder of my wife."

They stared at one another silently for what felt like hours, locked in a battle of wills, neither willing to blink first.

"We've both lost loved ones."

"Lost is not a word I would use." King Frederick ground out the words through clenched teeth as if it were painful to get out.

"No. I think taken would be far more appropriate." Cain's tone mirrored the king's, both raging for the losses they sustained.

King Frederick's eyes flashed. "She was an innocent," he growled.

"So was my sister, and your men destroyed her."

"Ingrid was innocent," he repeated, his eyes closing as he shook his head. He sighed. "She had nothing to do with it," the king murmured. His head sank into his hand, and he rubbed his temples softly.

"It wasn't about her," Cain said plainly. "It was never about her."

"I had no hand in those men hurting your sister. They were not acting under sanctioned orders."

Cain rose to his feet, his chains clanking around his wrists so he could look the man in the eye on equal footing. "They are under your command. They were working for you when I was sold to that ship and crew... and they were working for you when they did that to my sister." He took a slow, intimidating step closer to the king but he did not retreat. "At least death is swift, merciful. It ends. There is no end for my sister."

King Frederick's nostrils flared but he stayed silent, taking Cain in. A quiet rage bubbled under the surface, in control but visible. He let out a heavy breath. "I am sorry... for your sister. It is a terrible tragedy."

The words came as a shock to Cain, like a slap to the face. Despite everything, he could see that the king meant it. His eyes were soft, full of remorse.

Cain didn't know how to respond. He leant back against the wall, a scowl on his face. "It's rather late for that, wouldn't you agree?"

There was no denying the surprise on King Frederick's face, but it was swiftly covered with something unreadable. He took a breath and squared his stance. "Yes. I suppose it is much too late."

So much unspoken hung in the air between them. Resentment. Regret. Two lifetimes of actions that led to pain for the other. And now there they both stood, side by side. Cain might have been the only one in chains but neither looked free.

CHAPTER NINE

RISK & REWARD

P rudence woke early at the sound of movement. Feet shuffling past her as she breathed deep, the crisp morning air filling her lungs and bringing her out of the stupor of sleep. It was early. The sun was barely visible through the trees, the slight bit of light making the sky appear a very light blue, almost grey. It was still dark for the most part, but light enough that she could see everything.

The thieves all lay sprawled around the fire she and Khari had made the day before, their loud snores spoiling the otherwise peaceful glade. Khari slept soundly beside her, his chin resting on his chest, his mouth hanging open with a little bit of saliva dripping out.

She caught sight of legs heading into the woods to her right, and she turned to look. Jonah was sidestepping any sticks that lay on the ground as he carefully snuck away from the group a short distance. Prudence watched curiously as the boy walked a couple of paces into the treeline and then stopped.

He pulled something from his pocket. Prudence shifted around as much as her bonds would permit so she could see better. The boy dangled whatever it was in front of him, holding it up. It looked like a dead rodent. He held its tail between his fingers and Prudence cocked her head to the side. What on Earth could he be up to?

After a moment, Prudence heard the mewling cry of a bird overhead, and suddenly, it was there, landing on Jonah's outstretched arm, bending down to take the rodent in its beak.

"Good boy," Jonah crooned to the bird, stroking its head gently with a finger. It was a buzzard from the look of it. A brown head, mottled body and underside of its wings, each wing ending in five distinct feathers that spread out like fingers. A yellow beak and feet with long talons that could easily rip skin to shreds.

Prudence watched in awe. The large bird stretched up on its feet and spread its wings wide as it balanced on Jonah's arm. His fingers were clutching thin leather straps that hung from the bird's legs. The buzzard was solidly built and must have been quite a weight on his arm but Jonah only looked on fondly, murmuring to the thing like a childhood pet.

"Good boy, Arûk," said Jonah. "What will you fetch for us today? Hmm?"

The bird trilled happily in response and ruffled its feathers. Jonah raised his arm swiftly, lifting the buzzard into the air and it spread its wings, taking off. It flew upwards, flapping its wings in quick succession as it climbed above the trees of the forest until it broke through the canopy and out of view.

Jonah looked up, following the bird with his eyes as long as he could manage and then his eyes changed. The pupils rolled back in his head until his eyes were just white. A bright, brilliant white that looked inhuman.

Prudence's mouth fell open in shock. "Fucking hell." She must have been louder than she realised as her statement woke Khari.

He snorted awake, his head flying up at her words, and he looked around frantically. "What? What's going on?" He came too almost immediately as if, even while sleeping, he had been poised for any danger that might come their way. He followed her gaze to Jonah between the trees, his expression matching hers. "What am I looking at?"

Prudence glanced at Khari for a moment. "I have no idea."

"He's bonded to the bird." Mr. Sinclair had snuck up on both of them whilst they were staring in amazement. At their matching looks of confusion, he continued. "I don't fully know 'ow it works, but he's got some kinda connection to that bird'a his. Mentally, ya know? Can see what it sees through its eyes. Mainly uses it to keep us fed. It's 'ow we found ya camp."

Prudence was too fascinated to be angry that they had used this gift to prey on them. She couldn't take her eyes off of Jonah. The way he stood, legs braced, arms outstretched, head tilted up to the sky... what must he have seen through the buzzard's eyes? A long stretch of forest, and once he had flown beyond that, mountains to the west with miles and miles of farmland stretching out over the Isle beyond even that. To the north of them, more dense forest that expanded all the way up to The Great Lake by which Alwich Castle had been built.

Would Jonah and his bird have been able to see Cain? Travelling from the ship that took him to the castle dungeons? Would he be able to see where they kept him? How he was? The idea of using Jonah and his bird to aid in Cain's rescue fought its way into her mind so swift and strong that she couldn't help but think of ways they might be able to force it to happen.

Jonah was speaking now, his voice a low calm tone that they couldn't quite make out. He must have been talking to Arûk through their connection. It was both incredible and terrifying to witness. Such a power to be yielded by this young boy. It occurred to Prudence that he could be far more powerful than he currently was.

"Where did ye find this kid?" Khari asked Sinclair, looking just as impressed as Prudence felt.

"Dunno. He'd been with Mr. Gordon for years before I met him. Found him as a wee one all alone as far as I know. Took 'im in. Raised 'im."

Prudence's face softened. No wonder he was here. She knew better than most that bizarre feeling of duty to someone who's helped you, given you a life. He owed Mr. Gordon and this was how he paid him back.

She looked up at the sound of Arûk returning. His keening cry could be heard overhead long before she caught sight of him. The large bird soared through the canopy of treetops, gliding on outstretched wings, a dead rabbit in its talons which he dropped at Jonah's feet before landing on the boy's shoulder.

Prudence caught sight of the same brilliant white of Arûk's eyes—not quite bird-like—before they both seemed to return to their own bodies, their eyes going back to normal. Jonah's warm brown eyes and Arûk's, similar in shade but completely dark, all the white now vanished.

Jonah stopped to pick up the limp mammal, a little blood marring the pelt where the buzzard's talons dug into its fragile body.

"Couple more of those and we'll have ourselves a fine breakfast." Sinclair grinned.

P rudence woke to a sharp pain at the back of her skull, of hair being pulled. She came to thrashing, not knowing where she was or what was happening, only that it hurt. Her brain was racing to catch up to the events. Her hair was being pulled. She was no longer restrained. Instead, she was being dragged by the hair across the ground, through twigs and dirt, leaves and damp grass. Her fingers grasped at the ground beneath her, but there was nothing to get purchase on.

She flailed wildly, looking up at what was causing her pain. A thick, filthy hand was fisted into her black hair so tight it looked like it had ripped a few strands out. Barty had his back to her as he dragged her along behind him, away from the tree she had been bound to. Away from the safety of Khari. She yelped and clawed at his hand, trying to free herself from his grasp. Her nails tore into his hand, scratching so hard it brought blood to the surface.

But he didn't let go.

He yanked on her hair, sending pain radiating across her scalp. He didn't even look back at her. Prudence tried to force her head up off the ground, despite the pain to look around. Why was no one helping her? She caught a glimpse of the tree a short distance from her feet. Khari was still tied, his mouth now gagged, and he watched Prudence with a wild panic, straining to free himself.

It would do no good. Prudence could see he would not be able to break free.

Barty suddenly released her, and her head thudded against the woodland floor, bouncing off the ground. A hand clamped around her throat, cutting off her air momentarily. His face loomed close to hers, filling the range of her vision with his face. Despite the lack of breath, his stench filled the air, making it thick and clammy.

"Listen here, ye little bitch. Think yer safe jus' cause Gordon says so? Well, fuck 'im. He's not the boss of me," he spat. It landed on Prudence's face and she recoiled, swiping at it with a hand as the other groped at his gripping her throat.

He loosened his hold enough for her to suck in a ragged breath, and he smiled. The smell was even worse when he opened his mouth. He kept his grip on her neck as his other hand reached down to her skirts, tugging them up around her waist. It took him a minute to hoist them all up as Prudence kicked and fought against him, lashing out with her feet.

She kicked him hard in the gut and he folded. It gave her the briefest moment when his hand slipped from her neck and she was able to lunge forward, knocking him off balance. She hovered over him as he grappled for her, still trying to pin her down. Her fist met his face as they battled for dominance. If he caught her again... that couldn't happen, but her sole hand and ever-growing belly were hampering her.

Pure instinct took over as she fought him, fist flying, fingers gouging and scratching. One of his hands took hold of her hair tightly once more, the other finding her throat and grabbing tight. Prudence flailed, a wild animal caught in a trap, but his grip didn't loosen.

Driven by purely animal instincts, Prudence lunged forward, sinking her teeth into the man's neck as hard as possible. She felt the tough tear of flesh, the taste of blood filling her mouth, but she bit down harder. His garbled cry rang in her ears as she crunched down on his throat. It made her jaw ache, but she didn't pull back until she felt a chunk come away into her mouth.

She spat it out into the dirt beside Barty, both of his hands now clasping his neck in a futile attempt to save himself. His eyes were locked on her, full of panic, and he tried to speak, but all that came out was noise. A choking sound came from the gaping hole in his neck as the blood poured from it, coating the ground beneath them with a slick pool of red.

She retched and fought back the urge to vomit, her mouth dripping with saliva as she tried to rid herself of the awful taste. She felt a little slip down her throat and gagged. She couldn't think about it now. She didn't have time; she wasn't safe.

She felt Barty's body shudder underneath her, his blood pooling around both of them as he took his last breaths.

Khari gave a muffled yell and Prudence leapt up, racing for him. She bounded back to Barty as he lay dying only to retrieve the knife from his belt, which she used to remove Khari's ropes. He launched up and hauled her into him, swiftly embracing her, despite being covered in blood. She squeezed her eyes shut tightly as he held her trembling form for a moment.

Yells sounded from the thieves as they came to and caught sight of Bartholomew bleeding out just a short distance from their fire.

Jeremiah fell to his knees beside Barty and tried to staunch the bleeding, but it was no use. The light dimmed from his eyes as he choked, the blood filling his mouth, and then he was gone. Khari felt nothing but satisfaction. The bastard had gotten everything he deserved. If anything, he wanted to inflict more pain on him before he had died.

Sinclair flew at Prudence as she bent over cradling herself in panic, unawares. Khari pivoted, slamming a fist into the side of his face and sending him sprawling across the mossy ground. Prudence straightened within seconds, brought back into fight or flight mode. She caught Khari's eye, and he nodded at her. She wasn't in a position to fight. At least, not well.

They saw it all in seconds, how it would play out. They were outnumbered three to one, and Prudence wasn't at her normal strength. Even if she were, most of these men were twice her size. They locked eyes briefly and knew what was needed.

Prudence leapt on Sinclair before he had a chance to get up, and with a quick flick of her wrist, she had cut his throat with the knife she'd taken from Bartholomew. Everything exploded. Mr. Burke flew at Khari, his eyes wild as his fist collided with Khari's jaw with a reverberating crack. His nose dripped with blood and the taste filled his mouth, but he didn't back down.

"Yer dead," he hissed. "And yer little whore is next."

Khari met Mr. Burke blow for blow. He stood a full head taller than the man, despite his height and broad shoulders. If it weren't for the man's rage propelling him forward, Khari would have had no difficulty in taking him down. As it was, Mr. Burke was holding his own.

Prudence was caught in a tussle with Jeremiah, who had left Barty's dead body and gone straight for her. Khari saw the panic on her face, the struggle as she tried to fight him off, and he swung again at Mr. Burke, trying to knock him off balance. The man stumbled backwards, and Khari descended, hands grasping the man's neck, and with a sharp twist, his neck snapped.

Khari barely waited for his body to hit the floor before he moved for Prudence, only to be stopped by hands on his arms. Mr. Gordon flung Khari to the ground, his back smacking the floor with a solid thud that knocked the air out of him. He briefly caught sight of Prudence's knife slicing into Jeremiah's gut up to its hilt before a fist met Khari's face, momentarily blinding him.

Stars spun in his vision and he swayed, a bout of nausea filling him before he forced himself up. Gordon hit him again, but he withstood it, absorbing the punch. Khari spat and wiped his face with an arm, smearing blood across his cheek from his nose.

The pair tussled, on equal footing, each getting in painful blows to their opponent. Neither backed down. Khari caught a blow to the stomach, and he doubled over with a cough. Gordon's arms wrapped around his neck, trapping him in a headlock, and he tightened, crushing Khari's airways.

He clawed at Gordon's hands and bucked, trying to force him off, but his grip remained tight, arms locked together around his neck as his breathing became laboured. Black danced at the edges of his vision, and he sucked in half a breath.

Suddenly, the man's grip released, and Khari fell to his knees, pulling in as much air as possible. Prudence had come to his aid, ploughing into Mr. Gordon, forcing him to let go, but he now had Prudence pinned against a tree, his arm over her neck, crushing her.

"You little bitch," he spat in her face. "You've ruined everything!"

His face contorted in shock as Khari plunged a knife into the side of his neck. He pulled it out and blood poured. Mr. Gordon's hand came up instinctively, but it was too late; he was already dead. The body dropped and Prudence sank to the floor breathing heavily.

That was when Khari noticed Jonah standing frozen by their wagon, his eyes wide with terror. He stalked towards the young boy even as Jonah recoiled.

"Don't!" Prudence cried between pants. "Don't hurt him, Khari. He-he didn't do anythin'"

Khari stopped. He turned to look at Prudence before casting his glance back to the young boy. He looked much smaller than before, cowed half behind the wagon, shaking slightly. He hadn't uttered a word. Hadn't made any attempts to assist his fellow thieves. The boy looked up at Khari nervously.

"Leave 'im be," Prudence begged from her position on the ground, still leaning against the tree for support. She cradled her belly protectively, and Khari felt his resolve weaken.

"Ye run now," he said sternly, pointing the knife at Jonah's throat. "Ye run, and if I see ye again… I'll gut ye."

Jonah nodded frantically, his eyes almost popping out of his head before he was gone, running off into the forest as far away from Khari as he could manage.

"Thank ye," muttered Prudence.

King Frederick pulled a chair closer and sat down, only a short distance from Cain, separated by a table. He had permitted Cain to have a chair as well, at least for these moments they shared. He had come to visit Cain several times after their first encounter.

A few of these moments had been full of rage. Words yelled, threats uttered, but no fists thrown. Other moments had been sat in quiet contemplation, neither being the first to speak, sitting in silence for a long time before the king would rise out of his chair and exit, leaving the guards to remove both chairs with Cain once again sitting on the filthy floor. And there were moments, like this one, where they had found themselves engaging in a simple board game.

King Frederick moved a counter before leaning back in his chair, assessing the board. "You've got a good strategy, Mr. Morris, but I fear you will still fail."

Cain smirked. Their almost friendship amused him. The man who sat before him was worlds away. One rich, one poor. One a king, the other a prisoner, and yet... despite all of their differences and their natural state as enemies, they had found common ground.

Both were avid readers, relishing in the classics and poets of the previous century especially. Both were well travelled. In fact, they had found, over numerous conversations, that they had travelled to many of the same places over the years, although for wildly different reasons.

"I wouldn't be so sure of that, Your Majesty." Cain fiddled with one of his pieces before placing it. "I understand your thought process better than you think. I see your plan. Fret not. I shall not fall into your trap."

The king laughed softly. "You are too aggressive in your

approach. It will be your downfall."

They watched each other across the board, both knowing they were speaking about so much more than their game, and it was true. It would be his downfall. But he saw no point in regrets; no reason for them. Everything in his life had led him to this cell; to the noose.

He saw not a life of misery and pain when he looked back. It was there, but it wasn't what he saw. He saw his sister's giggle as she spun around and around in the meadow beyond their house as she made herself dizzy and fell down; he saw Prudence, eyes gleaming, cheeks flushed as she picked her first pocket. He saw a life of exceptional moments, astounding happiness... and freedom. He would not go back to exchange that for anything.

Cain moved another piece on the board, pushing the king's piece backwards. "Sometimes aggression is a necessary force. How else do we forge our path when an opponent is so clearly trying to beat us?"

King Frederick nodded slightly. "I heed your point. Still, it is not always the smartest way. It is not only about taking out your opponent." He watched his piece move back the five spaces he had just won. "But longevity. What good is defeating most of your opponent's pieces if you lose too many in the process? Then you are left still losing at the end. The slower, more controlled player taking the final blow for himself."

King Frederick moved another piece of his straight at Cain's. Slow, determined. He knocked Cain's piece off the edge of the board and it clattered loudly onto the tabletop, the sound echoing in the stone cell.

"I've arranged for you to do some work in the yard. It will give you a little bit of time outdoors in the fresh air," said the king, surprising Cain.

He looked up at the king curiously. "Why would you do that?"

King Frederick was silent for a moment, contemplating his answer. "Well, I wouldn't want you dying before your trial. You're looking rather pale and... emaciated, as it stands."

Cain smirked. "But of course. Might I ask... I came here with another prisoner by the name of Jed. Scrawny little thing. Mop of brown hair."

"I'm not personally familiar, but I can enquire. What is it you wish to know?"

"Would it be possible for the lad to join me?"

The king paused for a moment, thinking. "Not in this cell, but I could make arrangements for him to join you in your work."

"I'd appreciate that." Cain nodded gratefully.

He moved another game piece across the board, knocking another of the king's off the side. If someone had come in and seen them, they might assume the two were friends. Perhaps a brother visiting his more unfortunate criminal sibling in gaol. They also might have looked at the board and thought Cain was winning. He was, for the moment, but it was clear to both men that he would eventually lose his final piece to the king.

When Prudence and Khari finally stepped foot in the door of The Wayside Haunt, they both collapsed into the nearest chairs and breathed a sigh of relief. It had been a long walk from the camp and the bodies they left behind. Blood stained both of their clothes, and they had attempted to wash off as much as possible in a little stream. When that failed, they had covered the blood marks with mud.

They had taken the main road through the forest, heading north-east, closer to Eastcliff, when they came upon the inn. It had been a welcome sight. A lone building sat right where the forest tapered out and met the mountains, each window lit up with warmth.

The Haunt was, mercifully, mostly empty with only a few locals eating and drinking, dotted about the room. A high-backed settee had been placed in front of their wonky stone hearth, in which a fire roared.

Prudence rose on weary legs, feeling like her bones weighed more than ten men, and shuffled over to it, sinking into the soft fabric. It was the most comfortable thing she had felt in many moons. She leant her head back against it and sighed. Her body so wished to rest, but her mind was still reeling from what had happened. No matter how she tried to convince herself that the threat was gone, that she could breathe for the moment, her mind would not listen. It was on high alert, keeping her safe from any possible danger still around.

She felt the fabric dip as Khari sat at the opposite end. He too slumped into the settee and let out a deep sigh. Neither of them had anticipated any of this when they first set out. They had been somewhat naive, thinking the journey would be simple and only freeing Cain from his cell would be hard.

A young woman with bright eyes and mousy brown hair tied in a long plait down her back appeared beside them, holding a tray. "Can I get'cha anythin'?" she asked happily.

"Aye, ale, girl," Khari grunted. Prudence shot him a look and kicked his shin in warning. "Please," he added swiftly.

Prudence smiled softly at the woman. She looked a little younger than Prudence, though she was taller. Her hands were covered with what Prudence assumed to be food stains and burns from the hot oven. "Could we get some food as well, please?"

The young woman nodded, smiling. "O' course. Ma dad's got some stew cooking in the back, or we've got some breads and cheeses too." She paused to think, her nose scrunching up cutely. "Um... there's some pottage, salted rabbit and mutton, might be a fruit cake too."

She rambled on with endless options until Prudence jumped in. "The stew sounds good, thank ye. And some ale."

The woman grinned. "I'll get tha' for ya right now!" She seemed far too excitable for Prudence, but she couldn't hold it against her. "I'm Meg. This is ma dad's inn. Just holler if ya need anythin' else! I'll be right back with ya food." She was off quicker than Prudence could blink. She was a blur, buzzing about the room, collecting empty drinks and plates and piling them far too high on her tray.

Prudence thought they might fall, but she kept them balanced, despite the speed at which she took them back into the kitchen.

"Gods, she's loud," Khari complained and pinched his nose, a common habit of his when a headache was brewing, Prudence had noticed.

"She's sweet. Be nice to her," she warned.

Within moments, Meg was back, still grinning, with two bowls of steaming hot stew and two tankards of ale. She plonked them down on the low table in front of the settee and Prudence noticed a new burn on her hand, still bright red from the oven.

"There ya go! Enjoy!"

Prudence smiled. "Thank ye, Meg. We were wonderin' if ye've got rooms available."

"Oh, sure!" Meg beamed. "Two rooms?"

Prudence nodded.

"We've got a couple a' guests right now, but most of the rooms are empty currently. It's not the busiest time of year for us, but we get by. Mainly on travellin' folks like ya selves coming through town. Say, where are ya folks from? 'Av ya come far? Are ya staying long, do ya reckon? Ma dad'll be glad to have some more guests, 'specially if ya staying a while. It'll be good for business, tha's for sure." Her voice seemed to get faster the more she spoke, and it also got louder, rising in volume with every new thought she rambled.

Prudence found it endearing. Khari looked like he wanted to slap her.

"Two rooms, yes, please." Prudence nodded at her, hoping the interruption would slow the monologue.

"Two rooms. Got'cha. I didn't think ya looked like a couple. Ya walked in an' I thought to myself, 'now that there ain't a couple. They're too stiff with each other. Ya look at a couple and ya can jus' tell, ya know? Even if they're not touchin', ya can tell they're together, but y'two didn't look like that at all. I guessed ya'd be travellin' companions of some kind. Why are ya travellin' together? Are ya both goin' to the same place or jus' sharing for part of the journey? If ya goin' to the same place, are ya both goin' for the same reason? Are ya visitin' people?"

Prudence rose quickly at the sight of Khari about to explode and put a hand on Meg's shoulder, guiding her away from him. "Thank ye so much for the food, Meg. We're travelling up north together. We've, uh... got some people to see."

Meg nodded excitedly. "Oh, tha's so excitin'! I've never been more than a few miles from The Haunt. Ma dad has travelled a bit further, but he always leaves me 'ere in charge of the inn. Oh, how I wish to see the world. I want to see all of it! Have ya done much travellin' before?"

"I've done a little. I'm a bit like ye, Meg, wanting to travel to far-off places." She smiled warmly at the girl. "I should probably eat now. my stomach is growling and this child," she stroked her belly, "has me far more hungry than normal."

"Oh, sure." Meg nodded again. "Babies will do tha', I've 'eard, although, not seen too many meself, much less pregnant ladies tha' is. Not too many ladies travelling while they're with child, ya know?"

Prudence left Meg still rambling about food and children and the kinds of people she had met while working in the inn and returned to her food where Khari looked, if it were possible, even more grumpy than before.

As they sat around the fire that night, joined by some locals from the surrounding countryside who had come for a few drinks, they heard tales of a highwayman who had been robbing people on the main road that came right past The Wayside Haunt.

"They come this way to avoid the mountains. The mountain pass is too treacherous for most folk. Ye certainly can't bring any wagons or anythin' up through there... so they come this way. It's meant to be safer. Meant to be the easier journey, and now this." An older man, weathered with age, sighed.

"He's been terrorising the road for months. He stalks the road all the way from Holmston to here, attacking travellers, holdin' up carriages. I heard he even killed someone once," piped in another, younger man, who looked less scared and more exhilarated by this rumour.

"Don't be stupid, Harry. Don't you think we'd have had confirmation if that were true? Don't you think at least someone would know this person who supposedly died, hmm?" A small old woman named Bess didn't hesitate to put the rumour to rest.

Harry frowned, his chin resting in his hand. "Maybe not if they were travelling from far away," he grumbled. He took a long slurp of his ale.

"Point is, Miss..." The older man turned to Prudence. "...Ye both ought to be very careful travelling down this road, ye hear? Wouldn't want ye coming afoul of this bastard in the dark, that's for sure."

Meg appeared with a third tray full of ale, mead, and rum, and placed them all down on the table for the patrons before taking a seat on a small stool beside Prudence. She wriggled closer, forcing two of the locals to make room for her. She didn't speak, but Prudence watched her eyes bounce from one person to the next as they added their own opinions and tales to this legendary highwayman they were all so concerned with.

"If it's so dangerous," Prudence asked, "why are ye all willing to travel from yer homes to come for a drink of an eve?" It was an innocuous question, but still, Prudence felt a small ripple of something hum through the group before someone answered her.

"Nobody knows why, but this highwayman hasn't ever

bothered a local, besides... what are we meant to do, avoid leaving our homes for the foreseeable future? Ain't no soldiers in this middle of nowhere to help us. They don't care. They're too busy to pay attention to one little road being haunted by a robber in a fancy mask."

Bess nodded. "Fred is right. He's grumpy, but he's right. We're on our own out here, and as he says, he doesn't come for us."

"He's one of us, that's why!" Harry piped up again, slamming his drink down excitedly, spilling some over the table. "He's a local and he knows us. He knows we haven't got no money, no jewels. Why should he attack us? No... it's the rich travellers he wants. The fancy carriages and snooty people who only stop 'ere cause there's nowhere else, who turn their noses up at it." He sniffed, frustrated, and threw a glance at Meg. He looked annoyed, but there was something more... protective and caring underneath it. Prudence smirked. Meg seemed completely unaware of Harry's eyes on her, but Prudence could see there was something there, at least for young Harry.

He was sweet. Roughly Meg's age by the looks of him. A bit scrappy, but his eyes were bright and he had a lovely smile. Meg could most certainly do worse. He spilt a little more of his ale down his shirt as he took another slug and a loud burp erupted from his chest, but he didn't seem embarrassed. He grinned, amused, his smile making the apples of his cheeks more pronounced, and Prudence noticed a couple of freckles. It reminded her of Eleanora.

"Mark my words, one day he's gonna get caught. Someone is gonna fight back and he'll be in for it. Someone is gonna take off that mask and recognise him."

CHAPTER TEN

WHAT MIGHT HAVE BEEN

The first moment of sunlight Cain saw as he walked up and out of the castle dungeon almost blinded him. It had been so long since he had seen anything but the warm orange glow of lamplight. Shackles bit into his wrists and longer chained ones had been placed around his feet for the walk to the work yard. He shuffled along slowly so as not to trip, in a line with twenty or so other inmates, away from the dungeon that had become their final resting place.

They had walked up a set of stone stairs and come out just beyond the castle walls. The guards had escorted them away from the grounds, away from the people going about their lives in Alwich Castle, and towards open fields where many of the castle's crops were grown. They walked past many fields of wheat, corn, turnips, and beans, and stopped in an empty field of dirt.

The odd stone lay scattered across the ground and Cain nudged one with his toe. He watched as it moved, pushing dirt out of its way as he pushed it deeper into the soil. Earth, not stone floor, but earth. Rough, rich soil that smelt slightly sweet, the moisture in it offering faint whiffs of the rain that had previously fallen. It had been so long since he had been outside.

Tools were shoved into the prisoners' hands—hoes, shovels, and rakes—and their wrist shackles were removed. The chains attached to their ankles were joined together so that if one ran, he couldn't get more than a few paces with so many men's weight holding him back.

Jed was standing a few men down from Cain, and he caught his eye. The young man looked thinner than before, if that were even possible. His cheeks were hollow, his face gaunt. Still, his eyes brightened a little when he caught sight of Cain. His mouth quirked up at the right corner a little.

"This, you ingrates, is your one and only warning. Try to escape, start any fights, don't do your job, and I will shoot you without hesitation. Do you understand?" said a rather burly, broad-shouldered guard with not one but two rifles, one slung across his back, the other in his hands as if he were ready to shoot right then.

Nods rippled through the chained prisoners who stood in front of him.

He stepped closer, getting right up to the face of the prisoner closest to him. They were so close they were almost touching. "I'm gonna work you to the bone, you hear?"

The prisoner recoiled, nodding furiously, his eyes downcast at the ground. He clutched his rake tighter. He looked as if he might piss himself, Cain thought.

"Your task," the guard started pacing the line, "is to prepare this soil for ploughing. There are weeds to pull, rocks to remove. I want this full five acres done by the time the sun goes down."

They set a brutal pace. Multiple guards not only supervised the prisoners' work but walked up and down the line with a switch, lashing anyone who dared not make progress.

The summer sun beat down hard on them as they sweated through their labour. It was a hot day with no apparent breeze to offer them any relief as they worked. The soil was hard and unyielding as they worked to dispel any weed or rock underfoot.

Once the fields were cleared, they would be ploughed by horses, but that couldn't be done safely until there was no risk of damaging either the plough or the animals. The man beside Cain slowed to a crawl.

"Come on, keep working. Don't give them a reason to hurt you," whispered Cain harshly as he cut into the soil with his hoe.

"I- I can't," he panted, stopping working altogether. "It's too hot... there's no air."

"You can. Come on. In a little while, they'll let us stop to have a drink. You've just got to keep going until then." Cain nudged the man gently. "Let's focus on something else, huh?" He cut into the soil once more and hoicked a rock up off the ground into a bucket. "You have a wife at home? A family?"

The man slowly began to work once more. "Y-yes. A wife... my Abigail." The man smiled sadly. "She's lookin' after five kids all alone. Who knows if I'll ever see her again? Gotta wait an' hope they'll be lenient at the trial."

Cain nodded sympathetically. His own mind brought images of Prudence to his eye. "What's she like?"

He just had to keep this man's mind busy while they worked. If he was distracted thinking about his wife then he might be able to keep working until they rang that bell.

"Oh, she's beautiful. I've loved her since we were children. She's too good for a man like me."

"Aren't they all too good for us?" Cain smiled, and the man laughed.

"Yes, I suppose you're right. What about you? Do you have a girl somewhere?"

Cain nodded.

"Where's she then? Waitin' on you?"

"I hope not," said Cain mournfully. He pictured Prudence hidden in the dunes, held back only by Khari in the dark as he was arrested. Her face had broken him.

"Why would you hope such a thing?" the man asked. "Wouldn't you want to get back to her?"

"I won't be going back to her. This is it for me. I shan't see her again. Only when I sleep."

"You're giving up that easy, then?" The man paused his digging to look at Cain.

"I'm not giving up on anything," Cain retorted indignantly.

"Sounds like you are. You don't know what's gonna happen, but you've already decided that's it, it's over, and you're abandoning this poor girl."

Cain opened his mouth to speak then closed it again. What could he say? He wasn't getting out of here, he knew that. He was bound for the noose; his trial was merely a formality. But Prudence... would she ever know exactly what happened to him? Would she settle for hiding out somewhere, not fighting for him? Somehow, he doubted it.

"If she's worth it," the other prisoner said, "you'll fight for her."

Prudence sat beside the fire in The Haunt alone in the early morning just as the sun was beginning to wake. Birds chirped in their nests outside. A lone cat rose from its spot on the rug, stretched, and slunk off in search of food. The inn was silent, asleep, save for the quiet sound of Prudence's breathing and the fire crackling softly.

In such a remote place where no one else had yet risen, it was almost as if she were the only person alive. All alone in this roadside tavern as it waited for travellers to come and grace its halls. It felt like the world had stopped turning, that time had stopped passing and she were just there, existing, but frozen.

The sound of footsteps on the stairs made Prudence jump. "Oh, gosh. Sorry, Miss. I didn't mean to scare ya." Meg bounded down the stairs far too quickly, screeching to a halt at the foot of the staircase. "I was jus' coming down to prepare for breakfast, ya know? Me dad does most of the cookin', but he has me handle breakfast so he can sleep a little after being up so late. Do ya fancy anythin'? I can cook ya up anythin' ya want long as we have the stuff for it, which we probably do, the pantry is well stocked. Y'should see it! Absolutely brimmin'. The last time ma dad went to market, he came back with the wagon so fully loaded ya'd think there wouldn't be anywhere for 'im to sit!"

She continued her excitable pace through the room, turning in circles every few steps to speak to Prudence even as she walked in the opposite direction. She knocked backwards into a chair and stumbled, catching herself before she fell to the floor.

"Meg!" Prudence launched out of her seat. "Are you all right?"

"I'm fine!" The young woman leapt up, chuckling to hide any embarrassment she might have felt. Prudence moved towards her, but she held up a hand to stop her. "I'm fine, truly. What uh... what can I get ya?"

"I'm all right, Meg, really. Please don't worry." Prudence stepped a little closer.

"Nonsense! I'll fetch ya some eggs. My chickens will have some eggs for us; I didn't collect any yesterday. I was a little early, ya see, and they hadn't laid any, but there'll be some now! And how about some pears? Ma dad stewed some yesterday, and oh Gods, they are delicious, especially with cheese. Ooh! I'll bring out the cheeses too!" Meg chatted away despite Prudence's insistence that she didn't need anything to eat, and she hurried off to the kitchen to prepare food for the both of them, leaving Prudence mid-rebuttal.

Prudence sat back down, noting now how her bigger belly forced her to lower herself more slowly into the seat, leaning heavily on the armrest as she did so. Even such a short interaction with the exhausting but sweet Meg had left her wanting to rest. Being with child had really impeded Prudence. It slowed her speed, made her reactions less fast, and made her feel almost constantly tired. It was most frustrating, and Prudence could not wait until she was back to her usual self.

The front door of The Haunt opened, and in walked a group of people in the most bizarre clothing Prudence had ever seen.

They bustled in, a seemingly never-ending line of characters filling up multiple tables. Prudence watched, perplexed, from her seat by the fire. They didn't pay her any mind, too busy talking amongst themselves.

After a moment, Meg returned from the kitchen with a tray laden with porridge, eggs, cheese, and fruits. She spun around, trays in hand as she pushed open the kitchen door with her back.

"Oh, customers!" She hurried through the room, almost tripping over her own feet as she placed an over-piled plate of boiled eggs, sliced rye bread, stewed pears and apples, and a large bowl of porridge and hawthorn berries down in front of Prudence. "I'll be with ya in just a moment!" she called loudly to the newcomers. "Here ya go, Miss." She grinned at Prudence.

"Oh my. Meg, this looks delicious." Prudence's mouth was watering and her stomach grumbled.

Meg practically glowed at the compliment. "I'm so glad ya like it, Miss."

"Please, jus' call me Pru."

"All right... Pru." Meg's grin became even wider if that were possible, taking up all of her face. "I should probably..." She gestured to the group sitting waiting for her. "See to these new customers."

Prudence nodded at her, already in the middle of chewing.

No sooner had Meg left Prudence to eat in peace than the seat beside her was taken. A small elderly woman, birdlike in her features with dark hair and olive skin, sat down looking right at Prudence.

"You've travelled far," she stated.

"I have." Prudence eyed the woman but continued to eat.

"You've got a challenging task ahead of you."

Prudence put down her spoon and turned to the woman. "Do ye know me? For I am certain I don't know *you*."

"Oh, no." The woman smirked. "I'm Harriet." She offered a hand, but Prudence didn't take it. Harriet was undeterred. "Would you care to have your fortune told?"

Prudence's face must have looked reluctant because the woman pushed on.

"I shan't charge you, not this time." Before Prudence could even answer, the elderly lady took Prudence's hand in hers, examining her palm carefully. "Oh," she muttered, almost to herself, followed by an "mm..."

"What? What is it?" Prudence leant in as if she too might see what the old woman saw in the lines of her hand.

"You've had a lot of hardships, haven't you?"

"Yes," Prudence answered quietly, nervously.

"It seems you are not done just yet. You will have to make great sacrifices to avoid future hardships. It will cost you," she warned.

"Cost me? What will it cost me?" Prudence's mind raced with thoughts of Cain. "Will my husband be freed? Will he be saved from the noose?"

Harriet put Prudence's hand down gently but firmly before producing a small metal bowl from a coat pocket. "Your hands only tell of you, dear, but let's see what we can see, shall we?" She took Prudence's drink from the table, pouring it into the bowl, and she peered into the liquid's surface. "There are two paths ahead. Your husband must listen!. If he does, all will be well. He'll be fine."

Prudence breathed a deep sigh of relief.

"But be warned, child... your life is bound for further hardship, littered with loss and grief. You have a gift to give.

Don't waste it."

Prudence frowned. "I don't know what ye mean."

"You will, when the time is right." Harriet rose from her chair.

"Nana, stop tormenting this poor woman," a young girl with Harriet's same dark locks and knowing eyes called across the room.

"I'm not, child."

"Please don't worry, Miss. Nana foretells death and disaster for almost everyone and she's hardly ever right." The young girl smiled reassuringly, but it didn't settle the unease in Prudence's stomach.

She rubbed her belly comfortingly and felt a flutter of movement inside. What could it all mean? But she had said Cain would be fine, provided he listen. If only Prudence had some way of knowing what he had to listen to, or whether he did.

Khari had asked the innkeeper to draw a map, as best he could, from the inn to Alwich Castle. He was certainly no artist, but it was functional, and Prudence and Khari sat around this map splayed out across a table, making plans.

"Right, so we're here." Khari stabbed at the map with a thumb to the right, at the edge of the mountain range between Holmston and Eastcliff. Between the child in Prudence's belly slowing them down and the thieves who stopped their journey for a few days, they had not made as much progress as they would have liked.

Prudence sighed, her chin falling into her hand as she slumped forward over the map. "We're running out of time. How do we know they haven't hung him already?" She hadn't known before that it was possible to feel so fired up and energised, yet so weary at the same time. She wanted nothing more than to save Cain, and she certainly would never give up—that just wasn't an option—but this thread of hope on which she had hung all of her dreams was wearing thin. It frayed at the edges and threatened to break if tested any more.

Khari sighed. "We don't know, not for sure. But what else is there? Besides, he's the most wanted man out there. The king wants his head directly. Do ye really think if they had hung your husband it wouldn't have been talked about in every town from here to the other end of The Western Tides?"

Prudence chewed her lip. "I hope yer right."

"Me too, *keine*. Me too. We're not giving up." He nudged her shoulder with his. "We're so close now."

Prudence smiled reluctantly. "So... when do we leave?"

A loud ruckus erupted outside, and one of the travellers burst through the front of The Wayside Haunt. "He got Billy! The highwayman robbed Billy!" Everyone stood immediately and bundled out the door. Billy, the traveller who had been robbed, looked no worse for wear. He wasn't injured or bleeding, but his expression was less than happy.

"He stole the coin purse. All of the money we earnt in Braeburn and Acrine."

A loud grumble of complaint rumbled through the travelling performers.

"Damn bastard!" a bigger man with a rough beard yelled. "That was meant to last us all the way to Garendon! What are we meant to do now?"

"We'll be fine, Harlon. We've got a show in Bellanau on the way. We can get by," Harriet's granddaughter said calmly. She touched his arm gently. "Are you all right, Billy?"

"I'm fine, Marissa." Despite his answer, he looked rather pale. "I just don't... I'm not used to having a gun shoved in my face." Prudence smothered a smile in amused sympathy. The young man was cautious, nervous in his movements, and appeared a little shaken from his experience.

"What happened?" asked Khari.

"I was taking a walk. I needed to get some air. Next thing I knew, a man on a horse rode up to me, stopping right in front of me. Shoved his pistol in my face and demanded everything I had." Billy sat down on the doorstep, frustrated.

"What did he look like?"

"I don't know! He had a hat on, a black mask over his eyes, and a big cloak buttoned up his neck." Billy slumped forward onto his knees.

Just then, the innkeeper came out with his daughter scurrying along behind him anxiously. "This will not stand! I've had about enough of this bastard robbing people left and right. My custom has gone way down since this started. Half the people he robs are too scared to stay here and keep moving until they're out of the forest, and the rest have barely anything left to spend! If I could just get my hands on him." He pounded his palm with his fist.

"Dad, please!" Meg tugged at his arm attempting to calm him. The man huffed and his anger seemed to dull a little at his daughter's voice.

"I'm sorry, love, but it's not right. The man is a menace. Someone needs to deal with 'im."

Meg paled slightly but she kept her hold on his arm. "At least no one is hurt, right? That's the important thing, isn't it?"

Prudence smiled tightly at the girl. She was sweet, if a little naive. Prudence wondered briefly what would happen if this highwayman were to prey on Meg. Would she stay naively gentle, or would she fight back?

"Well, I've had enough," a tall man by the name of Jameson insisted. "We're leaving, first thing tomorrow. You all got that? We'll head for Garendon a little earlier than planned. Perhaps we'll have time to fit in a couple more shows before we have to move on. I want everyone packed and ready to leave at first light."

The performers all fell silent and nodded at the man's words before he stalked inside. Marissa crouched down to comfort the still-emotional Billy.

Prudence turned to Harlon. "Say... would it be possible for us to catch a ride with ye? Not too far. We jus' need to get as far north as yer able to take us on yer already planned route. Would ye mind?" She attempted to look as sweet and innocent as she could manage. Although she couldn't see her own face, she felt it wasn't quite as convincing as she had tried to be.

Harlon sniffed and shrugged his shoulders. "We're heading west but we 'av gotta head north just a little to get round the mountains before we head for Bellanau. 'Spose it wouldn't be too much trouble to 'av just two more people for the journey."

Prudence found herself uncharacteristically grabbing the man's arms in excitement. "Oh, thank ye. Thank ye so, so much. Ye don't know how much that'll help us. Thank ye... truly."

Harlon blushed slightly and shrugged her off. "'Tis really not much. No need to overreact." He escaped her grasp, following swiftly after Jameson into the inn.

Prudence turned to Khari. "Did ye hear that? We can catch

up. Maybe not all the way, but surely, this'll help, won't it? It'll certainly be quicker than walkin'!"

Khari returned her grin. "Aye, *keine*. It'll help. Ye did good." For the first time in as long as Prudence could remember, she felt some of the weight lift off of her chest, allowing her a deep breath of relief. They were close. So close now.

At the sound of a loud thud, Prudence flew up from her bed, now wide awake, and peered into the dark. She couldn't see anything save for darkness, but she managed to grope along the table until she reached the candle by her bed and lit it, providing a small amount of orange light in the night. Holding it, she rose, pulling her boots onto her already cold feet and she crept to the small window of her rented room.

The moon was mostly hidden by cloud that night, obscuring the view of the inn courtyard down below her, but Prudence saw shadow and movement. Human movement. Curiosity piqued, she snuck out of her room as quietly as she could, carefully holding the latch to muffle the click of it closing.

Khari was asleep in the room beside hers and she flinched as the floorboard creaked beneath her weight. Prudence faltered but he didn't emerge.

Once down the stairs, she quickened her pace, still cautious but not wanting to miss whoever was skulking about. She tiptoed to the back door and out into the night before creeping around to the front of The Wayside Haunt.

A shadow of a person was moving silently in the dark, making multiple trips from the front door out towards where the trees began by the road.

She caught sight of a sack of something—supplies Prudence guessed—in their hands, and as the shadow got to the trees, Prudence noticed the horse. Sat atop a tall, black steed sat another shadow. The highwayman.

Prudence clung to the wall of the inn to keep from being seen as she watched the pair. The person on foot wore a wide-brimmed hat, breeches, and riding boots, and a long red coat with a high collar around their neck.

It was then that a long braid of hair slipped from under the hat, and Prudence recognised her. Meg. She watched, stunned, as Meg gave sacks to the highwayman atop his horse. Prudence shuffled in her position and both heads spun to look at her. She sucked in a breath and slowly walked closer to Meg, arms raised.

The highwayman raised his pistol, and it was on her in an instant.

"No, don't!" Meg stepped in front of Prudence, and the highwayman immediately lowered his weapon away from her. "She's my friend." Meg turned around to face Prudence. "Please," she begged. "You cannot tell anyone." Her eyes searched Prudence's, asking for her assistance.

"But, Meg, do ye know what yer doin'? To leave your home? Yer dad?" Prudence looked beyond Meg to the highwayman. "He's..."

Meg followed her gaze with a soft smile and Prudence could see the love in her eyes. The highwayman pulled down his hood, and Prudence gasped. It wasn't a man at all.

It was a woman.

A thick head of blonde curls fell out over her shoulders. Prudence could just make out brown eyes over the top of a black handkerchief tied around the bottom half of her face.

"I love my dad, Pru. But I can't stay here, in the middle o' nowhere. I want to travel, to see the world... and I love her." She smiled at her 'highwayman' through the darkness. "You can't tell ma dad, you just can't. Please."

Meg's eyes were like saucers, pleading with Prudence, and she felt herself becoming soft.

Prudence sighed. "Oh, Gods. All right. I'll say nothin', but ye best be leavin' him a note to explain. He deserves that at least."

Meg broke out into another wide grin and sprinted back into the inn. Prudence wanted to deny it, but Meg's happiness was contagious. She returned swiftly and took Prudence by the hand. "Please make sure he gets it, and tell him I love him."

"Thank you." A firm voice came from the woman on the horse.

Prudence met her gaze, moving away from Meg towards the blonde woman. "Ye'll take care o' her?" she asked, giving a warning glare.

The blonde woman nodded. "I will, I swear."

Prudence sighed. "All right then." She turned back to Meg. "Be safe." Prudence startled slightly when Meg wrapped her in a tight hug, but after a moment, she relented and returned the affection.

"I will," Meg assured her, squeezing her tightly. "Thank you, Prudence."

Prudence watched her mount the horse behind her love and they took off at a walk until they got further away from the inn. And then they were gone, cantering into the night, leaving Prudence standing there alone in the dark, watching after them.

They left in the early morning, piling into their wagons amidst all of their belongings. Khari and Prudence climbed up, with him offering her a hand as she stepped over crates and bags, and they sat, squashed between Harlon and Billy and a number of other performers they hadn't met properly.

Prudence hadn't admitted to knowing anything about the sudden disappearance of the innkeeper's daughter the night before, but something in her face told Khari all he needed to know. She knew where the girl had gone, had probably watched her leave, but she dared not confess this fact to the innkeeper. The man had informed them that he had found a note, and whilst he seemed rather devastated, he didn't hasten to chase after her. Presumably whatever the note had said, it had been a sufficient answer for him. Khari suspected Prudence had had a hand in that as well.

The wagons pulled out of the courtyard slowly, wheels creaking under the weight, a little too heavy even for the large, stocky horses they had to pull them. The performers would drop them off in a place called Torrin Down on their way to the big city of Garendon, where they would perform for a couple of weeks before moving on further north, along the coast.

They passed through the forest on the main road, before the land opened up into fields and farmland and as they did so, they began to see more human life. Out of the dark vastness of the forest, there were more houses, more crofter's cottages, as they rode their way around the base of the mountain range.

The performers themselves wore colourful garb, stitched together with shiny thread with large hats and feathers, a most garish decoration to their already peculiar attire. The wagons were painted in vibrant patterns that reminded Khari of the body paint worn by his people on celebration days. They rang bells and shouted out to people in passing to get their attention. It was definitely working.

Many a person waved as they passed. A number of children caught sight of them and ran alongside the wagons for as long as they could manage before the wagons were too far away from home, and too much for their little legs to keep up with. It made Khari smile. It was rather like being back home with his people; the colourful dress, the sense of community. How he missed it sometimes. How he yearned for the life he used to lead with his family. It had been so many years since he had seen his homeland.

The wagon lurched into a hole on the road, and everyone tipped sideways. Prudence grunted in complaint.

"Are ye all right, *keine*?" he asked. He was mildly concerned about how much travelling would be affecting the child she carried inside of her, but whenever he brought it up, Prudence shot it down with a withering look and harsh words. She was too stubborn for her own good.

"I'm fine," she grumbled. "It's just bumpy is all."

Khari frowned. "Yer not a good liar, ye know. No one would judge ye for struggling a little. Ye know that, don't ye?" He stared at her until she conceded and met his eye.

"I'm… fine." She sighed and Khari let it go. If she wasn't ready to admit it then who was he to force her? Once they reached the castle, once he had helped her that far, it was no longer his obligation. They were travelling companions because he owed her, nothing more.

"So," he turned to Harlon, a rather large man with a pot belly and a kind face. "What kind of performances will ye be doing once ye reach Garendon?"

"Well, first we'll do a few shows in Bellanau since we'll be passing through anyway, and it has a decent number of people there considering the size of the town. It's the right time of year, it's sunny and warm. Everyone will be wantin' to spend more time outdoors in the open air. We'll set up just outside town. Marissa here will do some dancing; she's real good, you know. Brings in a good crowd. Her grandmother, Harriet there," he pointed to an older woman sat in the first wagon just in front of theirs, "she'll sit at a table nearby and read fortunes for anyone who wants one. Billy is our announcer and ticket collector. He also does the odd puppet show, would you believe." Harlon grinned and slapped Billy on the back, earning a sheepish smile from the shy younger man.

Khari smiled softly. It seemed like a fun show. It would be a shame that he and Prudence wouldn't get a chance to see it.

At Khari's disappointment, Harlon perked up. "Say, how's about we do a little show for you 'ere? Can't do it all, of course. Not sure dancing in the back of a moving wagon is advisable, is it, Marissa?" he called to the young girl, and she laughed, shaking her head. "But I'm sure we can make this journey a little more fun for everyone, can't we, ladies and gents?" He grinned, and Khari saw how everyone around him brightened at his words. He was a clear leader, and Khari could see why they all listened to him. His voice alone brought joy to life.

Khari and Prudence watched in quiet enjoyment as Harlon's booming voice sounded the start of their impromptu show as the wagons rolled down the dirt road in the direction of Torrin

Down and Bellanau.

CHAPTER ELEVEN

BAD BLOOD

The road didn't take them directly to Torrin Down. The wagons rolled to a stop where the dirt road they had been travelling on since The Wayside Haunt reached a fork.

"Now, if you head down this track, into the valley, you'll find you reach Torrin Down before dark... depending on how fast you walk." Marissa glanced at Prudence's belly and had the sense to look a little embarrassed when Prudence caught her.

"Thank ye, really." Khari smiled for the both of them and nodded at a number of the performers on the wagon before shaking Marissa's hand. He nudged Prudence gently with an elbow.

"Yes, thank ye. We really appreciate it."

They watched the wagons roll on away from them, Harlon and Marissa still waving from the back, and then they rounded a corner and were gone from sight. Prudence breathed deeply. They were so close now. Once they had found somewhere to stay for the night, they could begin forming the plan that would get her to Cain. Get him out of that prison cell and back safe.

"So... I 'spose, this is where we part ways," Prudence said quietly, reluctantly, wanting more than anything for Khari to stay. She didn't want to do this alone. Didn't want to have to find the castle, somehow work out where Cain was, and take on the unimaginable task of freeing him by herself. She wasn't even sure if she could. Now so close to her goal and to her husband, she was full of doubts and worries. What if she couldn't save him? What if she had to watch him die? Or worse, what if he never got to see her, never knew she'd come all this way just for him?

Khari sighed. "I uh, I thought I might stay."

"Really?" Prudence dared not hope.

"Yeah, I mean... s'not like you'll be able to do this yerself. Look at ye, so big already. How are ye meant to free a man from gaol?" His lip quirked up at the corner and Prudence scowled, although her pleasure at him staying made it hard to be mad.

"Ye like me, admit it." She smirked, giving him a smug look.

"Over my dead body."

Prudence laughed then, all worry and doubt escaping her for a moment. This might actually be doable. They might actually be able to save him.

They started walking. The long dirt track stretched down before them winding and bending as it sloped downward into the valley that lay nestled in the mountains. It was a difficult walk and Prudence found herself moving even slower than usual as she leant backwards, counteracting the weight of her large belly pulling her forward down the track.

The sun had now reached the middle of the sky and beat down on them ferociously. Prudence wiped sweat off her forehead with her sleeve and huffed.

"This is unbearable," she moaned.

"Here, *keine*, take this." Khari handed her a skein of ale from his pocket and she drank deeply, the liquid pouring down her throat providing a little relief in the heat. "Let's take a break. Sit for a moment." He guided her to a rock and she sat down on it, breathing heavily.

"Well, well. Look what we have here."

Prudence's head whipped up at the voice behind them. Julian and Vivienne stood there smiling cockily at the two of them. Prudence's mouth fell open in shock.

"I can't believe you didn't tell me you were with child, little one." Julian put a hand over his heart mockingly. "I'm wounded."

"What are ye doing here?" Prudence asked, fear heightening all of her senses. She didn't know why or what she was meant to fear... but she did. It was as if she could smell it on them. Vivienne's cat eyes locked on her belly, roaming her body, and Prudence wrapped an arm protectively around her stomach.

"Julian, listen." Khari took a step forward, hand raised, but Julian cut him off.

"Now, now. We're just here for the payment you promised. That's all. Then we can be on our way. We missed you at the meeting point, you know. We were meant to meet one another in Merton a few days after making berth... you remember that, don't you? Had to follow you all the way here." Julian's tone was laced with menace and all of it was aimed at Khari.

Prudence looked between the men, confused. "Khari... what is he talking about? What payment?"

Khari glanced back at her nervously. "Nothing, *keine*. I-"

"Hey, now. Don't go lying to the lady. She is pregnant and that seems awfully rude, don't you think?" Julian turned to look at Prudence, revelling in her concern. "Did your friend not tell you? He promised a bigger prize than your ring. Something he'd get to us after we reached Aelin. The ring was only a deposit, after all."

Prudence's eyes widened then narrowed at Khari. "Ye... ye told them what? Ye... you weren't going to be 'ere. Ye were going to leave me once we reached land. Ye weren't meant to come this way with me..." The realisation came over Prudence in waves, moment after moment. He had planned to leave her; that had been the agreement. "Ye were goin' to leave and find a ship to take you north. Why would ye tell them we'd meet them?"

Khari sighed loudly and ran a hand over his face. "I'm sorry, *keine*. I am. I'd planned to leave ye behind, to get on a ship and be gone long before they came lookin'."

Julian walked closer, moving between Prudence and Khari as he fiddled with his knife. "Tsk, tsk. You know we would have had to have killed her had she not been able to pay us. A promise is a promise."

Prudence's face drained of colour as she glared at Khari. "*You bastard*," she snarled. "Ye fucking bastard!"

"I'm sorry, *keine*. I'm sorry! I didn't know back then. Didn't think I'd come to care for ye." Khari looked apologetic and downright ashamed, but it didn't quell the rage inside Prudence's chest. She was now standing right in front of him, glaring up at him with such venom, chest heaving and if she'd had a weapon to hand, she might have used it, right then.

"*Julian,*" Vivienne whined. "This is boring. I'm bored."

"Patience, little dove. This won't take long, I promise," he cooed at her. "I hate to break up this little fight you two seem to be having, but I believe there is still the matter of our payment." He turned to Khari, hand outstretched, waiting.

"I- I don't have it," Khari said. "I can get it! I can get it for ye and we can hand it over in a few days and then it'll all be good."

"I'm afraid that won't work for us, will it, darling?" Julian flashed a quick smile at Vivienne over his shoulder and she glowed, an almost tangible spark of arousal between them. He turned back to Khari, knife now pointing directly at him. "If I don't return to my brother with the payment very soon, let's just say it won't be good." He took another step forward, poking the tip of the blade into Khari's sternum. "You've run out of time, friend. Should have thought about that before you tried to screw us over."

He pushed the blade further, and it dug into Khari's skin through his shirt, making him wince. When he pulled the knife back, the tip was red with his blood.

Everything froze for a second before Khari pulled his fist back, cocked, and slammed it into Julian's face. Vivienne gave an anguished yell as Julian stumbled backwards. Khari didn't hesitate as he advanced further, hitting Julian again, knocking him flat to the ground.

Julian coughed up a little blood, and his eyes flashed with rage.

Khari turned on his heel and grabbed Prudence's hand, tugging her down the track with him. "Prudence, run!"

They ran, half stumbling down the rocky track away from Julian and Vivienne as fast as they could manage with Prudence unable to run properly. Prudence didn't dare to look behind her, but she was sure that Khari's punch wouldn't have done more than merely give them a few seconds' advantage.

Khari's feet pounded on the ground behind her as he ran, casting glances behind them every few seconds. He tugged on her hand again, encouraging her to speed up, to just keep moving. Then he let go of her hand. "Go on. Keep going, Prudence. I'll be right behind you! Keep running until you find somewhere you can hide." He stopped in his tracks and Prudence instinctively slowed to match. "Go! I'll catch up!" Khari turned tail and ran back up the steep incline straight at Julian.

Julian had now got up and was coming ever closer, knife at the ready with a furious Vivienne at his back, looking like she was ready to claw Khari's eyes out.

Prudence looked back and forth between the open track in front of her, and at Khari heading back into the throng of danger for her. She hesitated for a long moment, the urge to help Khari at war with the desire to run for the sake of her child. She bounced back and forth on her feet as she debated before finally making the decision to keep running. Khari had told her to. She needed to for the sake of her unborn child, and if she were there, she most likely would only serve as a distraction to Khari, putting him at greater risk.

She ran at speed down the track, rounding a corner a little too fast, and stumbled sideways before catching herself. Falling over here would be dangerous; she needed to go carefully. Prudence kept running, but at a more cautious pace. She couldn't hear people behind her so she could only hope that both Julian and Vivienne were being kept busy by Khari for the moment. The thought of the two of them overpowering Khari flashed through her mind, but she pushed it down. She couldn't think about that now. There wasn't time.

She didn't know how long she ran, but after a while, Prudence had to stop. The added weight of the child in her belly was making it hard to breathe, not to mention putting an extreme strain on her ankles. She stopped, bending over to catch her breath for a moment, and while she did, she listened. There were no sounds to be heard except those of nature. No running footsteps. No yells of anger. It seemed as though she were completely alone.

Prudence allowed herself a moment to rest and sat down on the ground at the edge of the road in the grass. She kicked off her boots and reached forward, grabbing one of her feet. She massaged it gently, earning a little sigh of pleasure from her lips. They had walked so far these last few months and yet her feet were still not used to it.

Still keeping her wits about her, she tugged her boots back on after a moment, ready to run again if need be. She might not have been able to hear them now, but Julian and Vivienne had already snuck up on them once; she wouldn't let it happen again. If she did, she was dead.

She heaved her aching body up, leaning heavily on her left hand, fingers splayed in front of her as she did so. It was no easy feat with her belly in the way, but she stood and slowly began walking once more. She hoped Khari would catch up to her, that he would have dealt with the problem and that would be it, but even if he didn't, Prudence had to keep walking. Hours passed and Prudence's pace had slowed to a crawl as she made her way down the track into the valley. The sun had moved far across the sky and Prudence couldn't help but get worried. Khari should have been back already. She stopped and turned to look back the way she had come. No sign. She huffed.

"Gods damn it, Khari. Where are ye?"

Rocks skidded down the track behind her and she spun around, arms up braced for an attack. "It's all right, *keine*. It's just me." Khari came towards her, arms up like hers but in surrender, through the rocks and boulders of the mountains.

"Where the fuck did ye come from?" she hissed at him.

"I- I had to lead them away from ye. I lost them a while back, but it took me a long time to get back having to come over the mountain paths." He panted, clearly worn out from his excursions.

"Are they dead?" Prudence asked.

"No." Khari shook his head. "But I lost them. They won't be able to find us again, I made sure of it. I drew them towards the main road to Garendon and headed that way for a while then doubled back through the mountains. They won't be able to track me through there. We'll be fine, so long as we get somewhere safe for the night."

Prudence nodded, uncertain. "All right."

Khari took a step towards her, but she recoiled. "*Keine.*" His eyes were pleading and apologetic. "I'm... so sorry."

Prudence drew in a ragged breath, trying to keep her emotions from bubbling over. "Ye betrayed me," she muttered, not meeting his eye.

"I know. I know, I'm sorry. It was before we had spent all this time together. Before we had become friends..."

"I trusted ye! I trusted ye and ye betrayed me," she yelled, despite the tears falling down her face. The crying only fuelled her anger. "Why are ye even here? Ye planned to leave me for dead. Why the fuck did ye come with me? Why change yer mind? Why didn't ye just let them kill me, go off and head north alone like ye had always planned." She glared at him, eyes blazing with anger, but most of all, hurt. "How could you?" The pain in her words was evident to both of them, and she bit the inside of her cheek to try and force herself to stop crying. It was humiliating. A sign of weakness in front of an enemy.

"I-" Khari sighed angrily. "We didn't get on if ye remember! Ye threatened to kill me numerous times before all of this, do ye recall?" He rubbed at his scalp, frustrated. "I was going to leave," Khari muttered. "But I stayed, for you. And I'm gonna help ye get yer captain back, I swear it, *keine*." He took a hesitant step closer, an attempt at reconciliation, and Prudence permitted it, staying where she was.

She didn't say anything, just stood there, thinking. She didn't want to go at it alone. Didn't want to have to face trying to save Cain alone, but could she trust him? "I trusted you," she whispered. "And ye broke that trust."

"I know. I know, Prudence. How can I make it up to ye? How can I prove that it won't happen again? Please, what can I do?" Khari clasped his hands together as if in prayer, begging her. "I swear to ye, on pain of death, I will not leave yer side until Cain is free, safe and sound. Until he has made his way back to ye, I will be 'ere, lookin' out for ye. Please... what can I do?"

Prudence sighed and closed her eyes. "I don't know. I don't know if there is anything ye can do. Let's just get off this awful road before dark."

They made their way down the steep track into the valley, heading for Torrin Down. The path was difficult and they had to walk slowly to ensure they didn't slip on loose stones. Eventually, they reached the base of the valley, and the track became flatter.

The walls of rock from the mountains either side made way for fresh grass, and further into the valley, they could see the village of Torrin Down, lit now by candlelight in open windows, allowing the summer breeze into their homes even as the sun went down.

Such was the size of the little village that there was no inn or tavern, no shops to purchase goods from. Indeed, there was only a smattering of homes for the small population that lived there in the bosom of the mountains. Prudence and Khari walked hesitantly into the village, unsure of how their presence might be received in this tight-knit community.

A few children played outside their homes, tossing a ball to one another with loud shouts and giggles that promptly stopped at the sight of the pair approaching. One little girl ran alongside a large hoop as it rolled across the ground, a little stick in her hand to keep its momentum going whenever it slowed. She stopped as she ran into their path and the hoop slowed before toppling over.

They knocked on the first door that they came to and a small woman opened it. She was elderly, although not frail. She stood tall, with a slim build, somewhat taller than Prudence and with an air that she was still very much young in her mind.

"Yes?" She eyed them both, Khari more so than Prudence, evidently unused to visitors so far disconnected from the rest of the world.

"We were hoping," Prudence began, soft-spoken and sweet, "that there would be somewhere we might be able to stay for the night. Would you know of anywhere? I'm Prudence, by the way, and this is my friend, Khari."

The older woman's eyes flicked between Prudence's face and her large stomach. Her face seemed to soften at the sight of her pregnant belly. "Sybil," the woman replied. "You look like you've travelled quite some way."

"Aye, we have, ma'am, and it's certainly not been an easy journey. If we could just rest somewhere for the night, it would do us both the world o' good, and we could be on our way," Khari implored her.

Sybil sighed, but in her eyes, Prudence could see sympathy. "I suppose you could stay in my barn, just for the one night. Mind you, I lock all my doors and have a shotgun loaded and ready." She gave them both a warning glare.

"Understood. You have no idea how helpful that would be to us. Really, we're both very grateful. We only need some rest. We have no intention of causing you any harm." Prudence tried to assure the woman.

"It's not much, but it'll be warm and more comfortable than sleeping outside. Are you travelling north?"

Prudence nodded. "Yes. But how did ye know?"

"Well, no-one would be here if they'd been travelling south. There's no way through the mountains, not unless you're an experienced climber, and it certainly wouldn't be possible with you being so close to having that child." She smiled warmly. "I'll see if I can scrounge up some blankets for the two of you. Make it more comfortable in there. You don't mind sharing with a couple of cows, do you?"

Prudence grinned. "I can't thank ye enough."

"Yes, truly," Khari agreed.

"There's a well out back you can drink from if you're thirsty."

Prudence opened her mouth to speak once more but closed it again. The temptation to ask about Cain's home and family was strong, but she resisted. She didn't know this woman. Sybil might not even know of Cain's parents, but what good would it do if she did?

They had abandoned him and his sister. Worse, had gotten rid of them. If Prudence saw them now, she'd be tempted to deal with them herself such was her rage on behalf of the husband she loved and the sister he had lost. It had been so many years; they could have died or moved away. Regardless, finding out what happened to them wouldn't help her save Cain. They were inconsequential.

The old lady guided them towards her barn and opened the large door. It was stiff, and she gave it a good tug. Khari moved forward to assist her, pulling open the wooden door.

Inside the barn was warm and dark. Two cows stood munching hay in the middle of the room and they mooed softly at their entrance. The old woman stroked one of them lovingly and it nudged her hand.

"Rosie and Buttercup here will take care of you. Won't you, girl?" She scratched the cow's head affectionately. "She loves people, so don't be surprised if you wake up with a cow right in your face."

Sybil retreated to the barn door and gave them a brief smile as she pulled it back closed leaving them alone in the barn that was piled high with farm tools, hay bales, straw, and the two cows chewing noisily.

"We should probably get some sleep," said Khari, breaking the quiet.

Prudence nodded. "Yes, sleep. That would be good." Her body was exhausted, limbs achy and sore, feet crying for relief from so much travelling and running. All she wanted to do was lie down and rest, but her mind wouldn't quit. It whirred at speed, ploughing through thought after endless thought, refusing to give her any peace.

So much had happened since she had woken up that morning, and it was only now that she was actually acknowledging it. She couldn't sleep while Julian was still out there. Who knew if Khari had actually lost them? Julian was no fool and whilst Khari was perfectly capable… she feared Julian.

She could only hope and pray that Julian and Vivienne had found something… someone else to entertain their sick minds. That they had gotten bored searching for Khari after losing him, flighty as they were. She hoped that they had found themselves in another town, drinking and worshipping one another all the while most likely preying on some poor unsuspecting fool who hadn't known what danger he was in.

She carefully lowered herself to the floor, leaning heavily against the wooden wall for support as she did so. Prudence felt the flutter of a kick in her womb, and she smiled. It wouldn't be too long now until the child was with them.

By her rough calculations, it would only be just over one more moon until it was time. She only begged silently to the Gods that that would give her enough time to rescue Cain first.

The whip cracked against Cain's back and he bit back a yell. He was braced between two trees, hands tied to their thick trunks as the guard lashed him. He ground his teeth in an attempt to maintain some control. These guards were brutal; far too keen to dole out punishments to prisoners as they worked, even if they didn't deserve it.

His new companion, Nathaniel, had dropped a bucket full of rocks, spilling them all over the ground at the guard's feet as they were ushered off the field at the end of the day. The guard had lunged at Nathaniel, beating him into the dirt until he coughed globs of blood. Cain had acted upon instinct, getting in between them. Except now, it was his turn for a punishment.

The whip cracked against his back again and it was like all the air got sucked out of his lungs. Blood trickled down his back over his torn skin and it was all he could do not to cry. The pain was too much, too real. It was as if his skin was being torn from his frame lash by lash. It had been many years since he had last gone under the cat o' nine tails. Not since he was a child, and it was clear that he was no stronger now than he had been then.

His legs sagged underneath him and he hung between the two trees by his wrists. For the first time since his arrest, he was glad Prudence was far away. He didn't wish for her to see him like this. Brought down, beaten, weak. Another lash cracked against his back and he couldn't hold back the sobs anymore.

The prisoners had been lined up to watch this display of might from the royal guard, and now they stood, sombre, listening to him wail with every strike.

Despite his best efforts, and his promises to every god out there... they were winning, he was being cowed, his resolve crumbling. It seemed like there was nothing he could do to stop it all coming down.

After the final lash, a guard came to release his bonds and he slumped to the floor, exhausted. His face hit the ground with a solid thump but he didn't care. All he could feel was the scorching pain radiating across his back.

"Oi, you two. Bring him."

Two prisoners lifted him, one on each side of him, and carried him under the arms as they were all led back to the castle dungeon. His feet trailed as they carried him down the stone steps, the skin on top of his feet scraping against each one. They half dragged him back down the corridor to his cell and carried him inside. He barely registered their help as they lay him gently on the stone floor, face down so as not to hurt him further.

"Clean him up. Orders are to keep him alive and well until his execution. This one is not allowed to die before then," Cain vaguely heard a guard say from somewhere behind him, and then someone was kneeling beside him. A woman, he thought. Cold water and cloth dabbed at his back and he winced, a cry escaping him once more.

"Please," he sobbed, eyes screwed up tight, not even sure what he was begging for. Relief? Death?

The servant ignored his cries as she dabbed at his back, now in ribbons, cleaning away the blood as best she could. She rang out the cloth into a bucket before dunking it once again into the cold water and touched his back once more. The floor around him grew damp as the water dripped down his sides and onto his neck. His forehead was slick with the sweat of pain but the cold water made him shiver.

"Here," the servant murmured and tried to feed him something.

Cain turned his face away. "No," he whimpered.

She persisted, shoving something between his lips. "Chew," she instructed. "It will help with the pain."

He became aware of the taste of leaves in his mouth and he did as he was bid, chewing gently on them. They tasted slightly sweet and creamy, if a little floral. He didn't know if they would actually help with the pain but by this point, he was too exhausted to care.

The pain on his back continued to sing as she washed the wounds clean. Cain's vision swam, suddenly overcome with tiredness, and he closed his eyes once more, the feel of the cloth on his back, the sound of the servant humming softly as she worked all fading into the background as he drifted out of consciousness and into sleep.

By the time Khari woke that morning, Prudence was nowhere to be found. He sat up, rubbed his eyes, and looked around the barn, searching for her, but she was gone. The cows were still there, though, in the same place they had been all night, still chewing on some hay. Khari got up and headed for the door to look for Prudence.

Outside, the air was crisp but not cold, the sun hadn't quite started to rise, but the pitch black of night was gone, leaving a faint blue in its place that made it easy to see. The little hamlet of Torrin Down was quiet at this time of day. People had not yet risen from their beds, and animals were still quiet, either sleeping or grazing outside their owners' homes. The grass was still wet with dew, and a faint mist hung around the edges of the valley where the mountains blocked the rest of the world from view. It was a place all on its own, hidden, secret. The perfect hideout.

Khari found Prudence sitting on the edge of the well, looking a little out of breath after pulling up a full bucket of water from its depths.

"Are ye all right, *keine*?" He approached her warily, still unsure where he stood after the discovery of his deceit the day before.

"Fine." Her answer was curt and she refused to meet his eye.

"I am desperately sorry for what I did."

"I know." It was an acknowledgement of his remorse, but not acceptance.

"I hope we'll be able to jus' put this behind us?" His question hung in the air for a moment, Prudence allowing the silence to envelope them in a bubble of awkwardness. She cupped some water in her hand and took a sip. Khari's throat throbbed automatically, a reminder of how long it had been since he had had anything to drink. But he dared not move towards her.

"I'm not sure I can." Prudence finally looked at him then. It was cold, a look without any warmth or even tolerance. "How am I supposed to trust ye?" she asked, and her tone made him flinch.

Khari searched for the words. He wasn't sure how to answer her. How to prove to her that she had nothing to worry about, that she could trust him now. That he had been trustworthy ever since they left *The Wayward Damned* and he had agreed to accompany her. "I... don't know," he confessed. "But I am here to help ye, *keine*. I'll help ye get Cain back. I'll go with ye on this foolhardy suicide mission to rescue him. I promise ye, I'm here to stay now. Ye can trust me. I won't ever betray yer trust again, I swear to ye."

Prudence eyed him suspiciously. "Ye swear?"

He nodded.

"Ye'll help me get to Cain and free him? Ye'll help break him out of that prison even if it might kill ye?"

Khari swallowed once, then nodded. "Aye, yes. I will help ye get to him and I won't stop until he's freed." At the sight of Prudence's pursed lips and cautious eyes, he continued, "Besides... it's not like yer goin' to be able to get to him by yerself in this state. Ye need me and I'm here, offering my services. I am under yer command until yer husband is safe."

They stared at each other, unblinking as if waiting for the other to break first. Eventually, Prudence blinked, and she sighed. "All right, I accept yer apology. But if yer lying to me, I'll gut ye myself. Are we clear?"

Khari grinned. "Aye, *keine*. We're clear."

Just then, Sybil appeared, followed by her two cows. "Morning." She tipped her hat at them. "I don't suppose the two of you fancy somethin' to eat before you get back on the road?"

Both Khari and Prudence's stomachs rumbled in answer and the old woman chuckled.

"Come on in, I've got some eggs cooking, some bread that needs eating before it goes off, and there might even be some milk in it for you."

There was nothing quite as perfect as the taste of Sybil's cooking that morning. It had been almost a whole day and night since they had last had anything to eat and both were absolutely ravenous. Prudence tucked into four slices of bread and as many eggs as she could get from Sybil, and Khari polished his off with barely a word. It didn't take either of them long to clear the table of food completely.

"My, my. Looks like the house was invaded by goats!" Sybil exclaimed, amused. "Here." She handed both of them some fresh milk to drink. "So." She sat down at the table opposite them. "Are you going to tell me where it is you're travelling to now?"

"I- I don't know what you mean," Prudence stuttered.

"Oh, please don't try to lie to an old woman. We're far too wise to fall for that. It's obvious you're not just on some little journey to visit relatives. You come here late at night, dishevelled and exhausted. No one comes into our little village, especially not in such a state. And even if you weren't looking so out of sorts, you're about to burst, deary. No one in their right mind goes on a long journey this close to giving birth." Sybil locked eyes on Prudence and Khari saw her lip quiver.

Oh, fuck.

Prudence frowned down at her plate. She looked angry, but Khari had known her for long enough now to know that she was just trying to hide her feelings. She would probably kill him if he said so, but she was quite sensitive deep down. Prudence's lip quivered again and he saw a shimmer of a tear in her eye. Then the dam broke and she was sobbing.

"M- my husband... he was," she gulped loudly in between sobs, "taken."

"Maybe ye shouldn't, *keine*," Khari warned. Who knew who the old woman might tell? She might panic and send someone to fetch the royal guard and have them imprisoned for treason. Prudence didn't listen.

"My husband was arrested, I'm... we're going to rescue him." Her voice wavered, but she was resolute in her statement. Khari watched Sybil cautiously. He didn't relish the idea of killing a harmless old woman, but if he had to, he would.

"Don't worry, deary. I'm not going to tell anyone." She turned to Prudence. "Is he a good man?"

"What?" asked Prudence.

"Aren't ye wondering what he did?" Khari wondered. "Prudence, don't say anything else."

"I didn't ask what he did, I asked if he was a good man," Sybil replied.

"He is," insisted Prudence. She looked at Khari. "Cain would trust her. He is a good man. A great man." Sybil leant back, lips pursed for a moment. She assessed both of them with a critical eye. "His name is Cain?"

"Yes. Cain Morris... why?"

Sybil rose from her chair and headed for the door, pulling a jacket on as she went. She opened the front door and turned back to the pair at the table. "Come on. I think there's someone you need to meet."

CHAPTER TWELVE

TORRIN DOWN

The little hamlet of Torrin Down sat nestled in the mouth of the gaping valley. Surrounded by lush green grass, the homes were small, made of thatch and stone. They looked cosy. The cottage on the very outskirts, with a slanted roof and roses climbing up the side, had once been Cain's childhood home.

Now his parents had both passed, it was home to a kind older couple. They had taken one look at a rather pregnant Prudence as Sybil introduced them and ushered her and Khari through the door before they had even known who she was.

Phaedra was pure joy. If it weren't for her head of grey, she could easily have been a young lady. She certainly didn't look her actual age of sixty. She had known Cain as a child; had been a friend of his mother's when they were children themselves. She told Prudence of how she had mourned Cain and his sister; that their absence had been felt by everyone in their small community.

"When Mary came home without them, oh, my heart broke. I'd never had children, you see, and I adored those kids. They were the sweetest, and then when their little friends found out they were gone..." a small sob escaped Phaedra's lips.

"But why? I don't understand. Nor does Cain. He told me about what happened, but I don't think he's ever known why. It hurts him to this day. He had loving parents, and then one day, they just abandoned them. Worse, *sold them*." Prudence's voice rose swiftly in anger for poor little Cain, hurt and confused about why his parents had gone, and fury for older Cain so scarred by everything that happened after.

"Oh, sweetheart, it was a terrible time. I in no way condone what happened to those poor children, but I know they were desperate. There were crop blights, diseases that spread through families in days, the taxes had been raised so high that many starved. I'm sure Cain doesn't remember, it was such a long time ago, but we lost many children in the village that winter prior, those poor souls. They just didn't have enough. It was like they wasted away." She took a deep breath. "They were at risk of losing this farm, and their parents thought they might have a better chance at a good life if they worked for the fleet, where they could work their way up to good roles and good pay. To make somethin' of themselves."

"Did they know that their daughter was dead only a few years later? *Murdered* by the same men she sold them to?" Phaedra jolted at Prudence's words, tears spilling down her cheeks almost instantly. She felt a slight pang of guilt at the harshness of her tone, but she willed it away.

"I- I had no idea. Oh, Florence, sweet child."

"Fuck, that's... that's hideous I'm so sorry," said Khari quietly.

Prudence had forgotten he'd even been in the room; he'd been so silent. After a while, Phaedra's sobs began to quieten down and the tension in the room eased somewhat.

"Oh, poor, dear Florence. I'm so sorry to hear that. She was such a darling girl. I had no idea... no one did. Oh, Mary. What a fool you were." She scowled. "And now sweet Cain is in gaol." She shook her head. "Everything has gone so wrong."

Khari rose from his seat and offered Phaedra a reassuring pat on the arm. "We are going to get him out. I made a promise. He will not see that noose, I swear it." He nodded at Prudence, a silent confirmation of his previous vow.

This seemed to bring Phaedra's spirits up considerably, and she brightened. "Good, good. That wonderful boy shouldn't be in prison. Oh, but I am thrilled for him. I mean, he has you and this little bundle on the way, oh! It's wonderful." Phaedra moved closer to cradle Prudence's growing bump in her hands, but Prudence found she didn't mind. Her love and joy were infectious.

"He doesn't know. We were separated before..." Prudence looked down at her ever-growing belly. She couldn't help but imagine what the past few months would have been like with Cain at her side. Finding a home. Thinking about names for the child. She hadn't dared to think so far.

"Oh, my dear. Well, he'll be thrilled. I know it. The man you know was destined for fatherhood. Even as a child, I could see it in the way he cared for his sister."

"Oh, Dra, hush. You're overwhelming the girl." Another

woman breezed into the room with an armful of flowers. She planted a kiss on Phaedra's cheek as she passed on her way to a vase. She was a striking woman, tall and angular, with curls that fell down to her waist, tied up in a ribbon. She was somewhat younger than Phaedra, Prudence guessed around forty years of age.

Phaedra huffed. "Oh, don't be so silly. I'm merely making conversation, my love." She turned back to Khari and Prudence, smiling proudly. "This is my wife, Reesa."

Reesa laughed loudly. "My love, you are too curious for your own good. They've obviously come a long way. Let the poor girl rest." She handed drinks to Prudence and Khari, who drank hastily. "We have an empty room you can stay in. I'll sort the bed out now. Khari, I hope you don't mind sleeping here in a chair. I know it's not the most comfortable, but I can bring you some woollen blankets. After all, this one," she gestured to Prudence, "will be needing her rest. How far along are you, dear?"

"You're in luck," Phaedra added. "Reesa is well experienced in childbirth. She has delivered most of the village's babies." She smiled proudly at her wife.

"Eight months along," Prudence answered. The words were out of her mouth before she had realised. Had it really been that long? The kicks she had felt said yes, no matter how little she wanted to believe it. It would be even more difficult to get to Cain in this state. It was hard to picture a baby in her arms.

In another world, she was rotting with the fish in Highcliff Bay. There probably wouldn't be anything left of her now. But a mother… if her own mother could see her now.

"How marvellous! A baby in the house so soon!" Phaedra clapped gleefully. "Do we know what it is to be yet?"

"Uh, no. I haven't any idea."

"Oh, my dear, come. Let us see!" Phaedra took Prudence by the arm and hauled her over to a cabinet. She pulled out a needle and thread and held it out over Prudence's palm. It swung back and forth from fingers to her wrist.

"What? What does it mean?" Prudence asked. Her eyes flicked between her palm and Phaedra's face. "No... wait. I'm not sure I wish to know."

"Why?" Khari piped up from his seat in the corner.

"Cain's not 'ere. It doesn't feel right. Why do I get to know what it is?" She sat down in the nearest seat. "He doesn't even know it exists," she mumbled.

"Sorry, dear." Phaedra swept the needle and thread into her hand and tucked it away in a drawer. "I do apologise. I get ahead of myself sometimes."

"No, no. It's all right. I... I quite like being able to share this with you all. I've spent so long pretending it wasn't happening. But it is, and it's good. It's a good thing." Prudence stroked her bump and smiled.

"Come on, dear. Let us get you settled."

"I never wanted this as a child, you know." Frederick spoke casually as he moved a game piece across the board. "As a child, I wanted to be an explorer. I wanted to take off to lands unknown, to study botany and ornithology. I wanted to travel to different cultures and learn everything I could about them. I wanted to be anywhere but here."

Cain cocked his head. "Huh, I would never have guessed.

What had you so interested in exploration?"

"I could ask you the same question, could I not? You might not have been studying birds or plant life on your travels, but you learnt. You must have learnt about many different places and cultural practises. I have to imagine you saw many a great sight across the world."

Cain nodded. "Yes, you would be right. I've been to many different parts of the world. I thoroughly enjoyed the forests of Travore. They were magnificent. Trees as far as the eye could see. Some of them were as tall as mountains." He chuckled, reminiscing over the distant memory. "I remember, back in Travore seeing a group of strigoi. They were incredible. I mean... they were deadly, and we almost didn't survive, but still, it was an experience I'll never forget. I'd never seen creatures like that before in my life, or since. I would love to be able to witness them again, although admittedly from a safer distance than before."

King Frederick laughed loudly. "Amazing!" He clapped excitedly, the board game in front of them forgotten for the moment. "I have to say, I do envy you your adventures. I would have loved to have seen them."

"Well, perhaps you will one day, Your Highness." Cain moved a game piece forward before looking up at the royal in front of him.

"Perchance, although, my duties when it comes to travel usually have me in palaces meeting with other dignitaries and royals rather than traipsing through jungles or scouring the oceans for terrifying beasts... unfortunately."

The sparkle in the king's eye was undeniable, and Cain felt an odd sense of amusement. This monarch that sat before him, seemingly so regal and level-headed on the surface, dressed in the finest silks and fabrics, rings adorning every finger, and the family crest on every item that sat on his breast... underneath it all, he was nothing more than an excitable boy desperate for adventure. In many ways, it was a shame he had never been able to explore and see the world as he wished. He seemed to make a fine king, as far as kings went, but Cain tried to picture the man in front of him as an explorer, a researcher... it seemed to suit him.

How different both of their lives might have been had the man in front of him become someone else, rather than the ruler of The Western Tides.

"I would imagine you are most likely in need of some protection, mind you. A man of your position surely isn't prepared to battle some great beast out in the wilderness." Cain smirked and knocked a game piece of Frederick's over.

King Frederick returned his smirk and moved a game piece of his own, blocking Cain from making the winning move. "How wrong you are, sir. Indeed, whilst I may conduct a lot of business from behind a desk, I do also make sure that I am duelling with swords and pistols each day. I am quite the swordsman if I do say so myself."

Cain laughed. "No offence, your highness, but I think I should have to fight you myself in order to see whether you can call yourself an expert. I have spent much of my life at the hilt of a blade, and there aren't many who have been able to best me."

"Perhaps that could be arranged before your trial. I should very much like to see what you are capable of." Frederick grinned at the man who had killed his wife. Both his enemy, and yet also somehow his comrade in arms.

"I fear that is certain to end in a swifter death for myself, would it not? Taking down the King himself in a duel would be a fine way of sealing my own death only moments after."

It was surprising how swiftly Prudence fell into the stride of home life after so long running from place to place. Waking in the same bed each morning with the crow of the rooster. Helping Phaedra with the farm and making herself useful inside the home. She spent many hours cooking for the others, cleaning up, and overall homemaking.

Reesa called it nesting. Her body was like a mother bird preparing the nest for the arrival of her baby. She had never been much bothered with tidiness. Mess wasn't something that frustrated her, and since leaving Llynne, she'd hardly stayed anywhere long enough to truly settle in and make a mess, but now she regularly found herself tidying around the house.

It amused Khari to no end. He watched her as she ambled about the house, picking up things that had been left slightly out of place after use. Plates, knives, shawls, cups, anything that Phaedra and Reesa had used at some point during the day, Prudence was one step behind to put it away.

It made him laugh. "I've never known you to be so ladylike, *keine*. Isn't this what you women are meant to be doing in this part o' the world?" He chortled to himself and only laughed harder when Prudence threw a shoe at him. He ducked deftly. "Ah, *tsk*. Clearly, you're not quite as well trained as ye should be."

"Fuck yerself, Khari, ye cheeky shit." She threw another shoe across the room, managing to just skim his head.

He rubbed where it hit. "Ow. All right." He held his hands up in surrender. "You win."

She nodded. "Good." She continued her task until Phaedra entered the room.

She pulled on her boots by the front door and grabbed a crook from a stand in the corner. Phaedra was a shepherdess with a small flock that she grazed across the valley. "Do you want to come with me, dear? It would be good for you to get some fresh air, to get out of the house for a while." She smiled at Prudence and gestured to the door.

"Ye, tha' sounds good." Prudence smiled and followed Phaedra out the door. The flock was currently southwest of the village, high up in the mountains. They set out with Dolly the dog at their heels. It would be a long walk, a good chance for Prudence to stretch her legs and get out of her head for a little while.

It was a pleasant morning. The sun was slowly rising in the sky. Birds sang their morning ballads and the walk wasn't challenging. They walked the length of the valley before heading up a steep path in the mountainside. They walked for some way, with Dolly running ahead a few paces then turning to check on them and wait for them to catch up.

Eventually, Prudence could see white dotting the horizon. As they neared, little heads of black and white looked up at them in greeting. Dolly took to her duties, herding the sheep closer at Phaedra's command.

She looked over the sheep one by one, showing Prudence how to check their hooves and look for signs of flystrike. The lambs were Prudence's favourite. Their fleece was starting to come in thick and full, and they gambled about, chasing and jumping together, never straying too far from their mothers.

Once they had all been checked, they began a slow walk back towards home.

"Thank you for coming with me. We lost two last month to predators, and it's vital to check them regular," said Phaedra.

"You're most welcome. It was fun. The lambs are so sweet."

The return home was mostly in silence, and they opened the door to the mouth-watering smell of food. They scoffed a late lunch that Reesa had lovingly made and began to process the wool from the most recent shear. It had already been washed and sorted the day prior. Phaedra explained that the wool needed carding and combing before it could be spun.

"Now, you take these two paddles here." She handed Prudence what looked like two giant hairbrushes with sharp bristles and demonstrated transferring the wool from one to the other, working through it top to bottom. "Khari!" she called, summoning him from the other room. "Here, son. You take these, and I'll be on combing."

They spent a few hours working side by side, Khari and Prudence carding the wool before passing it onto Phaedra for combing and spinning. The spinning wheel sat in the corner of the room to turn all of the fresh wool into yarn, ready to be made into clothes or sold at market.

Reesa was a seamstress by trade, which made the couple a perfect pair. Phaedra's herd provided Reesa with an endless supply of yarn for her knitting. Between that and the loads Phaedra sold to other traders, they made a decent living. They had a comfortable life in their home in this quaint village.

Phaedra was lost in her work. Her hands focused on the yarn as it spun, eyes vacant as if her mind was elsewhere. It made Prudence smile. How blissful to get lost in a task that came naturally while her mind could explore wherever it desired. It looked peaceful. Her hands worked swiftly, and after some time, all of the wool had been processed.

"I thank you for your help, dears. It goes much quicker with extra bodies. We'll be completely ready come market day now."

"Aye, and when will that be?" asked Khari.

"Why in just two days, dear. Whyever do you wish to know?"

"Well, we need to be getting to Alwich if we have any hope of getting your beloved captain." He looked at Prudence. "Then we'll need to observe the area, where he's being held, learn the layout, check for guards and everything."

"My goodness, and you can do that? If you gather all of that information you need... you will be able to save Cain?" asked Phaedra.

Khari nodded.

"Then how might I be of service?"

With Phaedra's help, Khari mapped out the route from Torrin Down all the way to Alwich Castle. Reesa and Phaedra would take the pony and trap up to the market in Harnstead. Khari and Prudence would ride with them most of the way, then continue on foot to avoid tying them to the women. If there was any hope of them hiding out at the cottage then it was imperative no one could direct soldiers their way.

From the market, it would be a few hours' walk to the castle. They would go in amongst the servants to get the lay of the land.

"So, you two should get off about a mile before Harnstead, You can head into the forest there, then head north until you reach The Great Lake. Once there, you can head west around the lake until you reach Alwich," said Phaedra.

"Perfect." Khari slapped the map in agreement.

"We'll get what we need and then make our way back 'ere later in the day," said Prudence confidently. It had taken so long to reach this point, to be even this close to Cain, that it still felt surreal. He'd probably lost all hope of ever seeing her again, of being free. It was a cruel god who thought this was Cain's fate. It didn't bear thinking about what they might have done to him.

"That's an awfully long walk for someone in your condition."

They all turned to see Reesa in the doorway, watching them.

"It won't be long until you give birth, dear. It isn't good for you," she said, coming in. "It isn't good for the child."

"I don't have a choice! I cannot leave him to die. I won't!" cried Prudence

"All right, *keine*. Don't fret. We're not going to leave 'im to die." He turned to Reesa. "We'll take it easy. I assure you. We will stop and rest frequently. We'll bring plenty of water and food. I'll keep an eye on her, I promise," said Khari. "We'll be safe."

P rudence watched as Phaedra poured milk into a saucer and added a dollop of honey, stirring it in until the mixture combined. She picked up the little dish and carried it through the kitchen and into the living room, taking it to the hearth where she placed it on the little sill that sat just inside the chimney breast.

"Phaedra, what in the world are ye doin'?" she asked curiously, bending down to peer into the chimney. She was almost surprised to see the little saucer sat on the sill, full of milk, as if it must have had a greater purpose than that.

"Just a little offering, dear. We are not the only people living in this house, you know." Her eyes sparkled with amusement at Prudence's confusion. "What do you know of hobgoblins, dear?" Phaedra led her towards the chairs that were placed in the centre of the warm room, and they sat.

"Not much. They're pests, aren't they?"

"Oh, hush! Don't say such things. The poor little dear will hear you and become most offended. Whilst they might have a proclivity for mischief and practical jokes, they are most wonderful helpers if treated nicely. This little fellow has lived here longer than we have. Every night, I make sure to pop out a little treat for him, and once we are in bed sleeping, he'll come out and do a little cleaning. They enjoy it, you see, sweet little things. I can't say I feel as well-inclined to tidy as they seem to." Phaedra chuckled and patted Prudence's arm. "Come, dear. Let's head to bed and allow our little friend to go about his evening as he wishes." Phaedra rose from her seat, offering Prudence a hand as she guided her out of the room and up the stairs towards her bedroom.

Prudence's ears pricked up as they walked, and she could swear she heard the scurrying of tiny little feet behind them, followed by the clink of the saucer as it knocked against wood.

She glanced back, but all that could be seen was the hearth, the rug that lay before it, and the two chairs in the centre of the room.

Phaedra steered Prudence towards her room and gave her a swift kiss on the cheek as she bid her goodnight. Once inside her room, Prudence could not help but wonder about the creature supposedly moving about downstairs, cleaning, of all things. She quietly slunk out of bed and pulled on her robe, tying it around her large stomach, and crept out into the hallway. She just wished to catch sight of it.

The corridor was dark and silent as she walked, taking great care to avoid the creakiest floorboards. She crept down the stairs and hovered halfway, bending to peer into the dark of the living room. Through the gloom, she could just make out the broom that Phaedra kept by the back door, and holding onto it, a tiny creature no taller than a toddler sweeping the wooden floor.

It wore raggedy little trousers over boots that no longer fit, so much so that its toes were sticking out of the ends, a bedraggled red coat done up by a singular button sewed at its chest, and on its head, a tiny top hat that looked to have been made out of a pair of trousers.

The stair creaked as Prudence shifted her weight, and the hobgoblin caught sight of her vanishing back into the hearth, leaving the broom to clatter to the floor where it had once stood.

"Shit," Prudence whispered. "I'm sorry." She crept slightly further down the stairs. "Please come back."

The hobgoblin was nowhere to be seen as Prudence walked through to the kitchen and fetched the honey. With effort, she sat down on the rug in front of the hearth, jar of honey in hand and a spoon. She heaped the spoon with honey and held it out towards the hearth. "I'm sorry I startled you. That was rude of me." She spoke slowly, quietly, not wanting to spook it further.

She sat there for a long time, cooing in the direction of the hearth and trying to coax the creature back out. The sound of movement came and soot drifted down from inside the chimney. Prudence held her breath, waiting. After a period of silence, she caught sight of a tiny hand curled around the edge of the fireplace before a little face peered out nervously.

She remained frozen, holding out the spoon of honey towards him as he slowly came out of the fireplace. It crept forward out onto the rug and inch by inch got closer to Prudence, just enough to reach out an arm to grab the spoon from Prudence's grasp and devour the honey. He dropped the spoon instantly and retreated a few steps, still wary of her presence.

Carefully, Prudence picked the spoon back up and loaded it with honey once again, holding it out for the strange creature. This time, it only took a few seconds before it reached out to grab the spoon again. She couldn't help but smile as it gobbled the offering. She kept feeding it more and more honey, each time the creature getting slightly closer to her until it stood right in front of her. It seemed to begin to trust her as it moved forward, almost in her lap, waiting for the next spoonful of honey.

She blinked rapidly, the feel of tears welling in her eyes took her by surprise and she raised a hand slowly to wipe them away. The sight of this creature at her feet happily gobbling up the honey she offered forced a swell of warmth through her chest.

Its head bobbed up and down as it licked the spoon clean before shoving it back into the jar for another mouthful. Prudence felt the keen desire to reach out a finger and stroke its face, to take its tattered, old clothing and fix it up for him, to make it look brand new, but she resisted, not wanting to scare him away again. Instead, she let her hand fall to her swollen belly, softly cradling the curve of it through the fabric.

She sat like that for most of the night, feeding the hobgoblin and talking softly to it. It liked her as far as she could tell, and even came to continue its cleaning while she sat and watched. Just before morning came, Prudence bid it farewell, leaving the half-eaten jar of honey in its little sticky hands, and climbed the stairs once more to get some sleep.

The summer sun beat down on the village of Torrin Down with a merciless heat. With nary a cloud in the sky, it left the air oppressive and close on the skin. Sweat clung to the nape of the neck and limbs felt heavy, overworked.

Prudence was stuck indoors for the majority of the day. It was too stifling outside, especially when one was with child. The weight of her belly and the ache in her bones was felt even more keenly in the heat. She pottered about, trying to make herself useful cleaning up as Reesa worked on her knitting; preparing cheese and baking bread; collecting water from the well outside.

Once that had been done, she took to preparing for the following day. They would need water, supplies, and weapons. They didn't have their swords and pistols anymore; those had gone down with *The Maiden*, but they had borrowed a billhook from Phaedra's barn and a knife from the kitchen. It wasn't much, but it would have to do. The billhook's blade was wicked and could damage if need be, as could the knife. They needed to get Cain out as quietly as possible. To steal him away before anyone even noticed he was missing.

She took a deep breath. The uncertainty of their plan threatened to engulf her like a wave. The timing would be tight. They would need to get down to the dungeons and get Cain back out again between soldiers' rounds. And how would they get his cell open? Khari was certain there would be a key kept down there for easy access to prisoners for their work shifts and trials, and if not, he was familiar with the cell construction. They would bring gunpowder to bust open the door. Although, doing that would give them much less time to get out.

They would make do. They had to, or they would die trying. She wouldn't live the rest of her life without Cain. Soon, he would be free and they would disappear off into a new life together.

Slowly coming out of her thoughts, Prudence took to wrapping some supplies: bread, cheese, and dried meats. She tucked two apples into her bag and picked up a third, biting into it, the juices dripping down her chin. It tasted like summer.

A swift kick from the bump caught her off guard. "Oh, you like apple too, do ye?" She smiled. "Yer a bit small for it yet, little one."

Her mind still struggled to make sense of the idea that there was a whole person inside her. It was wild to think about. Even though she had seen the outline of a foot as it pushed against her skin, had seen the jolts of it moving as she lay down, it was hard to imagine that soon she would have an entirely new person to look after. Her responsibility.

How did other people manage it? One moment, you're only in charge of caring for yourself, the next, a tiny, fragile infant needs you. You're the only thing keeping it alive. Whichever god made it so had not been thinking clearly. Surely, someone needed to provide some training, to teach people how to care for a baby.

A real baby. One they had made. She couldn't help but picture a tiny baby cradled in Cain's arms, his biceps bigger than its little head. A little hand reaching out to hold his finger. It made her heart flutter. A mini Cain. With his blond hair and green eyes, little fingers and toes.

"You look happy." Prudence turned to see Reesa smiling at

her.

"Oh." Prudence blushed. "Yes. I guess I am."

"You've got a look of fond longing. He must be some man to get you all flustered like this just thinking about him."

"He is." Prudence smiled.

"A handsome one?" asked Reesa.

"Very handsome. And kind. Strong... brave... sweet..." Prudence seemed to get lost in her fervour.

"He sounds like quite a man."

"The best of men."

CHAPTER THIRTEEN

PREPARATIONS

Prudence and Khari were finally able to make the journey to Alwich Castle just a few days later. The King's Festival had arrived, giving them the perfect opportunity to enter the castle grounds and become familiar with the layout. The long track that led up to the outer gate had been lined on either side with colourful flags. Merchants strolled up and down with their goods, accosting anyone who passed them with convincing words and offers of great deals in celebration.

The two of them walked through the castle gate side by side, in amongst all manner of locals coming to the castle for the day of celebrations. No expense had been spared in honour of the celebration. There was dancing and joyous music from many musicians and bands set up all around the castle grounds to serenade the castle's guests. A great feast had been planned for the early evening, and many events were to occur throughout the day.

Prudence spotted a broadside pinned to the wall that read 'Hawking, dancing, music, and plays. Jousting to begin at noon in the north arena. Fireworks to begin after the feast.'

"Sounds like an exciting day, doesn't it, *keine*?" said Khari. "Oh, I do hope there's roasted hog. Nothin' I love more."

"Jus' don't forget why we're here." Prudence dropped her voice to a whisper. "We need to make note of *everything*. The number of guards, the route to the dungeon, where the barracks are. All of it. We leave nothing to chance, all right?"

Khari nodded. "Yes, yes. I've got it. Doesn't mean we can't enjoy ourselves too," he grumbled.

Prudence eyed the barracks as they walked past. They were so near the entrance and filled with a terrifying number of guards. To the right of them were the stables that housed the cavalry horses.

"Uh, *keine*, I think ye need to see this." Khari paused, his eyes on something pinned to the wall. He pulled down a sheet of paper and handed it to her. The likeness of Cain's face was staring back at her, inked in alarming accuracy. Underneath the illustration of his face read, *Cain William Morris is to be sent to trial for murder, treason, and crimes against the king*.

Prudence's stomach dropped. In only a week's time, he would be put on trial for his crimes, where he would most assuredly be sentenced to death. It was like she couldn't breathe. Her hand shook furiously as it clenched the paper, squeezing so tight it tore.

"We're out of time," she panted, her voice high and panicked.

"We're not out of time, *keine*. This is a good thing." Khari took the paper from her hands and guided her away from the throng of people so they could not be overheard. "This is good. Now we know when he's going to be sent to trial. All this time, we haven't known. We've been guessing. This king wants to make a spectacle of executing Cain, hmm? He's not going to just do it. He's going to make sure he takes the time so that everyone can be there. He'll want it done in such a way that hundreds of people watch him die. That gives us a little time. I promise."

Prudence started to calm a little at Khari's logic. It made sense. For all this time, they hadn't known what was happening. At least now they knew when his trial would be, and they could plan to get him out before he was executed. They would plan and find a way to get to him.

"Now, come on." Khari nudged her. "We need to be exploring, yes? Examining everywhere for guards, points of entry. We don't want to be left at a disadvantage." He pulled her along, and she allowed him to lead her forward, continuing on their mission under the guise of celebration.

From there, it was a long walk around the outer walls, past the outer courtyard and what could only be the entrance to the dungeons based on the number of guards that stood watch. They spiralled inwards towards the centre of the castle until they reached the Great Hall.

There, preparations were already being made for the feast that evening. Dozens of servants busied about decorating tables and placing flowers, decorating the room with bright colours and plenty of light for the celebrations. They were guided outside with the rest of the public towards the inner court where the hawking demonstration was taking place.

A falconer stood in the middle of the courtyard, gloved hand lifted, ready to act as a perch for the bird of prey that circled the sky. Its cry echoed across the stone walls and everyone looked up, taking in its beauty. Whilst the falconer kept everyone rapt with fascination talking about the birds he controlled and the way it hunted, Prudence caught sight of the king, sitting atop his throne on a dais at the far end of the courtyard, watching the event.

As she took in his face and frame, the gold crown that sat on top of his head, she felt her blood begin to boil. That was the man who had caused all of this. That was the man who had imprisoned Cain, who was going to have him killed. She wanted to walk over there and rip out his heart with her hands.

As Prudence and Khari made the long walk from the castle back to Torrin Down, they planned.

"All right, so we'll come on trial day. Everyone will be here anyway to watch the trial, so we'll blend right in with the rest of the public. We'll watch the beginning of the trial and make sure we know exactly where the guards are going to be, where they're going to be holding Cain." Khari rattled off the plan that they had been working on throughout the day.

Prudence heaved a sigh as she walked. Her feet ached from the long day they had had, and she wanted nothing more than to sit and rest, but it would have to wait. "I'll stick to the crowd for as long as possible before sneakin' away to cause a distraction." Prudence knew she couldn't keep up with Khari or Cain in her current state, and she didn't wish to risk the child she carried whilst they escaped.

Their plan was simple in theory. Khari and Prudence would enter the castle grounds with everyone coming to watch Cain's trial. Prudence would stand away from Khari so as to not be seen together. She would then wait for the opportune moment to cause a big distraction that would bring the guards towards the chaos and away from Cain.

They planned for Prudence to start a fire. Considering where they were in the castle, it would be sensible for a fire to start possibly in the Great Hall or in the officers' rooms—both of which would most likely be guarded to a certain extent, so they knew they would have to be flexible with their plans on the day. To have everything ready to start the fire so Prudence could do it at the right moment, wherever she would be able to that would cause a commotion.

Khari would position himself closer to the platform where Cain would be on trial. This way, he would be able to rush to Cain's aid, to fend off any guards that remained guarding him with Cain's help, while Prudence's fire drew most of the soldiers away. Ideally, if they planned it right, people would panic and run, causing even more chaos in which Khari and Cain could escape from the castle grounds.

"Once ye've set yer fire, ye need to be gettin' out with everyone else. Don't hang around for us. It'll only be suspicious, and whilst many of the guards will be fighting the fire, I'm sure the king will not make it easy to escape in the chaos. No doubt there will be guards still on Cain no matter how many fires ye set. So, ye need to walk or even run with the rest of the people. Get out of the castle in the panic, yes?" Khari's voice was insistent as if he didn't completely trust Prudence to follow through with leaving after her job was done.

"Yes, yes. I understand. I'm not stupid, ye know. I know I can't exactly fight like this." She patted her stomach half affectionately, half in annoyance. She already loved the child growing within her, but she couldn't deny that it was rather an inconvenience at the moment. "We'll reconvene in Harnstead once ye've gotten away and the coast is clear."

"And what do ye do if we don't arrive in Harnstead by the next evening?" he asked.

"I go on back to Torrin Down, to Phaedra and Reesa, and wait for ye there. I know this all already, Khari. Would ye stop talking to me like I'm a child?" she huffed.

Khari chuckled lightly. "I'm sorry, but if I'm to do this and I get yer captain to safety, the last thing I need is him killin' me because I couldn't keep ye safe. So, we're goin' to go over the plan as many times as necessary until I'm satisfied that ye won't do anythin' stupid and heroic. Got it?"

Prudence grumbled, frowning, but ultimately agreed. "I get it. Jus' know that as soon as this child is born, I shall go right back to not listenin' to ye," she said defiantly, making Khari laugh.

"Yes, all right, *keine*. That seems like a fine deal. Let's just get this over with first, hmm? We'll save yer beloved captain and ye'll have that child, and then we'll be free to go as far from this wretched country as possible. And I plan to go somewhere as far from ye as I can. Gonna find myself a quiet little spot away from all this nonsense. I fear I'm tired of lookin' over my shoulder now." He chuckled. "Ready for a bit o' peace and quiet."

Khari left the little cottage in the warm summer air of the evening and strode down the path that led through the village. The sun was starting to set and children finished up their games, having been called in to dinner by their mothers.

Chickens that had been roaming free throughout the hamlet clucked as they made their way back to their coops to roost for the night. Phaedra's sheepdog ran up to Khari, wagging its tail and darting around his legs as he walked, currently free to roam as she pleased whilst off duty from protecting her sheep.

The following day was the day of the captain's trial. When the man would be brought before the king and his council, his crimes read aloud, and where he would then be sentenced to death.

Prudence had been anxious all day, unable to be still for more than a minute, keeping herself busy with irrelevant tasks in a vain attempt to keep her mind from drifting to thoughts of Cain. Of what might happen if they did not succeed.

Khari stopped and bent down to scratch the dog behind the ears, and it woofed happily at the attention. "Yer a good girl," he crooned. Dolly followed him as he made his way through the village, running off every time she saw another person who might give her attention before returning to his side like a loyal companion.

It was a beautiful evening, peaceful and serene. It would be a stark contrast to the day that awaited them. Breaking Cain out of the castle would be no easy feat, and whilst he had never admitted it to Prudence, Khari frequently wondered whether it would be possible. No matter which way he looked at it, they would most likely not succeed in their mission, and worst of all, it would most likely end not just with Cain's execution but theirs too. It was why he had been so insistent upon Prudence only causing a distraction. With luck on their side, she'd be able to get away without anyone realising she had been helping them.

As for him and Cain... they would fight to the very end. And if that end came sooner rather than later, then so be it. He had made a promise and he would stand by it, even in death.

He dared not hope about the future, about what he might do if he did survive the coming day. Would he travel back east, home, to his family? Would he find new work aboard another ship, perhaps a legitimate merchant this time where he could merely focus on working and earning his keep before spending a peaceful night in his own home?

"What do ye think, hmm?" he asked the dog, and she looked up at him, tongue dangling out the side of her mouth happily. "Should I get myself somewhere nice to live? Maybe work as a fisherman or somethin'?" Dolly woofed again, and he laughed. "Oh, ye like that plan, do ye? Maybe I'll even get a dog jus' like ye to keep me company. That would be fun, wouldn't it." He patted the dog, feeling her long, soft fur in between his fingers.

He just had to get through the next day, that was all. Once Cain was freed and back with Prudence, once the soldiers had stopped searching for them, he could go wherever he wished. Live whatever life he wanted. The possibilities were endless and felt both exciting and overwhelming. He had never had such freedom before. He wasn't quite sure what to do with it.

He rounded the last cottage that made up the hamlet before turning on his heels back in the direction of their temporary home. The sun had sunk lower in the sky now, coating the whole village in a warm orange glow. It was like the sky was on fire. Maybe having a house like this one wouldn't be so bad. It had always seemed boring to him before, but perhaps there was more to life than death-defying excitement. He intended to find out. If he were wrong and the quiet life turned out to be unbelievably boring, he could always go and find trouble again.

It was up to him. He could do as he pleased and answer to no one. And that freedom alone felt more precious than any gold.

With every kick Prudence felt in her belly, the more and more accustomed to becoming a mother she had become. Despite her still lingering fears and her worry for Cain, she found herself getting excited for the prospect of having this child. Their child. She frequently found herself wondering who it would look like. Would it share Cain's blond locks or her own dark mane? Would it have Cain's vibrant green eyes or her icy ones?

She wasn't sure whether she wished for a boy or a girl. She could see Cain being delighted by either, and she found that so long as she was able to get Cain freed and the child was well, that was all that mattered to her.

She pottered about the cottage, tidying up as she went. Phaedra and Reesa were already very tidy people, but Prudence couldn't help but refold the blankets that were already folded, to rewash pans that had already been cleaned and were laying out to dry.

Multiple times she swept the floors in the kitchen, the living room, and throughout the hallway, even getting down on her knees to scrub the floorboards. When Reesa found her on all floors washing the same spot over and over, she had helped

Prudence up and insisted that she sit down and rest for a little while. Reesa fetched her some tea and sat down beside her.

"How are you feeling, dear?" she asked gently. Despite her sweet tone, her scrutinising gaze made Prudence feel a little foolish.

"I'm fine. Just trying to keep busy."

"You know, we appreciate the help, of course, but it's important that you rest as well. You won't be any good to that child if you're completely exhausted by the time it comes. The delivery itself will be exhausting enough." She smiled and nudged Prudence sweetly. "Don't make it even harder for yourself."

Prudence sighed and sipped at her tea. It was warm and soothing, and now that she was sitting, she found herself feeling tired almost immediately. "If I stop, then I end up..." she trailed off.

"Worrying about Cain?"

Prudence nodded. "Yes. I hate all of this sitting around. I feel as though we're out of time. That despite being so close, I'm going to lose him all the same."

Reesa nodded thoughtfully. "I understand, dear. But what else are you to do right now? Until the time is right for you to attempt this rescue..."

Prudence bristled at the word 'attempt' but said nothing.

"Then your only job should be to take care of yourself, for the sake of your child." Reesa patted Prudence's knee affectionately before rising from her seat, leaving Prudence alone to consider her words.

Prudence remained seated, sipping her tea as she stared blankly into the fireplace. She knew Reesa was right, but it was hard to just sit back and do nothing. As she looked around, she tried to picture what the cottage would have looked like some twenty years before, when Cain was just a small child.

She pictured him sitting on the rug before the hearth, toys in hand, playing with his sister as they waited for their dinner. Prudence saw a young Cain traipsing mud through the entire house after coming in from playing and being scolded for making a mess. She could almost see his blond hair as she imagined a slightly taller Cain running through the room at full speed, giving chase as he knocked into furniture, sending things crashing to the floor. It made her smile. Perhaps their child would be the same.

Prudence envisioned building a home like this one. With a thatched roof and climbing ivy that grew up around the front door. She pictured a chimney puffing with smoke as she baked bread and cooked for her family. There would be a stone walkway up to the front of the house lined with flowers, and a little barn for some animals. Perhaps they would even have a small garden where they could grow crops. She imagined a little child with beautiful blond hair helping her, with fingers all muddy as they dug up potatoes and harvested carrots.

She would have a comfy chair that looked out the window over the best view from their home across fields and trees that stretched for miles and practically sang when the sun hit it just right. And in the winter, it would snow, leaving their home a warm haven nestled in amongst a snowy blanket.

She felt the child kick once more and stroked it with her hand. "That sounds good, doesn't it? Ye'd like that as well, would ye?" She smiled. "I think it would be grand."

Cain was rudely awoken by the door of his cell slamming open as two guards stormed into the room. Still groggy from sleep and unaware of his surroundings, they hauled him up from the floor where he slept to standing and attached his chains to the wall as a couple of servants walked in. They brought buckets of water, cloths, new clothes, and a comb, and took to cleaning him up.

"Clean him up. Get him ready for trial. He's to be brought out into the courtyard in a few hours," said a guard to a servant.

She nodded politely and moved closer to Cain, somewhat fearfully despite him being shackled to the wall, unable to harm her. Between the two servants, they stripped him of his current clothes, which were now ragged and dirty. His shirt had been torn during the lashing and now hung off his back, barely a shirt at all.

They kept their heads hung low, focused on the task at hand, not daring to look up into the eyes of the criminal before them. Cain wondered what he looked like to them. Some vicious killer that might snap their necks? He stood a foot taller than one of the servants who couldn't have been more than sixteen. It must have made him seem like a giant. A dangerous man who deserved to die.

They cleaned off his chest and back as best they could with the cloths before dumping the full bucket of water over his head.

"Hey!" he growled.

The poor servant whimpered in front of him. "I- I'm sorry,

sir. I'm under orders to have you washed. and since there is no tub..." she trailed off, stuttering as her face turned a bright shade of red.

Cain felt an inkling of shame. "I'm sorry. I didn't mean to scare you."

"Rita!" hissed the other servant. "We're not meant to speak to him, for goodness' sake." The taller of the two servants scowled at Rita, and it was clear from the girl's reaction that she was used to being bossed around. Her face crumpled once again, and she hurried to continue cleaning him, eyes focused on the floor.

They combed out his hair, all manner of straw and dirt falling from his blond locks as they washed it. All this time sleeping on the cold stone floor and working merciless hours in the grimy fields, sweating and bleeding with no way to clean himself off had left him disgusting. He would be glad to feel clean for the first time in many months, even if it was to be right before his death.

The servant girls finished up their tasks, leaving his new clothes in a pile, neatly folded by his side before exiting the cell. Once the women were gone, the guards returned to unshackle him so he could get himself dressed.

The clunk of the chains as they released from him echoed loudly, and he rubbed his wrists, grateful for the brief moment they were free and no longer chafing.

"You've got five minutes. Hurry it up." The guards stood in front of him, a barrier between him and his freedom as he pulled on the clean britches and shirt. They were not new items of clothing, but they were clean and not stained with blood like his previous clothes, and in that sense, they were a blessing.

Cain tugged them on swiftly, wincing every now and then as his back twinged. It had mostly healed by now, but it still stung fiercely and certainly was not healed enough to sleep on. He couldn't even begin to imagine what his back would look like now. It had already been scarred from many years of previous lashings, but they had faded over time and weren't too hideous. Now, though, these new scars, he could feel, were raised. Scarred flesh over scarred flesh. They would most likely heal red and jagged. A horrible reminder... not that he was going to live long enough to see them.

"Time's up," the guard closest to him barked, and the man stepped forward, shackles in hand to clasp his wrists once more. The metal pinched as it closed around his already raw wrists, and Cain bit his cheek, hiding the pain. He would not give them the satisfaction.

"Now," the other guard spoke up, "we'll be back to fetch you in no time at all, lad, so don't you go anywhere." He grinned maliciously at Cain as they walked out of the cell, closing the barred door behind them with a bang.

Cain stood in the centre of the room, wrists chained, and waited patiently for his trial to begin.

CHAPTER FOURTEEN

TRIAL & ERROR

The day of Cain's trial arrived far too quickly, and Prudence woke with a sickening pain in her stomach. Sweat clung to her forehead and it took her a moment to orient herself. This was it. Now or never. She flung herself out of bed, almost tripping over in her speed to get to the door.

"Khari, come on! Ye need to get up! We have to go!" she yelled.

The sooner they left, the better. The trials were due to start at noon, and they had to get there first. Phaedra had convinced her neighbour to give them a ride on his cart as he was travelling to Harnstead anyway.

From there, they would need to walk, but it would be much

easier than travelling the whole distance on foot, and faster too.

Prudence raced down the stairs and into the kitchen, grabbing an apple and biting into it as she picked up their supplies.

She had packed a few morsels of food for the journey as well as a tinderbox, which she shoved into the pocket of her skirt, hidden but readily available when she would need it.

Khari appeared at the top of the staircase, still half asleep as he rubbed his eyes.

"If yer goin' to be this frantic the whole journey, I might have to go alone," he joked, and Prudence scowled.

She threw an apple at him and he caught it with ease. "Don't be a prick." She winced and hunched forward, and within an instant, Khari was at her side.

"What is it? What's wrong, *keine*?" he asked, concerned.

"It's nothing. I'm fine." Prudence brushed him off and continued preparing to leave. "Mr. Carver will be leavin' soon. We need to be ready."

Khari eyed her warily. "Ye don't seem all right."

"I'm fine," she snapped. "We need to go. We need to get to Cain."

She pushed past him, walking into the living room, and pulled on her thick boots, struggling as she bent down to tie the laces over her bulging stomach. Her stomach cramped, and she groaned, biting her cheek in frustration as she stood and headed for the door. "Come on."

"*Keine*, I don't think ye-"

"I don't think you'll be able to go, dear," Reesa spoke as she came into the room, heading straight for Prudence. "Seems as though yer child is on its way." She smiled at her, but Prudence just scowled.

"No. No, it's not. It's not coming, and I have to get to Cain before he... before he..." she panted, frantic, and her head rushed, making the room sway. "I have to get to him," she insisted, pulling open the front door and storming through it.

Khari and Reesa were right behind her. "You can't go, dear. Not now."

"She's right, *keine*. It's not possible. I'll be fine on my own. I'll get to Cain and get 'im out," Khari insisted, but she wasn't having it. "But I have to save him!" she insisted meekly, still trying to walk in the direction of the neighbour and his cart.

Khari and Reesa took her by an arm each and turned her back towards the cottage.

"No, I can't- I've got to go," Prudence insisted, but her legs moved with them as they guided her back indoors.

Another wave of pain swept through her middle, and she slumped forward, teeth clenched.

"See, you can't go anywhere like this, dear. I forbid it," Reesa exclaimed sternly. "For the sake of this child, you will go right back up those stairs to bed. Do you understand me?"

"But- but-" Prudence's objections fell on deaf ears as they steered her back inside and sat her down on a chair.

"I'll get 'im, *keine*, I promise ye," Khari swore. "Come on. Hand over the tinderbox, and ye focus on having that babe. All right?"

"What's going on?" Phaedra bustled into the room, cloth in hand as she dried a pan.

"Prudence here is in labour," Reesa beamed at her wife. Phaedra lit up instantly. "Oh my goodness, such a blessing. Quick, dear, let's get you back upstairs, hmm? Get you as comfortable as we can. I know it won't be comfortable per say, what with the pain but we'll do our best to make it nice and cosy for you." She swept Prudence up into her arms, and before she knew it, Prudence was being led up the stairs.

She stopped walking, digging her feet in as she turned to Khari and handed him the tinderbox from her skirt pocket.

"Get him back," she whispered earnestly and Khari's hand clasped over hers.

"I will, *keine*."

They returned for Cain quite quickly, two guards to walk either side of him as he shuffled along chained at both the wrists and ankles, one guard to walk behind and another to walk in front. All carried muskets and bayonets and stared straight ahead as they walked the criminal to his place on the wooden platform that had been set up for the trials that were to be done today.

A long line of criminals queued along the platform as each one was charged and promptly sentenced. The platform had been raised in the courtyard just above the dungeon cells and a large space had been left open in the centre of the courtyard for the public to stand and watch the trials.

A dais had been set up behind this area where the king and his council sat, table laden with food and drink as the proceedings went ahead. Most of the council weren't even watching as man after man and the occasional woman was brought before them for their crimes to be read aloud.

The speaker stepped forward and cleared his throat as Jed was brought forward to the front of the platform. His face was void of all colour, and the young lad looked as though he might vomit.

"The accused, Jed Woollsey, stands charged with the crime of theft and fleeing arrest. It is alleged that you unlawfully and with felonious intent did wilfully and wrongfully take and carry away the personal property of another, namely jewels and jewellery, fine fabrics, and one horse against the peace of King Frederick III and the Western Tides, and the law thereof. You are hereby charged with death and are to be hung by the neck until dead."

Jed quivered and promptly vomited over the platform and courtyard as people reeled backwards to avoid getting it on them.

Cain sighed. He watched as his friend was hauled off back to his cell and the next criminal was brought forward for their crimes to be read. He deliberately stood a little to the side of Jed's vomit that was now seeping into the wood and making the entire courtyard smell.

One by one, the people were dragged forward, crimes were read, and they were subsequently charged, until finally it was Cain's turn. The guards roughly pulled him forward until he was stood in the centre of the platform. Jed's vomit was now drying near his boot and he looked at it briefly before locking eyes with the king.

King Frederick was resolute in his attention. All of his focus lay on Cain Morris, his longtime enemy, being brought forth for the charges against him. Cain didn't think he imagined the small smile that played on the king's lips, nor the knowing glance he gave him.

The speaker stepped forward and cleared his throat again. "The accused, Cain William Morris, stands charged with the crime of murder. It is alleged that you unlawfully and with malice aforethought did wilfully and feloniously kill Ingrid I, Queen Consort of Aelin and The Western Tides by drowning."

A ripple of gasps ran through the watching public as the speaker read out the late queen's name.

"Kill him!"

"Hang him!"

"Have 'im drowned!" came the cries from the crowd.

The speaker coughed awkwardly before continuing to read the further charges. "The accused, Cain William Morris, stands charged with the crime of being a fugitive from justice. It is alleged that you, having been accused of a crime in Aelin, did wilfully and unlawfully abscond and flee from the authorities to avoid prosecution and justice."

The crowd was silent now, angrily watching Cain as he stood stoically in the middle of the platform, his eyes straight ahead watching the king.

"The accused, Cain William Morris, stands charged with the crime of piracy. It is alleged that you did wilfully and unlawfully engage in acts of robbery, violence, or other criminal activities for personal gain, thereby committing acts of piracy on the high seas. You, the accused, Cain William Morris, stand charged with the crime of treason against the crown. It is alleged that you did wilfully and knowingly conspire, levy war, and or engage in overt acts in betrayal of the king."

Angry jeers resounded as the charges were finished being read. The speaker rolled up his paper and faced the crowd. "You are hereby charged with death and are to be hung by the neck until dead."

As Cain was dragged from the platform back towards the dungeons where he would wait until his execution later that day, he caught sight of a face he recognised. Khari was in amongst the crowd, quietly watching the proceedings.

When he met Cain's eye, he nodded in greeting. Cain glanced around wildly for any sign of Prudence, but he couldn't see her before he was shoved down the stone steps into darkness. She had come for him.

Khari watched with trepidation as they read out Cain's crimes against the crown. The list of charges was almost impressive despite the angry crowd yelling for his death. In spite of it all, Cain remained poised up on the platform, hands bound in front of him, legs chained, he didn't look cowed or broken. Khari found it gave him a new level of respect for the man. He was facing death with a brave face. The face of one who has accepted his lot in life, consequences and all, and was ready for whatever came next.

Little did the captain know that Prudence had sent him to ensure he didn't have to face what was next. At least, not yet.

He glanced between Cain and the king as they stared at one another fiercely across the courtyard. Certainly, the distraction would need to be big in order for the king to lose sight of his captive, just for a short while. Khari looked around at all of the guards, taking in their weapons, the gaps between each of them, which ones were looking bored and downright tired. He could use that.

"You are hereby charged with death and are to be hanged by the neck until dead," said the speaker, and the crowd roared with satisfaction. They were hungry for blood, chomping at the bit to see the executions today.

The guards either side of Cain took him roughly by the arms and dragged him forcefully off the side of the platform and towards the dungeons down below.

Cain looked up as if aware of eyes on him besides the murderous crowd and caught Khari's eye. He nodded at the captain, a silent promise that he was here to help him before he was dragged down the stairs and out of sight. The speaker walked to the middle of the platform and held his hands out, quietening the ravenous onlookers.

"The executions will take place in just a moment, in order of the charges filed and sentences given." He bowed to his king and retreated from the platform as the people around Khari began talking amongst themselves. Cain had been the last of the charges filed; that would give him a little time.

Khari examined the courtyard again. Guards stood every few feet around the perimeter, weapons drawn and held upwards at their sides. The king and council were seated behind him, out of reach of the public. From his position near the front of the crowd, Khari could just about see the officer bunks to the left beside the dungeon stairs, and a gate that led through to the great hall.

Most of the guards were standing around the courtyard ready to deal with any prisoners and defend their king. Mercifully, as if a gift from the Gods themselves, the officer quarters themselves were mostly unmanned.

Khari began slowly inching his way back through the crowd in the direction of the officers' rooms as the first few prisoners were brought out and lined up along the noose that had been built towards the back of the platform.

"Charles Jackson, Thomas Wright, Turner Hill." The

speaker read off their names as guards placed the rope nooses around their necks.

The executioner stood to the side, already holding the lever that would drop these men to their deaths.

"You are hereby charged with death and are to be hung by the neck until dead."

The lever creaked as the executioner pulled and the trapdoors opened, dropping the men through the gaps, the only thing holding them up around their necks. Their bodies groaned with the weight. Two of the men were lucky enough for the sweet release of a quick death, their necks snapping audibly as they fell. The third writhed in pain as he struggled for air, his face turning a putrid purple as he clawed at his neck, hands still bound in front of him.

The crowd watched on silently until he finally stopped jerking and fell still.

Khari dodged a few people as he worked his way backwards, closer and closer with each little step. He moved slowly so as not to draw any attention. He just needed to get back there into that room. He fiddled with the tinderbox in his pocket, opening the lid and taking out the flint. It was smooth in his hand, sharp and cold. He inched backwards until he was at the back of the crowd watching the executions.

"Matthew Robinson, Martin Baker, Jack Smith. You are hereby charged with death and are to be hung by the neck until dead."

The bodies dropped instantly and the ropes creaked. Khari sauntered backwards, feigning drunkenness and the nearest guard paid him no mind. He leant heavily against the wall, slurring his words quietly to himself as if overcome with alcohol, all the while pulling out the flint.

Khari stepped backwards into the officer housing. The room was dark and empty, all guards focused on the execution outside. He quickly placed the tinder on the table and hit the flints together at speed to make a spark. A few sparks flew but didn't quite land. He tried again, feeling the pressure build as the executions continued outside.

Khari hit the flints urgently, sending sparks flying across the wooden table. A few landed on the tinder and the embers glowed. He dropped the flints, picking up the tinder carefully, and blew into it, bringing the small flame to life. It flickered and swayed in his hands, and he smirked. He looked around for the perfect place to put it to start a raging fire, and that was when he saw it. The munitions storage right next door.

Khari slunk out of the officers' rooms as innocently as he could and crept the few steps to the door of the munitions storage. He slipped inside with the little flame still protected in his hands. He opened a crate nearest the door and grinned. Gunpowder. He tore off the bottom of his shirt, trailing from inside the box out onto the floor. There, he placed the little tinder and flame and watched as it licked at the cloth.

Khari slipped back outside and retook his position against the stone wall. By the time the guard glanced his way again, he was back where he had been before, still looking drunk and out of sorts.

They led three more prisoners including Cain towards the platform and up the stairs as they cut down the previous three criminals.

Cain glanced briefly at him before looking away, deliberately not drawing any further attention from the king. The noose was placed around Cain's neck.

"Jud White, Aaron Ward, Cain Morris. You are hereby

charged with death and are to be hung by the neck until dead."

Cain felt his resolve shake as they tied the noose around his neck. Whatever Khari had planned... he hadn't seen Prudence. Was she not here? Was she all right? He thought for a brief second that Khari might have just been there to watch, as some kind of goodbye as he died. That was when everything exploded.

The platform shook as the building in front of him blew up, stone and other debris flying in every direction. It hit some people, but no one paid any mind. Everyone was frozen in shock as they turned to see the great fire that was now billowing out of the destroyed roof.

Cain scanned the crowd for Khari and spotted him at the far wall, coughing slightly from the smoke, but he locked eyes with Cain and gestured for him to move.

Cain didn't hesitate. In the chaos and confusion, he flung off the noose from his neck and dove off the platform, ploughing into a row of people in his way. He shoved through the crowd, trying to get as much distance as possible from the platform and guards.

After a moment, everyone seemed to come back to themselves. People screamed in panic and many ran straight for the nearest exit. People fell in their rush to get away from the fire that was now spreading to the next roof and were trampled underfoot, just not quick enough to get away.

"Seize that man!" he heard King Frederick yell from

somewhere to his right, and he ploughed forward even faster as guards began to descend upon him.

He lost sight of Khari in the crowd but continued on. He was the one they were after; he needed to get out. He shoved through the crowds of people and darted in the direction of the inner castle. He dodged panicked people as they ran, getting as many terrified onlookers between him and the guards as possible.

They made chase, following him through the throng as he surged forward. A shot fired out, missing his head narrowly as the lead ball embedded in the wall beside him.

Cain ducked around a corner and hesitated for a moment, catching his breath. As the nearest guard approached, he stepped out, slamming his foot into the guard's knee before he had the chance to fire. He dropped to the ground clutching his leg as Cain snatched up his musket and fired, shooting him in the face.

He didn't wait for more of them. He ran as fast as his lungs could bear, looking in every direction for some way to go, somewhere he could lose the guards.

He ran past the chapel and turned right. The castle gardens were unmanned, and Cain ran inside, looking around wildly for a way out. The walls were high and he could see to his right, in the distance, a thick trunk of smoke billowing into the sky from the explosion. Flames licked at the far walls as they climbed. That should give them a little advantage; some of the guards would have to be trying to put the fire out.

Cain caught sight of a gnarled apple tree growing against the far wall and ran to it. It was tall and looked sturdy. Most of all, it grew to the top of the garden wall and he grabbed hold of the trunk as he stuck a foot on a low branch and began to climb.

A deep groan escaped Prudence's lips as she bent over at the waist, clutching her side. It was a deep pain she'd never experienced before, something she couldn't quite explain, there was nothing quite like it. She clutched the bed frame so tightly her knuckles turned white and she clenched her teeth.

"Oh, that's it, dear. Let it out. No good holding in the screams, it'll only ache ye more," Reesa crooned at her, a hand on her back, rubbing in what she knew was meant to be soothing circles, but it only added to her discomfort. Another feeling on her already uncomfortable skin. Her skin prickled at the touch and she forced herself not to shake the sweet woman off.

Prudence growled softly. "I don't need to scream, I need it out!" Her voice rose in a mix of annoyance and pain. She didn't wish to admit it, but without Cain there, she was terrified.

"It's coming, dear. This little one is ready to meet its mama. Don't you fret. Bit of pain to be sure, but once you're holding that babe in your arms, you'll forget it all."

Prudence huffed and moved away from Reesa's touch, choosing to stride the room at a fast pace in hopes it would speed the process up. She grit her teeth harder, a solid ache in her jaw but she didn't let up. Her breath came out through her nose, fast and laboured as she paced the small bedroom. Her strides were long and purposeful, pausing only every few moments as another bout of clenching in her womb rippled through her.

Phaedra entered the room with a bowl of warm water and some blankets. "Oh, deary, look at you," she breathed softly, looking awestruck as she took in the sight of Prudence.

Prudence rolled her eyes. "Do not humour me, Phaedra. I am aware of how I look." Dishevelled. Hair stuck up in areas from sweat and gripping it tightly in frustration. Her face, she could tell, was red and clammy and she panted like a dog as she insisted on maintaining a speedy pace back and forth across the same creaky floorboards each time.

"Darling, you look radiant. Just look at what you're doing. It's Godlike." She winked at Prudence and it did momentarily make Prudence swell with warmth. "Nay... not Godlike. No God has the countenance to birth a child; this is Goddess born."

Prudence did break out into a smile then, as did Reesa.

"Aye," Reesa agreed. "We women are made of strong stuff. I should know, I've helped hundreds of women birth babes over the years. You'll do fine, dear. You're made of hardy stuff. Look at what you've done already."

It was true. Prudence had faced tougher hardships than this. And none with such rewards after the fact. This pain was more than worth it. She smiled briefly at both women, the expression cut short by another bout of pain in her gut, and she sank onto the bed for a moment.

"Deep breaths, Prudence." Reesa stroked her head gently. "I'm going to fetch you some tea to help you relax, all right?" She left the room, giving her wife a quick kiss on the cheek as she passed.

Phaedra joined Prudence on the bed and put a reassuring hand on her knee. "Won't be long now, not really. It might take a while until this little one is ready to come out, but Reesa is well-versed in this. She's the best midwife this side of the mountain pass. She'll keep a good eye on you and your child." She smiled and patted Prudence's knee gently. Her hand was warm on Prudence's knee, a comfort.

Just then, Reesa reappeared in the doorway, holding a steaming cup of tea. She handed it to Prudence. It smelt sweet, and Prudence eyed the colour warily. "What is it?" she asked, peering into the mug.

"Red raspberry leaf tea, dear. Should help to ease the process for you," said Reesa.

Prudence glanced at her, hesitating before taking a sip. It wasn't bad considering. She wasn't particularly fond of tea, but if it would speed up labour, she would drink buckets of it. She licked her lips then looked up at Reesa. "Is there anything else we can do?"

Reesa smiled softly at her. "I have some willow bark you can chew on that will provide a little bit of pain relief." She moved over to a box she had placed on the bed and rummaged around in it. It smelt strongly of herbs and such when she opened the lid. Prudence knew it was most likely tinctures and dried plant medicines, but still, with the pain she was in... it promised magic.

Reesa pulled out a stick of genuine bark and Prudence found herself surprised. She had called it bark, from a tree she was very familiar with, but it was still a little odd to take the rough bark in her mouth and gnaw on the wood. She may as well have been chewing on a twig she'd found outside for the taste. There was no way to tell if it was helping at all, and if it weren't for her faith in Reesa, she might have stopped.

Another contraction of the womb struck her then, and she arched her back, her teeth grinding down on the willow bark still in her mouth. Her brow was slick with sweat, and she shifted uncomfortably many times, unable to find a position that was even half comfortable for a minute.

"All right, dear. Let's take a look to see how you're doing." Reesa's hand stroked her shoulder and guided her to lie down on the bed for a moment. The older woman lifted her skirts and moved her knees apart to examine her. "I'm going to check how you're progressing. See how far the child has descended, all right?"

Prudence nodded, leaning back on the bed. Her breathing slowed somewhat as she lay there quietly. Any embarrassment she may have felt at being this exposed was squashed by the need to know this would be over soon. That she would be giving birth any time now.

The momentary relief from pain allowed her mind to wander and lead her away to thoughts of Cain, of Khari going to him now. Would he make it in time? Would Cain be able to escape? Her heart clenched at the thought. She needed to be there, finding him, not here giving birth. This wasn't the right time. She wasn't ready. There were more important things going on right now.

A wash of pain came over her once more, sweeping through her entire body, folding her up into a ball, and she yelled.

"It's time, dear," Reesa said softly, removing her hand and pulling her skirts back into place. "Let's get you ready, hmm? Why don't we try kneeling here," she guided Prudence to the floor as she knelt beside the bed. "And you can lean against the bedpost here, yes?"

"Your babe is coming, child." Phaedra smiled warmly at Prudence.

Prudence tried to smile back, but it came out more like a grimace as another contraction struck her and she doubled over the bedsheets. She groaned loudly and clutched the sheets.

"It's time to push now, love," Reesa encouraged.

CHAPTER FIFTEEN

REUNITED

Khari surged forward, shoving through the throng of panicked people in search of Cain. He pushed past people as they ran away from the explosion, ignoring the shouts as they tripped and knocked into one another. His only goal was to find the captain.

He rounded a corner, straining to see over people's heads, but he couldn't spot him. He searched for that knot of blond hair, but no luck. He followed the soldiers running after the escaped prisoner, but it seemed they had no idea where he had gone either.

One of them yelled instructions at the rest, but there was no clear plan. They fumbled with their weapons as ordinary civilians ran past them, blocking their sight and path to the exit. Cain would be heading for the castle gate, and so would Khari.

He surged forward with the people running in terror, allowing their wave of panic to help him forward as well. He managed to get past several soldiers and pushed on, running hard, keeping his eyes peeled for any sign of Cain. They passed the stables, and that was when Khari spotted it.

A head appeared over a wall just ahead, crouched low, keeping a look out for soldiers as he climbed over the wall.

Khari raced ahead, throwing a glance back over his shoulder to watch for the guards. They were a little ways back, caught up with the sheer amount of people panicking over the fire and smoke. "Cain, quickly!" he hissed at him, and Cain's head flew up.

He broke into a surprised grin at the sight of Khari before hopping down from the wall. "What the fuck are you doing here?" Cain asked incredulously.

"We really don't 'av time for this now!" Khari shoved Cain forward and they both broke into a run, dodging servants and public alike as they made their way to the castle gates. There would be more soldiers at the gate, but most of them had been at the execution and were now somewhere behind the two men, trying to fight their way through crowds in search of Cain.

Khari pulled two knives from his belt and thrust one into Cain's hands. "Here, take this." As they reached the courtyard, the few guards who were stationed around the gates caught sight of Cain and lunged for them.

"Stop!"

"I command you to stop in the name of the king!" One guard raised a musket at Cain and fired, and they both ducked just in time. The lead ball erupted from the gun with a loud bang and people froze, dropping low to the ground, screaming.

Cain and Khari didn't hesitate. They advanced, heading straight for the castle guards. Multiple other shots were fired off, but they all missed as Khari knocked one musket out of a guard's hands, jamming his blade into the man's throat where his armour and helmet left a gap. He dropped like a stone.

Cain took a shot to the arm, but it didn't slow him down. He ploughed into another guard, knocking the man to the floor. They grappled for the sword as another guard descended on them.

Khari leapt at him, slamming his fist into his face, but the guard was large and strong. He shook off the blow, hitting back with double the force, and Khari was knocked to the floor, stunned. Blood pooled in his mouth, and he spat it out.

The guard loomed above him, sabre raised at Khari's face, and it was all he could do to hold his hands up in a feeble attempt at protection. Suddenly, the man collapsed onto Khari, pinning him to the floor. Khari shoved him off as Cain offered him a hand, pulling him back up.

Together, they raced for the gate as it was swiftly coming down. The gate spikes caught Khari's shirt as they ducked underneath, running at full pelt as it tore his clothes away from his back. Shots fired as they ran, hitting the ground near them as they raced for the safety of further distance.

Behind them, the gate creaked as it opened again, soldiers hot on their heels.

"We've got to get somewhere we stand a chance of fighting them. If we fight here, we'll be dead in no time," Cain panted as they ran.

Khari looked around for any sign of shelter, anywhere that they might be able to get the drop on these guards individually.

If they had to face them all at once, Cain was right, they stood no chance.

"There!" Khari pointed at a small patch of trees in the distance and they aimed for it, running as fast as their legs could carry them. It wasn't much, but it was their only hope.

They surged ahead, racing across the open heathland towards the patch of trees. They needed to get the soldiers separated if they were to stand any chance of getting away. Cain rounded a tree, diving out of sight of the guards, and kept running. With Khari to his left, they dodged trees and hopped over roots in the ground.

His chest heaved with the effort. His arm screamed at him, pain radiating from the shot in his bicep. It wasn't bleeding too badly; the bullet seemed to have gone straight through. But still, it was another disadvantage.

Another shot sounded from somewhere behind them, and Cain ducked his head instinctively. More soldiers spilled out of the castle gates in chase. Khari dashed around a large oak and ushered Cain to follow.

"We've gotta take some of them out. They're only going to keep coming," he whispered to Cain urgently, peeking around the thick trunk to count their opponents.

"I know, I know," Cain murmured, following the man's gaze. "If we can take out the first few and get their weapons, we might be able to hold enough of them off to get some distance between us."

"I count fifteen men so far. There's only going to be more on the way. It's now or never."

The two fugitives nodded at each other, silently agreeing on a plan of action. Cain moved away, sprinting quickly through the undergrowth to hide behind another tree a short distance away, and they waited. Within minutes, they heard the scurry of feet in the dirt, making their way through the trees.

Cain peered out from his hiding place. One soldier to his right, another to his left between him and Khari. He glanced at his companion and held up a hand. *Wait for it*. They allowed the guard to creep nearer, his eyes skirting the trees, searching for them. *Just a little more*. The guard crept up so close he was directly between Khari and Cain. If he looked to his side, he would spot them immediately. *Now*.

Cain nodded at Khari, and he surged forward, knocking the guard off balance. He stumbled sideways but kept his grip on his blade, swinging at Khari, narrowly missing his torso. The guard yelled out for his fellow soldiers and more footsteps could be heard, louder now and faster, heading for them.

With the guard's focus on Khari, Cain lunged out behind him, shoving his knife in between the man's shoulder blades. He ignored the cry of his arm, pushing it as far in as he could manage as Khari cut the guard's throat.

The body fell to the floor as they released him, and they grabbed every weapon he had on his person. A singular musket with an additional shot, a sabre, and a small dagger. It would have to do.

Cain cocked the musket and fired at the oncoming soldiers. One shot met its mark, hitting a guard square in the chest, and he dropped like a stone. The other kept advancing, and Khari met him halfway, taking him on one to one, blade to blade. They clashed and parried, but it was over within moments.

Khari's sabre slashed through the man's arm, and his own weapon fell to the floor as he yelled. It only took one further thrust to finish him off. He rounded up the weapons, taking another musket for himself and shoving multiple blades into the belt at his hips before he took off towards Cain, and then they were both running again, away from the further onslaught of soldiers.

They defended as they ran, each taking brief pauses in running to shoot at the soldiers coming for them. Khari hesitated, waiting a dangerously long time as the guards got ever nearer before shooting once more, taking down another one.

Once they had managed to gain a little distance from the soldiers, they took the time to be more strategic. They worked off each other, luring the soldiers closer and lying in wait to take them on and dispatch them as efficiently as they could manage.

They could not head straight for Prudence; it would lead the soldiers right there and so they moved about across acres of king's land for hours, hiding out where possible until the immediate threat was mostly gone. They had managed to lose the soldiers that had come after them, but no doubt, there would be more.

By the evening, Cain had no doubt that the king would have every soldier at his disposal roaming the countryside in search of him. By morning, he imagined that every person living within ten miles would know his face and his name, and they would be at risk of being caught.

They needed to get to Prudence as fast as possible, and when it was clear, head for the nearest ship they could trust to take them away from this country for good.

Cain cleaned the blood from his split forehead with a torn piece of shirt as they hid out in an old storage shed on the far side of a farm. He licked the cloth, dampening it before putting it back on his head, and winced when it stung the wound. The blood came away easily, and by now, it had stopped gushing, but it left behind a nasty gash across his forehead that would most likely scar. The wound was too wide for the skin to knit itself back together, the cut, despite his best efforts, not clean enough to heal properly.

He had bandaged his shot arm as best as he could manage with another piece of torn shirt after heating one of their blades to seal the skin. Khari had done his best to wrap the cloth around his arm, tying it tightly over the wound that had, for the most part, stopped bleeding. Khari himself had multiple injuries.

A soldier had managed to catch him in the face whilst fighting, and he was now sporting a vicious black eye. He walked with a slight limp due to the stab wound in his upper thigh, although he insisted he was fine. Blood covered his shirt, both his own and the guards', and his lip was swollen, showing a rather impressive split that must have stung fiercely.

Khari sat nearby, knife still in hand, prepared to pounce even though it had been a few hours since they had come across anyone. The man looked poised for danger. Cain wondered if he was even breathing.

"You're sure she's all right?" Cain asked, touching his forehead gingerly.

"Aye, she's with yer old friend. She's fine."

Cain had asked previously why Prudence had not been with him when they found one another in the castle. He was sure that she would have insisted on being there. Indeed, she must have been a driving force to make Khari come for him—it certainly wouldn't have been his own decision. But Khari had remained mum on the subject, keeping vague with his answers, only implying that she had been held up for some reason or another. It must have been pretty serious to keep her.

"And you're not lying to me?" Cain dropped the cloth he was holding, his hand instantly at Khari's collar threateningly for the third time.

Khari looked up at him placidly. "I swear to ye. She's alive. She just wasn't well enough to make the journey, tha's all, I promise ye. I can't tell ye any more than that. I jus' can't."

Cain's eyes narrowed, but he released his hold. There was something going on. "She's not well… but she's going to be fine?" he asked warily. He didn't even know if he could trust the former smuggler, but there was also no other reason for him to be there helping him, other than doing it for Prudence.

"Aye. She'll be well. She's a strong one."

Cain sat back on his heels. "Yes… she is at that." He breathed deeply and gave Khari's shoulder a light punch. "I suppose I owe you thanks for doing this."

Khari smiled at the captain. "She's a hard one to say no to. Practically forced me 'ere all the way from Vaerny." He chuckled.

Cain's heart swelled. That was his wife. She'd never been the type to accept fate. She fought it every step of the way for those she loved. He wasn't quite sure what he had done to deserve that love, but he was damn sure he would do everything in his power to keep deserving it. He was so close now. Just a little ways farther to go and he'd be back to her.

"We should make a move. The sooner we get as far from the castle as possible, the better." He rose alongside Khari, and the two of them took off walking once more, taking quieter, less travelled routes, but it would take time for word to get out, and for now, no one around there would be looking for an escaped prisoner aside from the soldiers, and certainly no one would know Cain's face.

The closer they got to Cain's childhood home, the more trepidation he felt. A whirlpool of emotions raged inside him—hope and excitement to see Prudence once more, worry that she was not already there with them, worry for her health. He also didn't relish the thought of seeing his home again after all these years.

The last time he had laid eyes on Torrin Down and his beloved cottage, he had been a child full of joy, with loving parents and an annoying little sister... he had thought their tiny village the most amazing place in all the world. Now, it just brought pain.

As they took the steep mountain track down into the valley, he caught sight of the first few homes. It took his breath away. Cain came to a standstill, his eyes on the village ahead of him. Khari clapped a hand on his shoulder.

"Ready to go and see your wife, Captain?"

Prudence laid the baby in the basket and gently stroked his head with a finger. His little pink face was so soft, so fresh, and he smelt sweet—of milk and an indescribable scent that drove her new mother instincts wild with love and protection. He was *hers*.

It had only been a couple of hours, but already she couldn't be apart from him, couldn't imagine her life without him. It was an all-consuming feeling she'd never felt before. A feeling she could never have even imagined. She watched the rise and fall of his little chest, breathing steadily as he slept.

The door swung open slowly, and in walked Khari, covered in blood.

"What happened? Where is he?" Where's Cain?" All the questions came pouring out of her mouth simultaneously in a panic. Her voice dropped to a nervous whisper. "Khari... who's blood is that?" It was like all the air had been sucked out of her lungs. The blood... so much blood. Her own blood pounded in her ears so loud she couldn't hear anything else. Suddenly, the doorway was no longer empty behind Khari. And there stood Cain. Bloody, beaten, towering in the door frame despite the weight he'd lost.

Prudence crossed the room in a blink, crashing into Cain at full force. He grunted in pain, and then they were wrapped up in each other, clutching one another earnestly. Cain's hand found its way into Prudence's hair, holding her tight, and she buried her face in his chest, inhaling the scent of him.

"Cain." His name came out breathless and quiet as if he might disappear into thin air if she spoke too loudly.

"I'm here" he murmured into her hair before pulling back to take her in. She ran a hand over his face, gently caressing the new cuts and bruises that dotted his face. His gaze swept slowly down from her head, pained eyes lingering on her own before sweeping down and catching sight of her still large belly. Instantly, he seemed to become aware of the room and the baby in the corner.

A breath rushed out of him, and he dropped into a chair, gripping the arm for support. His eyes darted back and forth between the basket and her stomach. He ran a hand over his face and sighed, leaning back in the chair. "Is that...?"

"Yes," Prudence choked out, smiling. "He is."

The silence was deafening as Prudence stood watching Cain sit immobile. He barely breathed for the longest time, and doubts plagued Prudence's mind. The sudden relief that he was here was being flooded by the anxiety of awaiting his response.

The minutes ticked by until finally Cain exhaled happily, and Prudence broke out in a grin. He rose on unsteady feet and moved over to the basket that sat on the bed. Prudence came to his side and he slipped an arm around her middle as if unwilling for any space between them ever again. "He's... beautiful."

"His name is William... after his father," said Prudence, and she noticed the shimmer of a tear well in Cain's eyes.

Baby William wriggled in his sleep, sucking on his bottom lip, completely oblivious to the world around him.

"He's perfect." Cain reached a hand down to touch his son. His face was a mixture of serenity and sadness. "I can't believe you did all of this alone." He turned to Prudence, pressing a firm kiss on her forehead. She felt him quake slightly before he regained his composure.

"Ye can't?"

"I can. I hate that you had to." He held her close, the pair of them leaning on each other for support, and Prudence sighed happily.

Prudence rested on the husband she had been apart from for the entirety of their marriage as they stared at their son. It could almost be a dream. The delusional hallucination of a desperate mind. It was too perfect.

Despite the ache she felt all over, the blood slowly pooling between her legs, and the exhaustion that kept tugging at her eyelids, she wanted nothing more than to embrace her husband. She looked up at him. At his soft eyes, his chiselled jaw, at the scar across his cheek. She had to reach up on tiptoe to press her lips to his. Her eyes closed instinctively as he moved closer, leaning into her as his hands cradled her head. She sank into him.

The roughness of his lips... the faint taste of blood and sweat in her mouth was a welcome one, grounding her in reality, confirming that he truly was standing in front of her, kissing her, and soon, she was drowning in him.

His lips and hands blazed a trail of fire across her skin. It had been so long she had almost forgotten the feel of him, but with every breath, every touch, her body remembered. He fit against her like they were two parts of the same whole. Moulded for one another.

She wrapped her arms tightly around his neck, clinging to him as he kissed her face, peppering kisses across her cheeks, along her jaw, down her neck. He took her hand in his, bringing it to his lips to kiss each finger, one after the other.

When he ran his hand down her other arm, down to the stump of her elbow, she flinched.

"What happened, my love?" He took her face in his hands, pushing her hair back.

"I-I had to. I had to get rid of it," she whispered.

His gaze softened and stayed on hers as he planted kisses

down her arm tenderly.

"Oh, my darling, you've been through so much." He enveloped her in an embrace. It was like he was trying to absorb everything she had experienced, all the pain, all the worry, all the hurt. To take it and feel it for her, but all she could think about were the injuries covering his skin. The thought of him locked up, abused, sent to die. All of the things he had to suffer through himself. She would rip her own heart out if it would heal his.

She hadn't realised she was crying until Cain wiped the tears away with a thumb. "Don't ever leave me again." She fixed him with a serious expression.

He smiled then, cheeks creasing at the curve of his mouth. "I promise. You'd have to kill me."

"Even then."

He nodded, kissing her deeply. "Even then."

The docks were blissfully quiet in the early hours. The birds were awake and singing, but the sun had not yet broken through the clouds, lighting everything in a soft haze. They hurried down the docks as inconspicuously as they could manage.

Cain gripped the tiny bundle of William wrapped in blankets in his arms, their few possessions strapped to his back. Prudence strived to keep pace with him, still waddling slightly from the soreness.

Khari and Phaedra followed in their stead, Khari to board with them to this new world, Phaedra misty-eyed, mourning their departure before they had even left. It had taken no time at all for Phaedra to reconnect with the boy she had once known, and Cain had welcomed the warmth of a mother figure from his past. He had been eternally grateful to her for taking Prudence in, and of course, Phaedra had promptly fallen head over heels for their darling son.

Prudence could not help but feel an even bigger rush of love for Cain as he stared doe-eyed at William. The baby had his features, as clear as day, all except for Prudence's blue eyes and her mess of dark hair. He was a little blend of the pair.

They had lay low for a fortnight, keeping hidden from the soldiers that searched for Cain. Torrin Down was a quiet village, out of the way, and soldiers had only passed through twice, both without incident. Whilst Cain's face still plastered the walls and patrols still walked regular routes, it seemed that the royal guard had decided Captain Morris must have moved on. It made no sense for him to stay.

Still, they were cautious as they travelled from the village to the docks at Merton. Phaedra had insisted on coming, leaving her herd in Reesa's capable hands for the few days' journey. She was forlorn to see them go, but she knew they must if they were to live.

They had made arrangements with a local fur merchant for passage to The Northern Border on his next run for skins. He had looked at Cain for a long while, analysing his face to the point where Prudence thought her heart might burst from her chest. But then he agreed. They shook hands, and for an exorbitant sum of fifteen silvers kindly provided by Phaedra and Reesa upon their insistence, he would take them all the way to Atwood Province.

Prudence didn't know what to expect from this new world,

other than it was extremely cold, but it didn't matter. They would make do. They were all walking away; something she hadn't thought possible. Wherever they found home, it would be perfect, because it would be theirs. Together.

They reached the quay mooring *The Georgiana*, her captain, Mr. Rogers, already waiting for them. Phaedra pulled Prudence into a crushing hug, and Prudence hesitated before embracing her. She would miss the old woman, so much the mother they had both deserved. It hurt to leave her behind.

"Well, dear, I suppose this is it." Phaedra sniffed.

"Thank ye... for everythin'. I owe ye so much."

"Pssh." Phaedra waved the comment away. "You owe me nothing. It's what we do for those we love. We may not be blood, but we are family." Phaedra squeezed her one more time before she reached for baby William. "Take good care of this precious bundle, you understand me?"

"Yes, ma'am." Cain grinned, handing him over for a moment. "With everything I have."

Phaedra cupped Cain's cheek and smiled. "You're a good boy. Look after them."

"I will." He kissed her cheek softly.

"Come on, we haven't got all day." The merchant captain huffed, hurrying them onto the ship.

Prudence grasped Phaedra's hand, planting a kiss on her palm before following Khari up the gangplank. She stood on deck for a long time, watching the distance for any sign of soldiers until *The Georgiana* was heading out of port.

Eventually, Khari appeared at her side. "Ready for this new life, *keine*?"

"I am." she sighed contentedly. "But why are ye heading to this frigid north? Why not head east back home? Back to yer mother." She turned to look at him.

"Maybe I will one day. Right now, though, I'm content to begin a new adventure."

Acknowledgements

This book wasn't meant to exist. When I first 'met' Prudence and began scribing her story, it was only meant to be a standalone. She certainly wasn't meant to get married or have a child… it's very true that we writers aren't fully able to control our characters. We are at the mercy of their whims. But for that I am grateful, this story and these lives are greater than I could have possibly imagined.

Firstly, I'd like to thank my wonderful son Lincoln, to whom *The Bloody Maiden* was dedicated to. He's been a spectacular help in working things out for this book - including coming up with the solution for battling the morgawr, and naming a few animals along the way. Despite being years too young to read my work, he is my biggest cheerleader, proudly telling anyone who will listen - teachers, strangers, friends, that his mummy is an author. He's even gone so far as to show my website and bookmarks to people in class. No matter how proud I am of these books, it will never compare to how proud I am of you, and at the risk of embarrassing you terribly, you are my reason for living, much in the same way that Prudence lives for Cain and William.

ACKNOWLEDGEMENTS

To Karen, my amazing friend and wonderful editor - I still can't quite believe that we've not known each other our entire lives, it certainly feels like we have. The series wouldn't be what it is without your skill and keen eye, not to mention your ability to listen to long-winded, incoherent voice notes at all hours of the day about the most minor of story details.

To Lizzie, for being a fantastic proofreader and even better friend. I've always believed in soul mates and I'm fairly sure you're my platonic soul mate. To think we existed in passing for years before ever really speaking is both hilarious and maddening. We missed five years of potential friendship, but at least we're making up for it now.

To James, both my illustrator and brother - thank you for being part of this series. It means so much more to do this work with my sibling by my side. You've made the inside of these pages absolutely beautiful with chapter headings and scene breaks [not to mention designing numerous tattoos for me]. It makes all the difference.

To Kristin, once again you've done wonders making a cover so beautiful [and fitting with book one] that I may cry. I honestly couldn't imagine a better artist to encapsulate my words. I can't wait to see the entire series standing side by side on my bookcase. They'll be the most beautiful books in my entire library.

I'd like to thank all of my family for their support. Many of whom have been the first to read the final product; to buy merchandise and wear it proudly; to show off my books any chance they get [even so far as approaching big name authors at public speaking events to tell them my entire life story - thank you Tom, it's greatly appreciated, always].

Finally, I'd like to thank my readers. This book series is a quirky little thing, a big niche, and often I'm beaten down by the dreaded imposter syndrome. It's all of you who buoy me back up. Hearing or reading your thoughts, your feedback and fierce love of these characters is *everything*. The right words simply don't exist, thank you certainly isn't enough.

As I write this, I've already started the beginning of the end… the final part of Prudence's story. And whilst I'm so excited to get it all down on paper, I'm also mourning. I have numerous projects in the works that've been neglected the last eight years in order to focus on this series, but it feels like I'm hacking off a chunk of my own soul to put out into the world, and with the final 'the end' coming, I fear it's a feeling a might never feel again with other stories. Prudence is so close to my heart we are essentially one person. I just have to keep reminding myself that she'll always be a part of me.

ABOUT THE AUTHOR

S. M. MITCHELL is a swashbuckling night-owl pagan, whose love of pirates, the gothic and all things historical led to her starting her career as a literary fantasy novelist back in 2015. She has a degree in English Literature and Creative Writing and runs Little Crow Marketing, working with kickass female entrepreneurs. She lives on the stunning Jurassic Coast in England with her crazy family and myriad of animals. When she's not writing she can be found baking, gardening or bingeing Netflix.

WWW.SMMITCHELL.COM
Facebook & Instagram @SMMITCHELLAUTHOR | Twitter @SMMITCHAUTHOR

THE
WICKED REDEMPTION

COMING SOON